JADE:
The Law

To Jeanne and
Don, long time
friends are the
best.

Also by Robert Flynn

The Last Klick
North to Yesterday
In the House of the Lord
The Sounds of Rescue, the Signs of Hope
Seasonal Rain and other stories
Personal War in Vietnam (a memoir)
When I Was Just Your Age (with Susan
Russell)
Wanderer Springs
Living With the Hyenas
The Devils Tiger (with Dan Klepper)
Growing Up a Sullen Baptist
Tie-Fast Country
Slouching Toward Zion
Paul Baker and the Integration of Abilities
(With Eugene McKinney)
Echoes of Glory
Burying the Farm
Jade: Outlaw

JADE:
The Law

Robert Flynn

JoSara MeDia

ISBN: 978-0-9843049-6-7

Published by:
JoSara Media
Tomball, Texas

Cover illustration © Deirdre
FlynnBass

1st printing, October 2011

To the Shirley and Bob Huffman family
...from the beginning

Chapter 1

Law Comes to the Settlement

Rain grieved Jade as she had grieved Skull Cap and Brave Little Bear but without slashing her face and breasts. She had endured loneliness before but there was no happiness in it. She had heard the grandmothers tell of a bird whose song was so sad and so sweet that the very singing of it required its life. She thought she had become that bird. Then Jade returned.

When she heard Jade riding through the brush and under the trees of Moccasin Street leading his horses to her house what she felt wasn't entirely joy. It also tore old wounds so they could bleed again.

Rain was standing on the porch when he saw her but she didn't speak. If Jade had hoped for a smile or a greeting he was disappointed. She assayed his face.

Jade's hair was wet and plastered to his head when he took off his hat to speak. He wiped his brow with his shirt sleeve. "I'm not offering two horses for you but I aim to marry you," he said.

Did he expect her to deny who she was? become what he was? Her people had left her because her father and mother, brother, husband, son had been killed by soldiers and Texas Rangers that seemed to follow her. Her people had left her at the springs to placate the palefaces but palefaces could not be placated.

"That will take time," she said.

"I have time," Jade said, sitting easy in the saddle.

"What will you do?"

"I don't know other than try to stay alive."

"That won't be easy either."

"No. I'll have to work in the settlement or with one of the cow outfits. No more escorting freight wagons or cavalry patrols."

"I'll stand beside you in the settlement," Rain said.

Rain didn't want him to be gone for months with a freight wagon train or weeks with an army patrol. She knew no way she could live with a cow outfit without putting both of them in danger. Jade knew she meant stand beside him with a gun.

"If the Indians come back?" Jade asked.

"I'm not killing anyone I don't have to."

"But you might torture a prisoner to catch other suspects?" He had seen men beaten, choked, their hair pulled, their arms twisted until they confessed, until they betrayed friends, brothers, mothers, wives, children.

"Squaws don't torture for information but to see if a man has the fortitude required of a woman," Rain said.

"I won't ask to marry you until I think it's safe for you."

"I've never been safe," Rain said. When Indians didn't plague her palefaces did. "Marriage won't change that."

"Do you think you can be a white wife?" Jade asked. "Cowboys won't shoot a good woman but a redskin squaw would be no problem."

Could she return to the people of her birth? Mattie had been one of them but they had lynched her with no understanding of what she had done. "I can try," Rain said. "Can you be a husband who accepts his wife as she is?"

"I'll try," Jade said. "Maybe you could get a dog to warn you of prowlers." There were no dogs in the settlement. Cowboys shot barking dogs and freighters gutted them with their bullwhips. Outside the settlement lobos lunched on dogs. "You could keep it in the house until I come to check things out."

That kind of routine would get him killed. "I don't want to be slave to a dog," Rain said.

"Do you reckon we'll ever agree on anything?" Jade asked.

"We agreed to a courtship. That's enough," Rain said.

"As long as we shoot the same people," Jade said.

Rain smiled and when her face lightened, her lips relaxed, for the first time he saw how pretty she was. What had he loved before? Her strength. She was as much an outcast as Mattie had been but she had been brave enough to claim Mattie as a friend, steadfast enough to protect Mattie by holding the mob at bay with a gun.

This was the woman he needed. The woman he dared not lose. Jade named something he had not known since Linnie, composed equally of joy and sorrow. Joy that he had found her, sorrow that he was not likely to have her for long.

"I'm keeping my horses," he said. "I'll fit one of the saddles to you in case we have to ride for the Rio."

He got off his horse and she came to him. For a moment they clung together, trying to melt through their clothes and into each other. Jade felt young again, but also old. Wary, suspicious, holding his fragile future in increasingly clumsy hands. Once he had seen death as redemption and escape. Now he wanted to live. "I need to borrow a shovel," he said.

"It's rusty," Rain said, fetching him a pick and shovel likely taken from a dead surveyor or prospector. "Come inside and I'll cut your hair."

"Scalp me? Give me braids?"

"Better you cut your own hair," she said.

⌒

Jade skirted the settlement, shed the pick and shovel in his shack, hobbled the extra horses, then rode to the store to buy oats for them and an old newspaper to burn out the wasp nests he had previously tolerated. There were no new newspapers. When newspapers arrived with the freight, everyone in the settlement who could read read one, sometimes the same one.

The wild kids from Barefoot Street scurried to tell everyone that Jade was back. He had scarcely deposited his plunder in his shack, his soogans on the bed, lighted the paper and burned out the wasps, and fed his horses when the committee presented itself. Ruth, Iowa, Curly, Smitty, Parson Wilbur and his wife, Hannah, who carried Belle, followed by the wild kids. Cletis, freckle-faced with the boyish look of a cruel kid, stood ajar. He was not one of them and maintained the separation. Jade met them outside his door.

"You're back," Ruth said from under her bonnet, turning to her husband to give him the floor.

"Do you intend to accept our offer to be the law?" Iowa asked.

It signified the end of his freedom as much as marrying Rain would. He would never be far from danger, and alone except for Rain. If he didn't prescribe the law in the settlement the cow outfits would. "I don't know much about the law but I'll try to keep you safe in your homes." They received that with murmurs of appreciation. "If I'm the marshal, you're the posse," Jade said.

They nodded agreement except Parson Wilbur. "I'll do anything short of taking a life," he said. Hannah nodded approval. For the first time in Jade's memory, Belle wasn't fretting. He thought perhaps it was an omen but Wilbur had bought a nanny goat from Pancho to provide a better diet for Hannah and the baby. He and Hannah were the only ones who didn't call Pancho Pan-cho.

"We got a deal," Jade said. Talk of money would come later and depend on how necessary he was.

"Maybe the parson could be Justice of the Peace," said Smitty, the blacksmith, blowing flies from the harelip inadequately covered by his brushy mustache. Smitty, no one had bothered to learn his name, nursed a grievance against Parson Wilbur and this was a way to invite trouble on him. Smitty had made another iron cross for the church house but Wilbur would not accept it because he never wanted to see another body hanging from a cross in front of a church house. Since Wilbur wouldn't use it Smitty placed it atop his shop to advertise his skill with ironwork.

"I second the motion," Curly said. Curly owned the saloon but Wilbur had saved it and Curly's life during the Indian raid.

Wilbur looked at Jade. "I don't know much about the law," he said. "None of us knows much about justice but I'll be as fair as I can."

The wild kids ran through the mesquite, cactus, catclaw, Spanish Dagger, sage and other low brush down the dirt trail called Barefoot Street to spread the news. The wild kids were an amorphous group of varying ages with parents too sick, too defeated by brutal work conditions and cruel nature to care where their children were or what they were doing.

"Come down to the saloon and the drinks are on the house," Curly said, searching for a long hair in his nose.

"Dractly," Jade said, mispronouncing directly and meaning when he got around to it.

Curly found a hair, pulled it, examined it and discarded it.

Jade watched them walk back toward the settlement then began digging a hole as long as his body in the dirt floor of the shack. The general's son, Cletis, would tell any Augur hands in the settlement to carry the news to his father that Jade was now the law. If none of his father's cowboys were in the saloon or the shack behind, Cletis would ride for his father's headquarters at first light.

Jade dug until the hole was deep enough to protect him from anyone shooting through the shack walls. He would finish it later.

He rode to the saloon for the obligatory drink that turned out to be three beers before riding back to his shack. Jade didn't know how long he would have before the shooting started. He took his soogans off the rope bed where they spent his waking hours and spread them on a bush and put his guns outside the door, except the one on his hip. He finished digging the hole then spread the dirt he had removed around the dirt floor, hauling the excess outside on the tarp and scattering it where it wouldn't be noticed. With the tarp thrown over the hole, no one would know it was there.

The digging had left the shack dusty and Jade opened the door and the wooden window, cleaned his guns, and hunkered outside until the dust settled. Then he put his rifles in the hole, spread a bandana over the end of the barrels, placed his soogans beside the hole, and with his six-shooter at hand lay down as secure as he had ever been.

At the first nicker from a horse, the sound of a bootheel or a weapon being cocked, he would roll into the hole, safe from ambushers who would shoot at the corner where his bed was. He would shoot at any flash he saw through cracks or any hole that appeared in the wall of the shack hoping to trace the bullet back to its owner. If they set the shack on fire they could drive him out but otherwise he was safe.

Feeling safe didn't make Jade sleepy; it gave him time to worry. He was the law and the first bronc he had to ride was justice for Mattie, the whore they called "Killer" before they lynched her. He was bogged to the saddle skirts in how to do it. Who should he arrest when the whole country was guilty? Everyone had an active or passive part in the crime, except for Rain, Parson Wilbur and his wife Hannah who had tried to save her.

The general, the jefe, the dutchman could have stopped it but did nothing to control their cowboys. There was no way he could arrest them because he was the law in the settlement, but they were the law in the country. Their cowboys would burn down the settlement if he tried to hold them there. He would have to take them miles across open country with their cowhands looking for them to get them behind the control of the soldiers at Fort Clark. Even there, the state would probably take their side. The cow bosses weren't present at the hanging.

The leaders of the mob were Sarge, Segundo and Cody. Sarge was straw boss of the T over Z, mistakenly recorded as the Augur because the brand looked like an auger. Sun-and-wind ravaged Sarge told Parson Wilbur that the lynching was cattle business and the church had no part in it.

Sarge, tough as a rawhide steak, considered himself the chaplain to the general and his former Rebels. Sarge's God was a stern Master who expected his slaves to live hard lives filled with want, sacrifice and cheer. "Shuck yourselves," he ordered them when they were boy soldiers crying over the nibbling fear, the uncontrollable rage, the red lust to deal pain. "Pull away the rough, ugly husk of war and you'll find the sweetness and goodness that is still there. When you sleep you return to God and are in His care."

Brine, a private as loyal and ferocious as a one-man dog, had bad dreams. He saw a woman in an abandoned house, forced her on the floor and had his way with her. She didn't resist but she cried. A blue belly came in and kneeled over her, crying with her. "I raised my rifle and drove the bayonet through him, killing both of them. They scrabbled around for a while, arms and legs flailing like a crab but I had pinned them to the floor."

"Yankees, both of them," Sarge said. "When you send an enemy of God to hell you take another step up the ladder to glory."

Segundo was Jefe's near partner of the Skillet. Their intricate stamp brand didn't look like a frying pan but a hot skillet of snakes. Jefe did nothing to stop Segundo or the pistoleros. Cody rode for Dutch but Dutch had also been at home with his family, unlike settlement folks who watched the entertainment. Cody was assisted by cowboys of mixed brands who barged into the church house or fought Mick and Pancho into uselessness.

It might be possible for Jade to pick them off one by one by living the way he lived when killing Indians. He could bushwhack Segundo and the pistoleros would scatter. However, Jefe and his Tejanos would come to the settlement looking for him. He could backshoot Sarge but the general and his former Rebels would scour the Devils River country for him. It would be easy to goad Cody into a gunfight the next time he was in the settlement. Dutch's scrub kids wouldn't face him but he didn't know what Dutch would do. Or what they would do to Rain.

⌒

Jade took Rain to teach her how to shoot the Sharps and trapdoor Springfield but she wanted to use the weapons she had, the 1861 Springfield army rifle and 1860 Army Colt revolver. They weren't the best but she was familiar with them and when he watched her shoot them he knew she had shot at something before.

"Have you ever shot at someone?" he asked.

"Yes," she said.

"I'm not going to ask who."

"Thank you," she said.

He told her he knew no way to bring justice to Mattie.

"The whole country is guilty," he said.

"Does that mean that no one can be punished? What about the man who put the rope around her neck?"

"If I let the big ones go, the bosses who authorized it or condoned it, how can I punish the little ones who just cheered, or maybe just watched?" It was simpler when every Indian was a red devil. Killing all of them was at least theoretically possible.

"Violence is never redemptive," Parson Wilbur said when Jade told him. "It may be necessary for some men to be removed from common people but killing them brutalizes everyone. You'll turn this settlement into a war zone. You'll start something that can never be set right."

"I don't want to fail that tormented woman," Jade said. "That seems the cruelest act of all."

"In this life some things can never be set right. God said that vengeance belonged to Him alone. Only God can do justice."

"Do you really believe that?" Jade asked.

"I have to believe it. I'm a Christian. God help my unbelief."

Jade wanted to roll up his soogans, gather his horses and ride into the setting sun. With Rain if she would go.

***

Rain's heart sang with memories of Jade saying he intended to marry her. Jade was her first chance at happiness since Brave Little Bear died, her first hope of a future since she was a child. Yet she faced a boggy crossing with quicksand and water moccasins at every step. Jade was a warrior.

Skull Cap had been a warrior also. After saving their hunting ground proved impossible Skull Cap fought for her, for their son, for the grandmothers and grandfathers, for honor. And he was killed as was Little Bear who wanted to be like his father. Jade would fight for justice that was as impossible as fighting for the Indian way of life. How could he bring justice for Mattie? While Mattie was hanging by her neck they had violated her during her death throes.

When Mattie had first brought her clothes to be washed they had been wary of each other. Both were aliens but Mattie feared that Rain might scorn her the way white people did. Mattie's laundry told Rain the kind of woman Mattie was and she knew that if she befriended Mattie she would never be accepted by the settlement.

"Do you speak English," Mattie had said on her third visit.

"Yes," Rain said. "Let's go inside." Inside they shared coffee and cold biscuits.

"Are you Indian?" Mattie asked.

"Yes. My first parents were white but I am Indian."

"Do you ever wish for someone you could talk to?" Mattie asked.

"Yes," Rain said. "I would like to listen to your story."

"Would you really?" Mattie asked, as though Rain had offered to restore her baby. Mattie recounted her story of how Lovie had smothered at her breast as Mattie tried to quiet her to prevent Indians from discovering and killing them all. She looked at Rain for disapproval. "You lived with Indians. Did I do the right thing?"

"I replaced the little girl my Indian mother sacrificed for her village because the soldiers were close, the girl had a fever and they couldn't stop to cool her in the shade or bathe her in the river."

"My family thanked me for saving them but I would have watched them all die to save Lovie. They said it was an accident but I don't know. My husband never forgave me. I knew God would never forgive me because he never gave me another child, no matter how hard I tried, how many men I used. Now I am forsaken by everyone."

Mattie was the only paleface Rain understood until she helped Hannah bring forth Belle, her baby. Then Hannah knew the fear that had filled Rain's heart with dread. The inability to save your child from danger, disease, death. Ruth, and those like her, she would never understand because of their contempt and fear of those of a different tribe. Like Rain, Mattie had been discarded by the community as waste.

Rain's people called Jade "paleface with hell in his neck" because once he fixed his sights on an Indian one of them was going to die. Whether it was a friendly Indian, a young boy larking on a horse, or a brave on the warpath was irrelevant. Would he be the same way with those who broke the law? Pursue them until one of them was in a grave? Could she abide a man whose every thought was about punishment? who every day brought death to her table, to her bed?

Rain loved Jade. She wanted to marry Riley, the man Jade had been before he was a killer, to share that life, but she could never become one of his people unless he denied Rain her past and she denied Jade his future.

***

Having accepted a job, Jade didn't know where to begin. Whatever he did would have to be done by the littles. He rode through the settlement leading another saddled horse. The settlement seemed quiet enough but it was still early. Iowa came out of the store and nodded at him. Curly was still asleep in the shack behind the saloon and he had rolled the barrel and carried the bottles of whiskey into the shack with him. Smitty was outside his blacksmith shop working on his first chaw. "Everything seems quiet, Marshal," he said.

Jade rode up Moccasin Street and interrupted Rain's washing to ask her to try the saddle on the extra horse. His arm brushed her thigh after she mounted and he laced the stirrups at the proper length. Both pretended not to have noticed but when she stepped down he kissed her until she paused for breath. "I have washing to do," she said.

Jade rode back to the store and told Iowa to order two shotguns by the first freight wagon train to San Antonio. "Ten gauge side by side," he said. "And a dozen boxes of buckshot. And charge it to the settlement."

Iowa looked up from his studying and considered but reluctantly did so. Iowa was learning by book how to be a gunsmith because guns were his most profitable commodity.

When Smitty learned that Iowa was going to charge the county for two shotguns, he made a tin star for Jade to wear and also charged it to the settlement. Iowa informed the other citizens that there had to be some organization to levy taxes and pay for services that he had rendered, and called for a meeting at the church house.

Wilbur agreed to moderate the meeting that quickly became fractious. Everyone wanted law and order but no one wanted to pay for it. Wilber pointed out that both the Old Testament and the New Testament, both Jesus and the Apostle Paul said believers should pay taxes. The believers present believed the Bible was God's Holy Word but that the Almighty was wrong about taxes.

Curly believed a tax should be collected from items Iowa sold at the store since settlers headed west, freighters, the cow outfits, even soldiers sometimes bought supplies there. The squatters, Mick and Pancho, said they bought only necessities and the tax was unfair. If Iowa ever agreed to sell their produce Iowa could take the tax out of the money he paid for their produce and tax them again for everything they bought, and living outside the settlement they didn't have the same protection.

Iowa, with the sad-eyes, drooping mustache of a store keeper who pretended his customers took advantage of him, said the same outsiders who traded at the store patronized the saloon and the shack behind. And Curly's revenue was greater than his. And came from what good people called sin. The two men argued which was better able to charge taxes but neither would disclose their revenue.

Shep, who represented this son, the general, said it wasn't fair to hard-working cow folks to make them pay for luxuries wanted by the settlement, and taxes would drive the cow outfits to take their money and their cattle elsewhere. Iowa said the taxes paid for county necessities and if one business paid taxes all should, including the blacksmith shop.

Smitty claimed that he was as hard-working as cowboys. Mick and Pancho said they too worked as hard as the cowboys, but with biddy bridles. The lungers, old soldiers and broken-down freighters from Barefoot Street said they were reduced to begging for bread, medicinal whiskey, and shoes for their barefoot children. Taxes would mean choosing between food, medicine, and clothing for their children.

Wilbur arranged a truce by which the business owners contributed to a fund to pay settlement expenses. Curly complained that the store and blacksmith shop charged inflated prices for reimbursement from the general pot. The lungers, freighters and those who had shucked their spurs agreed.

Jade said he had some old business he wanted to bring up. The committee warned him against trying to set right things that had happened before he became the law. "We can try to do justice," Jade said. The committee insisted it was too late. "That's like a dog returning to its vomit," Shep agreed.

"We can tell the truth about Mattie's lynching," Jade said. Mattie shot the man who beat her and threatened to kill her.

"At least, we can face the truth about what we have done and allowed to happen," Wilbur said.

"Don't look back," the committee warned. "We need to forget the past and move forward into a better future."

The settlement was taking on the aspect of a city, segregated by danger, fear and taxes.

⌒

Jade didn't make a practice of riding up the trail that was quickly becoming main street. He tried to avoid all routine. Sometimes at night he circled around the settlement listening for trouble, suddenly appearing on the scene. When the general complained that the wild kids pilfered from his house when his wife and family were at church, and threatened to burn one of their homes as a lesson, Jade slept in the low brush along the dirt trail called Barefoot Street, abruptly appearing to frighten wild kids starting a prowl.

When five Augur cowboys with unlighted torches tied up their horses to slip up on the house of a disabled Confederate veteran, Jade untied the horses and fired a shot to scatter them and the cowboys. He fired shots after the horses and cowboys to speed them on their way to reunion.

After the shotguns arrived, Jade gave one to Rain. Sometimes he sat with the shotgun in the store or the saloon, always with his back against the plank wall of the half-shack, half-tent saloon so he could not be shot through the canvas side.

Sometimes Jade cut firewood for Rain's washing pot, fed her guineas, slopped her hogs, laid newly washed clothes on brush to dry. Rain hadn't asked him to plow her field or milk her cow and he hadn't volunteered, but he did clean her rifle and six-shooter and he had poked at the clothes in the boiling cauldron while she cooked his breakfast, dinner or supper.

Those were the best times, watching the quiet, graceful way she moved, sharing a meal, lingering over coffee, biscuits, butter and mustang grape jelly, enjoying the quiet until some sound, some intuition, some impulse caused him to jump on his horse and ride into the settlement from an unexpected direction.

⌒

The new whore came to the settlement with a freight wagon train escorted by some Augur cowboys. Previous whores had been pretty at one time in their lives and most had known a moment of love. This one was of mixed parentage, maybe Indian-Mexican with a dash of buffalo soldier. Dark skin, black hair, a moon-shaped face, high cheek bones, thick lips, and uneven teeth. She was young, shapely, but there was no spark in her eyes and she seemed to be of low intelligence and monosyllabic in two languages. "Good thing no one goes to a whore for conversation," said Curly, her new boss, tugging at a long hair in his eyebrow.

Jade watched the cowboys crowding around the frightened girl to be the first. The freighters seemed to have already had their fill. She was so cowed and spiritless that to see her was to pity her. Jade feared she was so pitiful she would inspire violence on herself.

Jade backed-up Curly who assigned numbers to the cowboys so they could line up. They wrestled, shouted insults at those who took more time than they should have, but there was no gunplay. The shoves and insults would get worse when the cowboys spent the rest of their money on whiskey. Curly rolled up the canvas sides of the saloon and Jade took a seat against the wall behind the bar for a long night, the shotgun across his knees.

Jade moved his chair frequently so those waiting their turn in the shack behind the saloon couldn't be sure where he was. He also stepped outside into the darkness where he could see without being seen.

There were some fist fights around the shack but the only serious incident occurred when two cowhands reached the shooting stage and Jade cocked both hammers of the shotgun from the darkness. Both men recognized the sound and gave Curly their guns and rode for the wagon. Their guns would follow in the hands of their riding mates.

The sun was up when the last of the line left, some of the cowboys lining up twice. Curly dragged the girl out of bed to cook some breakfast for the two of them. "What do you call her?" Jade asked over eggs wrapped in Ruth's tortillas.

"Girl," Curly said. Failing to find a long hair in his ears and eyebrow he searched his scalp with his fingers.

～

News of the whore's arrival spread and other cowboys rode to the settlement for a look-see but singly or two or three at a time. There was some horsing around but no fights. Jade rode to the store where Iowa reported little business but no problems. Iowa hoped that when the newness wore off the saloon and shack would offer less competition. Ruth eyed with disgust the cowboys who bought a twist of tobacco for the ride back to the range. "She's got the brown skin of a Mexican, the nose and high cheekbones of a savage, the thick lips of an African," Ruth said. "I don't know what she is. You should be ashamed," she called after them, knowing what they had been doing in town.

Ruth was ashamed of her part in the lynching of the woman they called Killer. Still the woman had brought it on herself. She had made herself useful for any man who paid her. The thought made Ruth shudder. Old cowboys, soldiers, politicians served their purpose and were left with only their story. But females were useful as long as their aperture remained, sometimes after death. That had been Killer's fate. At least one cowboy rode her after her last breath while others cheered him on.

⌒

One muggy morning, so humid Jade thought he could slap water out of the air, Jade saw Cletis slip around the canvas that had been rolled down to keep out the damp. Then he saw Cody ride straight for the shack and tie up his horse at an iron hitching post. Jade followed. Cody and Cletis were the same age but Cody was a teenage man and Cletis was a teenage boy.

Cody was born with a swagger although he had to leave home because his mother could no longer feed him; his father had died in the war. He was small in stature with a smooth, simple baby face and almost girlish hands that fascinated women and spooked men who would have ridiculed him if he hadn't had the cold eyes of a killer. Cody believed killing was the bronc he had to ride to acceptance as a man. He was good at it, perhaps his only skill.

"I got here first," Cletis said.

"Get out of the way, milk sucker, or go for your gun," Cody said.

"I don't have a gun," Cletis said.

"You're wearing one."

"It belongs to one of my father's cowboys. He's laid up sick at my house," Cletis said.

"If you're man enough to wear it, you're man enough to pull it," Cody said.

"No, please, I've never shot a gun. I just put it on to impress the girl."

"Then you ain't man enough for a woman," Cody said. "She'll chew you up and spit you out. Draw or drift."

"If you shoot me, my father or one of his hands will track you down and kill you," Cletis said, hoping it sounded like a threat.

"Like I reckoned, you're still sucking your mama's tits," Cody said.

"Don't talk about my mother."

"Then run for your house titty-boy. I'm counting to three and I'm drawing whether you do or not. One."

"No, please. You can have her. I want to go home," Cletis blubbered, putting his hands on his head.

"Two."

Jade slipped behind Cody and as Cody began to drawl "Thiiiirrrr" Jade pulled the six-shooter from Cody's holster. Cody turned on him in fury.

'No one takes my gun," Cody said. "Give it back."

"Get on your horse and get out of the settlement," Jade ordered. "One of your pals can pick up your gun for you. And don't come back looking for trouble unless you aim to find it in a grave."

"No one talks to me like that," Cody said, but he got on his horse and left in a lope, not fast enough to look like he was running but fast enough to look for another gun.

"Don't tell my mama where I was going," Cletis said.

"I don't work for your father," Jade said. "If I see you wearing a gun again you'll have to back it up like everyone else. Now go home, get out of that six-gun outfit, and if I was you I'd lay low when Cody is around."

Cody was furious at being humiliated before Cletis, having to ride back to the wagon and explain how he had lost his six-shooter, having to ask someone to bring it to him. He had already killed one man, a pistolero who had called Homer, one of Cody's friends, some names in Spanish. When Homer punched the man, the pistolero shot Homer, mounted his horse and raced away. Cody shot him in the back, also his horse, but he vowed his second kill would be face to face.

Before Cody reached the wagon he met one of his riding mates and borrowed his gun. When they reached the settlement, Cody learned that Jade was in the store and he tied his horse to a ring on an iron post at the saloon and walked to the store. His friend watched from astride his horse, ready to ride. When Jade came out of the porchless store, Cody yelled, "Draw, star puncher," pulled his pistol and fired, missing Jade and the store. Jade took aim and before Cody could get off a second shot, shot Cody in the foot. Cody hopped around in pain, trying to shoot at Jade again.

"Drop the gun or die," Jade said. Cody dropped the gun to grab his foot and fell to the ground moaning in pain.

"If I'd had my own gun you'd be eating dirt," Cody said. "I'll kill you for this."

Jade told Cody's pal to go to Wilber's house, tell Hannah what had happened and ask for her help. Jade got a bucket of coal oil from the store, pulled the boot off the screaming Cody and stuck Cody's foot in the bucket. Hannah dressed the wound as best she could and soaked the bandaged foot in coal oil. Jade put Cody on his horse and sent him back to Dutch.

The general's wife was insulted by a pistolero who whispered impertinences to her in Spanish. No Augur hands were in the settlement so her father-in-law, Shep, strapped on a six-shooter. "I may be old but I ain't pulled in my horns," Shep said. He stood outside the canvas that had been dropped to keep out a cold north wind and called the "cowardly sidewinder" out. The pistolero shot him through the canvas siding of the saloon, walked outside, shot him again, jumped on his horse and pulled for the Rio Grande.

The wild kids scattered to find and tell Jade. Cletis rode to tell his father that Shep had been shot and the shooter escaped. Jade considered the pistolero's absence a good thing. The general would send his hands to lynch anyone riding alone but it would keep the gun smoke out of the settlement.

The next time he came to town, the general invited Jade to supper. The general had lost everything save the loyalty of his soldiers and the coins his wife had hidden when the slaves he had mortgaged to fight the war had to be redeemed with US dollars.

The general's house was off the trail and faced the hills. The ground was kept clear of brush and weeds by Augur hands or Shep when he was alive. Not knowing what he was riding into Jade hid Rain in the low brush facing the front porch with her rifle.

Then he rode up to the house and went inside. Jade hadn't met Caroline, the general's wife, but he would have known her. Southern lady holding her head high, accustomed to looking down on servants and other inferiors. Partial to silk and silver but managed pewter, Winchesters and waste. Jade wondered how she had begot Cletis.

She set a crock of son-of-a-bitch stew and a skillet of cornbread on the table. Jade knew that she disapproved of the poor tableware but also defiant, challenging him to disparage or trivialize what the Yankees had compelled her to do. Seeing the Yankees coming she buried gold and silver, built a fire over it and ordered slaves to clear the brush nearby and pile it on the fire. The Yankees added fence posts, doors, furniture, planks from the cow lot before they burned down the house. After they left, Caroline dug up the disfigured coins and gave them to her husband, all that was left of his fortune, family, heritage. Save the silver spoon still showing traces of black in the filigree that Jade had been given.

They ate in silence after the general had offered grace and Jade had complimented the food. Then the general and Jade retired to the front porch with good whiskey and cigars.

The general was thankful that Jade for "let bygones be bygones" and not wake up trouble about that woman that was hanged. The general was also grateful that Jade let the cow outfits settle the law outside the settlements. Some Augur hands, led by Sarge, had caught Shep's killer and left him decorating a tree. Jade was not convinced it was the shooter. When the man saw cowboys riding after him he turned and rode toward them rather than racing away. Probably a Tejano trying to oblige. It didn't matter; one of them had been lynched as a lesson to all of them.

"How long do you expect to be here? the general

asked.

"I figure I've got one, maybe two years," Jade said referring to his life expectancy.

"Cletis told me what you did for him," the general said. "I thank you for that and for allowing me to take care of my pa's killer. I don't approve of you being here but I can abide it as long as there is no Yankee government. But it's coming, as inevitable as Yankee carpetbaggers. They burned our plantations, slaughtered our livestock, stole our forests to destroy our livelihood, and now they want to destroy our culture. This is not the kind of life my wife is accustomed to. And now some Yankee fool quarantines my cattle? Tells me what I can and can't do with my own cows? It's going to make me and my kind small. Mark my words, they will come for our guns."

The general showed open hands. "The government can't be defeated with guns. That was a hard lesson but we learned it. Courage to attack better arms and equipment in the midst of disaster cannot defeat those arms and equipment. The South must rise again with subtlety."

The general had been a captain in the cavalry during the war and most of his cowhands had ridden with him. None of them was reconstructed. "Nesters can't be stopped by us. We know that too. Those battles will be fought in the courts, the congress, the legislature and I want a gun there to fight for me. Cleet is no good with cows or guns but he can be a back-shooter there."

The general refilled their glasses and lit another cigar. "There's a school in Waco, and I'm going to send Cleet there to learn the law and become a politician. I don't know how far he'll go but he can start here. I expect you to support him. When the county government is formed, cowhands will be able to vote for the sheriff, and you can go as far as he does.

"His mama approves. She has been teaching him the traditions and ways of the Glorious South. He will be a politician and he and others like him will undermine the Union from within. Cleet and others will restore the mudsill people under the foundation of those meant to lead civilization to prosperity and refinement. Those who were slaves and the Micks and Chinks we import will become wage slaves and debt-slaves and America will become the most productive and powerful nation on earth if we can keep them out of the political process. If we don't they will destabilize the economy. You can ascribe that to the Bible."

"I don't know that I'll be sheriff when Cletis does all that," Jade said. Or alive, he thought.

"They've already given black bucks the right to vote. Next, it'll be the other nonwhite aliens. That's why I want Cleet to get there as soon as he can to take the spokes out of their wheels," the general said. "You can be part of it or be buried by it."

Jade had to ask Parson Wilbur what "mudsill people" meant.

"It's the theory that there is no such thing as a classless society," Wilbur said. "When you sell your labor you sell yourself and become a servant to the aristocracy. A mudsill people are required to do the menial work under the foundation of skilled workmen with the propertied class at the top."

"The general said that landless people must be kept out of the political process or they will threaten society, the economy, government itself," Jade said.

"Yes. That was the justification for slavery. A Confederate politician said that when you put your labor in the market and take what you can get for it, you are essentially a slave. In the South slaves were hired for life and compensated for it with food, shelter, clothing. They were allowed, sometimes required, to have families. None was a beggar. In the North wage-slaves were hired by the day and often hungry, homeless, ragged. If they had family, their wives and children begged on the street. Southern slaves had no dreams of sharing some of the wealth their labor created. Northern workers did want to share in the wealth of their labor, but one man was helpless against a corporation unless he could persuade others to join him. In the South, former slaves are denied the right to vote by whatever means possible. In the North, wage-slaves are denied the right to collective power by any means possible. And usually the government and the churches have been on the side of the powerful."

"And that's bad?" Jade asked.

"It's abominable. It's the philosophy that fostered secession. The North won the military war but I fear the South is winning the philosophical and political war."

⤶

One of Dutch's brothers in Germany sent the treasured family music box to Otto, his father, who lived in Dutch's house in the settlement. When it arrived the intricately inlaid wood, silver and ivory top was splintered and the silver and ivory missing. When wound up the music box played but the sound was off-key. Otto, who spoke no English, confronted the muleskinner.

The skinner pulled off his hat and wiped his nose and his receding hair line with his sleeve. Above the hat line his skin and hair were white. Below it his face and hair were sun-chapped and dark with days-old dust. The freighter shrugged off the complaints. He didn't understand the words but he did understand the tone. It had nothing to do with him. The freighter had brought the box from San Antonio and if there was something wrong with it, it happened at sea or maybe between Galveston and San Antonio.

Otto continued to complain. Everything Otto said sounded like an insult to the teamster who couldn't tell the curses from the rest of Otto's German. The exasperated freighter wound up the music box to show that it still played. "Das ist ja kaputt," Dutch's father said. The freighter took the box and tossed it aside. Otto slapped the freighter and the freighter shot him.

The gunshot brought Jade who confronted the freighter. "Why did you shoot him?"

"He's a damn foreigner. Can't speak English. I don't know what the hell he was yelling at me for. I give him his damn music box."

Jade arrested the freighter and put him in the stone roundhouse, built as defense against Indian attacks, and braced a log against the outside of the door so that the freighter could not open it. That night a visitor called the freighter to one of the loopholes built into the roundhouse. When the freighter looked to see who it was, the visitor shot him in the face, then again where he thought the freighter had fallen, and rode away.

Everyone knew that Dutch had shot the man but no one had seen him in the settlement and Jade had no proof. Going to Dutch's wagon to bring him to town for questioning would be certain death. Jade knew he couldn't put another suspect in the roundhouse unguarded but neither could he take a suspect to the Fort Clark guardhouse and leave the settlement defenseless.

Jade told Smitty to make an iron latch for the door of the roundhouse and to charge the county for it. The county also bought the most expensive padlock Iowa had.

⤳

When Dutch came to town in daylight he left his cowhands at the saloon and went in search of Jade. "I know I told you to take the slack out of Cody's rope but I didn't intend you to maim him," Dutch said. "He was no good as a cowboy before you warped his foot and now he is totally worthless. He's laid up at the wagon, can't get his foot in a boot or a stirrup. He walks with a crotch-stick his friends cut from a tree but that makes him one-armed. You'd a done me a favor if you'd killed him. I can't send him home and if he gets in the way of Jefe or the general, they'll plant him."

"That's not your problem," Jade said.

"When you can hire and fire a man you can control his life," Dutch said. "Some need that kind of control over others. Some want that kind of control from others and are happy when someone else decides their right or wrong. The general needs that kind of control and his hands want to give it to him. Like Brine. Few skills, no ambition, no curiosity, but obedient to whoever brands him.

"Jefe has that kind of control over the Tejanos. No one has control over the pistoleros. Segundo has the reins when he's with them but when he's out of sight they choose their own trail. I don't need to control others. I don't want to. I want to hire a man because he is of some use to me and to let him go because he might be of better use to someone else. Nobody wants Cody deciding what's right or what's wrong."

"Did you shoot the freighter in the roundhouse?"

"Who says so?" Dutch asked.

That was the burr under the saddle. No one had seen him and if they had they wouldn't have said so. "I'm riding back to the wagon with you," Jade said. "Just the two of us and I'm riding behind you with the shotgun on your back both barrels cocked. If I see anyone with a rifle or a shot is fired I'm pulling both triggers, even if it's a death twitch. If you run, the Sharps is hanging from the saddle horn."

On the way to Dutch's wagon, Jade studied his situation. He needed a deputy. He had already put Rain in more danger than he wanted. With a deputy he could have thrown the freighter in the roundhouse, propped the door closed, and put the deputy in the suicide hole on top of the roundhouse to discourage visits. With Smitty's latch he could throw a prisoner in the roundhouse, bolt the door and the deputy could throw his soogans in front of the door.

Cody was a fool but he was fearless and he was a shooter. He was going to work on one side of the law or the other, maybe both sides as Jade had done. Why not start him on the right side? He might grow up.

Dutch's young hands watched Dutch ride to the wagon with a shotgun pointed at his back. None of them moved, waiting for orders. "Squat," Dutch said. "We got business with Cody and it ain't no concern to you."

"You shot me," Cody said.

"I probably should have killed you," Jade said.

"Not if I had my own gun, you wouldn't of. Worthless hunk of tin couldn't hit a barn if you was inside and the door was closed."

"You're no good here but Jade can get you a job in the settlement," Dutch said.

"I ain't no counter jumper," Cody said.

"I can use a deputy," Jade said. "It will be no loss to anyone if you get shot."

"Ride over that again," Cody said.

"You can work for me or you can get out of the territory," Jade said. "I'll shoot you on sight."

"You no longer ride for the V under W," Dutch said. V under W was for Von Werther but Augur and Skillet cowboys called it the Rat's Ass. That caused a few fights between cowboys who would fight over whether the wind blew dust or dirt. "I don't want to see you around my wagon."

"How much does a deputy make?" Cody asked, caught in the crowding pen.

"Nothing at first." Jade didn't have permission to hire a deputy.

"How long will I have to live on what Dutch owes me?"

"That money you owe to Pancho for his dog that you shot and any damage you did to his ewes," Jade said.

Cody looked at Dutch. "He ain't riding my horse out

of here without paying for it," Dutch said.

"I'll give him one of mine and send yours back," Jade said.

Dutch nodded and gave Cody's wages to Jade. "He's got his own saddle."

"You're going to get down on your knees and apologize to Pancho in front of his wife and kids, and you're going to promise to protect his family when they're in the settlement," Jade said.

Cody chewed on that trying to swallow it.

"Cletis is going to learn the law and he will be mayor or judge when government comes to the settlement. If you have ambitions to be the law in these parts you need to get straight with Cletis before he leaves for schooling. Or get out of the territory before I kill you."

"How do I get straight with him?" Cody asked.

"That's your lookout," Jade said.

"How will I live?" Cody asked. "I won't even be able to buy a beer."

"You'll sleep on the ground like you've been doing, in the roundhouse if the weather is bad," Jade said. "I'll see that you get something to eat. You can wash up at Smitty's or in the creek."

"Can I keep reward money?"

"You can keep reward money but you won't start trouble and you will, by God, shoot the right people," Jade said. "I will cut you no slack and I will arrest you or kill you for a single mistake. You will get no second chances. Think it over. Then come to the settlement or dust out of here."

"And get away from my wagon," Dutch said.

"Do you think you could have shot me if I'd had my

own gun that you took?" Cody asked.

"Yes," Jade said.

"Did you intend to shoot me in the foot?"

"Yes."

"If you'll help me on my horse I'll ride back with you," Cody said to Jade, fetching his bedroll and saddle, and hobbling to his horse.

Jade made Cody carry his saddle and bedroll and hobble to his horse unaided. Cody threw his saddle on the horse but dropped his crotch stick. "Ain't you going to help me?" Cody asked.

"You built this noose by yourself and now you can decide whether you want your head in it or out of it."

Cody tied his rolled soogans behind the cantle and painfully pulled himself into the saddle. His misshapen foot dangled outside the stirrup and Cody grimaced at the sting shooting up his leg. Jade pretended not to notice.

***

Before approaching Pancho's house Jade took Cody's gun, gave Cody the wages Dutch had given Jade for safekeeping and rode in front of Cody to protect him. Pancho was working in the field and unarmed. "Let's go to the house," Jade told Pancho. "And call your kids."

Cody kneeled, gave Pancho his wages to pay for Pancho's dog, apologized for any trouble he had caused, and promised his protection in the settlement. Aurora, and Pancho's sons, Miguel and Tomas, watched in amazement.

"I'm going to take the wagon to Fort Clark to get me a sheep dog," Pancho said.

"Get me a guard dog while you're there," Jade said. "I'll watch your house at night while you're gone."

"I'll ride to the fort with you," Cody said, wanting to collect reward posters. "Help you pick out a dog for Jade."

Jade studied Cody, figuring a wagon's bumps would be easier on Cody's foot than bouncing outside a stirrup. Cody also might want to visit the surgeon at the fort. "If Pancho doesn't come back I'll hunt you down the way I did Indians. You'll never sleep good until you sleep forever," Jade warned Cody.

~

The wild kids came to tell Jade that a black man had gone into the saloon. "Who was inside?" he asked. Sarge, Brine and Skeet. The canvas sides were down in a cold north wind and Jade would be walking from bright light into dimness but he had a shotgun and a star. He stepped through the opening into the dim light and walked to the bar that was planks laid over two sawhorses.

Jade recognized the black man at the bar as a buffalo soldier he had met while scouting for the army. The soldier had bought crackers, a chunk of rat cheese and a can of sardines at Iowa's store and wanted a beer to wash them down.

Curly had his shotgun on the soldier and the three Augur hands were backing him up with six-guns. Iowa and Smitty were weaponless but Jade knew which side they were on. He asked for a beer to assay the probables. Sarge was hard as a hawk's lips and dangerous as kissing a rattlesnake. Brine was a cocked gun ready to fire when Sarge or the general pulled the trigger, great courage but little understanding of what he did. Skeet was a walkaway.

"We ain't drinking with no blue belly 'freedman',"

Sarge sneered.

"I'd rather serve a savage," said Curly, who had sold alcohol to Indians.

"You a deserter?" Jade asked quietly.

"Discharged," the black man whispered.

"Give my friend a beer," Jade said.

"This is private property and I got a right to say who gets served and who don't," Curly said. A man had a right to follow the gold and his customers didn't want black freedmen in the saloon. That meant they had no right to be there. "And he don't," Curly declared.

"And I got a right to call for two beers," Jade said. "Bring them to that table in the corner."

"I ain't serving no blue belly and no freedman," Curly said.

"The Bible says he's supposed to serve us," Sarge said.

"This is my new deputy," Jade said, "And the law will be served whenever he says so."

"The committee didn't authorize no new deputy," Curly said.

"He hasn't been sworn in because the committee hasn't met," Jade said, "but I hired him because I need him. Now put down the shotgun and serve us two beers or the law is riding out of here and shaking the dust off our boots. As the Bible says."

"We didn't authorize hiring no deputy," Curly grumbled but he stood the shotgun against one of the sawhorses that supported the plank bar.

"Get ready," Jade warned the black man, then holding his shotgun he turned to face the others. Iowa and Smitty had abandoned the fight. Sarge, the general's top hand, holstered his six-gun and the other two followed suit.

"This settlement is going to hell and the law is holding the gate open," Sarge said.

"We'll have our beers at that table," Jade said, leading the black man to the table. Jade laid the shotgun on the table and the black man kept his right hand under the table. "Don't look directly at them," Jade said quietly.

"I'm looking them dead in the eye until I see dead in their eyes," Jubal said loud enough to be heard outside the canvas walls of the saloon.

"Are you here to start trouble?" Jade asked under his breath.

"This fracas didn't settle nothing. Trouble is coming and I'd rather be facing it than having it come at my back."

"As long as you work for me I'll be behind you," Jade said.

"I've heard that before," Jubal said. Jade was a hard man but fair. Fearsome but as comforting as a repeating rifle. "This time I think I believe it."

Sarge got up and left. Skeet followed him. Brine stood up, his hat brim rolled up over his ears and pulled down above his close-set eyes, thick mustache and prim mouth. He was called Brine for his salty character some thought. Others thought his name was Bryan but unsure whether that was his first or last name. Brine spoke to Jade but faced Jubal, his sun-bleached eyes, faded to near invisible, focused on what was before him. "I like you, Jade," he said looking at Jubal. "But I ride for the general and if has-to-be I'll kill you." Then he followed Sarge outside.

Jade picked up the shotgun, motioned for Jubal to follow him and put the wall of the saloon at their backs. "What happened between you and the army?" he asked.

"Hit a white officer who gave a stupid order. I carried

it out but lost two good men."

"Your horse carries an army brand," Jade said. It was almost a question.

"I bought it."

"It's trouble any time some soldier or lawman sees it," Jade warned.

"Do you aim to put me afoot?"

"I'll give you a good horse," Jade said. "As long as you take care of it. Sell that one to Smitty and don't sign no papers. And get out of that blue uniform." Rebs riding for the Augur hated the blue uniform. The buffalo soldier was wearing the uniform blue pants, boots and belt.

"I aim to wear parts of it until it wears out."

"Are you looking to get yourself killed?" Jade asked.

"It don't matter what I wear, there'll be a showdown. I aim to say when it happens. After I prove myself things will be what you folks call normal."

Jade liked the soldier's confidence. He nodded his okay. "I don't remember your name," he said.

"Jubal."

"What's your other name?"

"I don't have no other name," Jubal said.

"I've already hired one deputy the committee don't know about. I don't know about two but you can pick up some reward money. There's wanted men passing through. Some of them work for the cowmen but don't go looking for them."

"I need money," Jubal said, without complaint. "Things cost me more than they do other folks."

"The other deputy is a young hot-head and I don't know that he can be trusted," Jade said. "You'll need to ride herd on him without him or anyone else knowing it. And look out for yourself until you know whether he will stand with you."

"I been wet nurse to white officers who saw me as a shield," Jubal said.

"Okay. Cody is his name. Don't hit him or hurrah him unless you intend to kill him," Jade said.

"I'll work for you, I'll die with you if has-to-be but I won't call you sir."

Jade nodded. He had never been called sir.

"That goes for everybody," Jubal said.

"Okay inside the settlement. Outside the settlement the cow outfits are the law."

"I've been outside the settlement most of my life," Jubal said.

"Don't kill no one unless you have to."

"Yes sir," Jubal said.

⤺

Jubal's earliest memory was of a black woman who took care of him. Then she disappeared. He remembered white children who teased him and a white woman who gave him extra food and clothes. He emptied chamber pots, ran errands, sometimes trick errands by the white children, and carried messages to black men who always seemed angry to see him coming. Then the black people went away.

He had to work harder for less food and then he was told to leave. Where would he go? he asked. Look for your mother. That was the first time he knew he had a mother. Was it the black woman who took care of him? No one knew. What was her name? Poppy. Pinky. Prue.

How will I find her? You'll know her when you see her.

He thought when she saw him a spark would ignite in her heart. Sparks did ignite in his heart but not in the heart of the women. Don't be claiming me, boy. I done got my own chillen to find. He found work, food, clothes, a bed wherever he could, sometimes in the woods, sometimes killing rabbits for food, eating roots and berries, stealing chickens. He picked cotton, chopped wood, carried chains for a surveyor, dug post holes.

The Army offered three meals a day, a bed, clothing and money besides. He was in an all-black unit officered by white men. It was the first family he had known.

With that family he tormented hostiles, killed them, killed their horses, burned their teepees, destroyed their food and weapons. His family destroyed a hostile village leaving children crying over their dead mothers. Other mothers had fled with the children who could run, with those they could carry, leaving some behind. He killed braves armed with nothing but knives for skinning buffalo, old men with weapons almost as old and worn as they, boys with bows too big for them to flex. He shut out tendrils of kinship with them, closing his mind to their bravery and their suffering.

Jubal rose to a position of leadership but leadership meant responsibility, something he had never had before. His soldiers did as they were told as he did what he was told. When stupid orders brought calamity on his men, he told the officers. Each time he pointed out an error he was told it was not his job to ask questions. Thinking would be done for him.

When he followed the orders of a fool that sent him and his soldiers into an obvious trap causing the death of two of them and wounding of most of the others, he did what a leader would do. He told the colonel the lieutenant was responsible for their deaths. When the lieutenant followed an insult with a slap to the face, Jubal hit the officer. Just once. He did not lose control; he represented his men. For that he was dishonored and discharged. He could get along with any man but he would take disrespect from no one.

~

"I brought Rain a dog," Cody said when he and Pancho returned to the settlement. He had what looked like a real bandage on his buckled foot.

It was a mangy, yappy dog that was as cowed and beaten as the new whore and looked no brighter. "It's not a fighter," Cody said. "I figured you wanted an alarmer."

"How did you pay for it?" Jade asked.

"It was a giver," Cody admitted. "They gave me a beer to take it."

When Jade had hunted Indians he had trained dogs for warning and companionship but had to choke to death one dog, lying on it so that its kicking didn't further betray his location. It hadn't growled but had bared its teeth and licked and snapped loud enough to be heard a long way in a stilly night. He spent the rest of the night bellying through the brush to escape and never recovered one of his horses. One dog he shot after it had been mauled by a bear. One he shot because it scattered horses he was trying to round up. One he lost to lobos. Others had died when shot by Indians for food or were trampled when he was on the dodge.

This was a brockled, mid-sized humble dog that fawned, barked, rolled over, tucked its tail and wet itself when someone made a quick movement. Jade took it to Rain. "Don't tell me if you eat it," he said.

"What else will I do with it?"

"Feed it, encourage it to hang around your house. You'll know if there's a prowler."

"The guineas tell me that," Rain said. Rain kept guineas instead of chickens because guineas were better alarms and survived longer. Rain washed the dog in coal oil, rubbed it down with tallow, fed and watered it, made a bed of straw for it and tied it outside her house.

The first prowlers were wild kids drawn by barking. Rain ignored them but untied the dog and they frolicked with it, rolling on the ground, chasing it, being chased by it. The dog left with them when they looked for other excitement but soon returned to Rain who fed it. In a few hours the kids were back. Rain gave them buttermilk and biscuits and welcomed them to the pecans falling to the ground that were hard on the outside but sweet inside like the wild kids.

The wild kids were everywhere in the settlement and they knew everything that was knowable. Few adults knew them by name and when the kids drifted away, the boys to work with freighters or cow outfits, the girls to follow freighters or cowboys they were not missed.

"We ain't scared of you," one of them said.

"Good," she said. "You can come whenever you want, pick up pecans when they fall, but never come after dark."

"Can I have a biscuit to take to my sister?" one boy asked. "She's sick and I ain't found no food all day."

Rain spread butter and honey inside a cold biscuit and

gave it to the boy. "If I hear that you ate the biscuit instead of giving it to your sister, I'll never give you another one. And you will say 'Yes, ma'am' to me."

Rain dug screw worms out of wild kids who had skewered themselves on Spanish dagger and sealed the area with jell squeezed from an aloe vera, washed their scrapes with coal oil, treated ringworm with sap stolen from the fig tree that Ruth watered diligently, gave them bark from the tickle tongue bush for toothaches, and applied a mad stone that she had carried in her medicine bag to their snake bites to draw out the poison and to their mouse, rat, ground squirrel bites to prevent hydrophobia.

⸜

When Cody met Jubal, Cody told him to get rid of whatever was left of his Union uniform, to buy a better weapon and to steer clear of cowboys, especially former Rebs. If they needed ironing out, Cody would see to it. Jubal respectfully ignored him.

When Jubal went into the saloon for a beer, Cody publicly reprimanded him. "If you want a drink you tell me and I'll ask Curly to take you one outside," Cody said.

"If you want a drink you tell me and I'll tell Curly to take you one," Jubal said, poking Cody in the chest with a finger.

Cody went for his gun but Jubal caught his arm and said. "If you want to fight let's take off our gun belts, step outside and do it. If you want a shootout let's take it outside the settlement so we don't shame Jade." Jubal towered over Cody and Cody's only chance of success was with a six-gun.

"Outside the settlement," Cody said.

"You ride out that way, I'll ride out this way," Jubal said. "Start shooting when you're clear of the settlement."

"Where will you be?" Cody asked.

"Oh, you won't likely see me. If you're lucky you won't likely hear the bullet that kills you," Jubal said.

That wasn't the kind of fight Cody wanted or expected. Furious, he went to Jade. "That deputy you gave me is worthless," Cody said. "He won't do what I tell him and when I insisted he wanted to fight me outdoors at night."

"He's not your deputy, he's my deputy," Jade said.

"I ain't taking no orders from him," Cody said.

"He will get his orders from me and so will you. If I tell you to take an order to him you will take it. If I tell him to carry an order to you, you will obey the order and complain to me afterwards."

"You hired me first," Cody said.

"You will both be approved or disapproved by the committee at the same time."

"No white man is going to take orders from him," Cody said.

"Jubal will enforce the law or he will no longer be deputy," Jade said. "The same goes for you."

Cody was not happy wearing the same brand as a black man. He and Jade would lose all respect. At least he would.

⌒

Jade was invited to a committee meeting. Before going he talked to Rain. "I can't control this country by myself and if they won't accept deputies then I'll have to quit. I need to know whether you'll ride with me if I quit."

"I've never had a place to call home," Rain said. "Even before I became an Indian my folks were always moving. I live in this house because the man who built it is dead and his widow abandoned it. Folks in the settlement treat me better since you staked out a claim. If we marry this will be our place."

⮌

Linnie was a good woman, of that he was certain. Would she have been a good wife or would she have been a buzzard like her mother, a circling symbol of death?

Rain would be a good wife. Of that he was certain. Was she a good woman? A squaw who had shared a bed with a savage? Maybe every night? How many redskin bucks? Jade knew enough about Comanches to know that when a warrior died his property was destroyed or given away, necessitating another brave, especially if she had a child. Had she loved it? Jade had rather she slept with a Mexican bandit. There wasn't much difference between them. What else could she do? Her helplessness troubled him as much as her submission.

And she gave him a choice between riding away without her or taking on the Devils country with only her at his side. He was a starving man sucking bear tits, not knowing which would get full first.

⮌

The meeting was held in the church house because there was no other building in town that would accommodate them except the saloon, and the saloon was always occupied with cowboys and teamsters getting drunk or sleeping off a drunk, and Curly didn't want to lose profits for a community cause. Wilbur insisted that the benches he had constructed be arranged in a large square. Wilbur sat between Pancho and Mick who weren't invited but also wanted Jade's protection. The committee, already unhappy at the thought of more law costing more money, were unhappier that plow chasers were present.

Jade laid out his proposition. "I've hired two new deputies and I need a shotgun for each of them. And we've never talked about my salary."

"If the stores charge taxes the stores are the ones who will be blamed," Ruth said. Ruth planned to open a small cafe next to the store, maybe with a room in the back for some decent person needing a place to stay. The settlement was getting crowded and revenues were up.

"You're the ones who want law and order," Jade said. "You're the ones who have something to lose. No one is going to break in and rob the folks on Barefoot Street. Bandits will hit the saloon or the store, maybe the blacksmith shop. Maybe all of them." Jade paused searching for a synonym for cowboys.

Parson Wilbur supplied it. "Raiders are more likely to hit Mick and Pancho." He used a soft A hoping the others would hear it and learn, but they never did. He had told Mick and Pancho of the meeting.

"Fighting, stabbing and shooting are going to be around the saloon," Jade said. "I can't guard one place without leaving the others unguarded. If you're going to keep me you're going to pay me, you're going to pay my deputies, and you'll pay for the equipment that we need."

"How are we going to pay for all that?" Iowa asked, concerned about the security of the store but not wanting to pay for it himself. "We'll have to tax everyone in the settlement. The cow bosses have homes here and they're worth breaking into."

"We have to have something to say to the folks who don't have nothing worth stealing and ain't likely to be involved in shootings," Curly said. He searched his eyebrows for a stray hair to expel.

"We'll tell them they need us," said Smitty, who planned to open a livery stable next to his blacksmith shop. "The store, the saloon, the blacksmith shop. A livery stable. Barefoot Street has to pay taxes to protect us." Curly, Ruth and Iowa looked doubtful.

"How about the church house?" Wilbur said. "There's nothing to steal in the church house and anyone shot there will be hit by a stray bullet."

"Or seeking refuge," Jade said. He did not want them to forget Mattie.

"That's old business," Iowa warned. "New business is hiring and equipping two deputies so that Jade can get back to his job."

"Tell folks that fines and half the reward money the deputies collect in the settlement will go to the settlement," Jade said. "I don't want deputies running into trouble outside the settlement. Except protection for Mick and Pancho."

That seemed to placate the committee that had a greater concern. Jade had won a battle as serious as a gunfight. He could tell Rain they had a place. "One other thing," Iowa said and looked at Ruth.

"We don't care what you do on your own time," Ruth

said. "But this settlement won't accept you marrying a squaw." Ruth laid down her opinion as though it were a shirt to be ironed into submission.

"Rain is as white as you are," Jade replied.

"She looks like a savage, she acts like a savage, she claims she's a savage. That makes her a savage," Ruth retorted.

"They are an inferior people," Iowa threw in. "Some folks don't even believe they're human and marrying one is like marrying an African."

Jade looked at their faces. They all nodded except Wilbur and he said nothing. Jade turned on his boot heel and left without speaking. "We still want you to be the law," Curly called after him.

Jade was already on his horse when Wilbur asked him to stop. "I expected you to speak up," Jade said.

"Come to the house and let me explain. Things are worse than I imagined," Wilbur said when they were inside. "The whole country has gone mad. It's like now that the war is over they miss the killing and destruction. I don't know if you and Rain can live here."

"What happened?"

"There will be no more treaties with the Indians. The government is subsidizing railroad construction and the army will kill or drive out the Indians so railroad magnates can grab their land at no cost.

"Sherman and Sheridan are going to destroy the Indians the way they devastated the South. Total destruction of property, entire villages including horses and dogs. Indians that survive will be driven into isolation and starvation."

"What are you going to do about it?" Jade asked.

"It's national policy and newspapers are supporting it."

"You talked about running for Congress and fighting for the Indians," Jade reminded him.

"A foolish dream. Politicians and newspapers have demonized the Indians. Those who regard them as children of God are mocked by those who call them savages. I would be ridiculed as trying to gain attention by pretending to prefer vermin to my own people. The only thing I know to do is to try to enlighten the people where I am. The richest and most powerful men in the nation are behind this national murder and plunder and nothing but the people can stop them.

"Indians refuse to be indentured servants so the government is importing Irish, Chinese, and other despised people to take the dangerous, difficult jobs at wages that deny them advancement or families. And newspapers support it."

"How can Rain and I marry?" Jade asked.

Wilbur sighed. "Educated people use the Bible to condemn marriage outside the circle the way they used the Bible to support slavery. If you want to stay here the only way I know is for Rain to convince everyone that she is white. She should come inside the church house. She should be baptized--"

"She has been baptized," Jade exploded. Rain stood outside the church house during services because she didn't have the appropriate clothes.

"She must do it again so that these people can see it. Tell her to buy clothes from Ruth to show that she wants to be like Ruth."

"She doesn't want to be like Ruth. I don't want her

to be like Ruth."

"I don't mean that she should be like Ruth but show that she wants to be. Dress like Ruth, ask Ruth's advice on what she should wear or how she should look, and ignore anything Ruth says about how to be."

"Isn't that hypocritical?"

"Yes, it is," Wilbur agreed. "You didn't ask me the right thing to do but for a way to do it at all. It's the way people have gotten along for centuries. The way communities and churches are formed. Everyone has to pretend a little."

Jade tried to imagine how he could persuade Rain to take advice from Ruth. A midget minute before frogs could fly.

"Rain wasn't born Indian," Wilbur said. "She became Indian by doing the way others did until she was able to think the way they did. Doing white should be easy for her. Neither of us wants her to think white if it means being like Ruth."

Jade shook his head, knowing no way he could make that possible.

"Toleration won't happen overnight," Wilbur said. "I didn't speak up at the meeting because they would have rejected anything I said and me with it and my work here would be finished. But I will make my opinion known from the pulpit. In church their thoughts are loftier. They feel kinship with each other for a little while. In political meetings every man is fighting for his own advantage. To have spoken there would have made me your partner rather than their parson trying to speak to the conscience of the community."

Jade went directly to Rain's house. "They will pay me and hire two deputies," he said.

"Should I plan a wedding?" Rain asked.

"We need to talk about that. Give me a couple of days to figure out how to say it."

"Say it now."

Jade faced her directly. "I can't stay if I marry an Indian."

"To this place I will always be an Indian."

"Not if you try to be white," Jade said. "We can make this work."

"How?"

"You showed them your white belly once to prove that you weren't an Indian. You have to show it to them again, but in a different way. Be pretty in an American way. Make your face as white as you can. Show less skin. Wear lace around your neck, long sleeves to cover your arms, and stockings. And shoes."

"When I am washing and ironing?" Rain asked, incredulous.

"When folks are around, leaving clothes or picking them up and such."

"What's wrong with my neck?"

"Men will be attracted and women will think you are advertising yourself."

"Advertising is bad."

"Advertising is necessary but using parts of a woman's body for advertising is bad."

"Attracting men is bad?"

"You can smile. Whisper. Look at them from the

corner of your eye. Bat your eyes. Pay extended attention to them. Require their assistance when sitting, going up or down steps, carrying things. Be afraid of snakes, frogs, grasshoppers so men can defend you. Pick foreign objects from their clothing above the waist. Give them a playful slap. But not too much of any of these."

"Attract attention without advertising?"

"Yes," Jade said, pleased that she understood. "And don't be outspoken in public. Tell me what you think and let me tell them. Show deference to men, even to me when we are with others. Stand at my side and do whatever I tell you." He could see that she rejected all of it. "Only when others are present."

"That's the way white women act?"

"Well, most of them act like that at home too."

"What about Ruth? She says whatever she wants."

"They have accepted that. They allow it because Iowa allows it. After we marry I will allow it if you still want to do it."

"Why wouldn't I want to speak for myself?"

Jade believed it best not to respond to that. "Don't point a gun at someone unless you mean to kill them."

"I don't. I would have killed anyone who tried to enter my house to harm Mattie."

"Try not to point guns at men. It's not lady-like."

"You wanted me to stand beside you with a shotgun."

"I still do," Jade confessed. "When necessary."

"Who is this woman you are talking about?'

"It's you. Can you try? Once they accept you as white then you can go back to some of your ways."

How would she become one of the white people when there was no place for her in the settlement? "I need to be alone," Rain said. "I need to think what the grandmothers would say."

⟜

With the crotch-stick, Cody hobbled to the general's house to see Cletis. "What do you want?" Cletis called, refusing to go out.

"I don't have a gun," Cody said. "I thought we'd go to the saloon, get things straight between us."

"Step up on the porch so I can see if you're armed and have a seat if you're not."

Stepping up on the porch was a strain on his swollen foot but Cody did as he was told. Cletis came out. "I ain't armed but my mama is inside and she knows how to shoot. I ain't wearing a gun because I don't know how to use one."

"If you need someone to back your play I'm your man," Cody said.

Cletis was surprised and suspicious. "Why would I trust you?"

"Because I work for the law now. You're going to learn the law and you may come back here and say what the law is and tell the law officers what to do about it. Your daddy's cowboys will protect you outside the settlement but your trouble will come from those inside it. I don't plan to be a deputy forever. I want to work for someone who's going places."

Awkwardly, Cody stood on one foot. "Come with me to the saloon and I'll show you how things will be."

Cletis thought that over while Cody waited. "Mama, I'm going with Cody."

Cletis' mother came out of the house with a rifle and the will to use it. Cody wondered how she had begot Cletis but he didn't doubt she could use a rifle.

"I've shot savages," Caroline said. The cruelty and brutality of the West repelled her but it didn't shock her. She had watched Yankees burn down her home, sack and pillage their plantation. Some of the soldiers had led female slaves into the woods. She wanted to tell the women they didn't have to obey Yankees but she could not. "If something happens to my boy I won't wait for his father to set things right. He'll shoot you dead but I'll shoot you to pieces starting with your manly parts."

"Yes, ma'am," Cody said, his hat in his hand.

On their way to the saloon, Cody picked up the six-shooter and gun belt he had hidden in the brush. "I'm on the job now," he told Cletis. In the saloon, he rearranged chairs, pointed Cletis to one and took one facing him, placing the six-shooter on the table. "Don't worry about no one behind you," he told Cletis. "You tell me if someone gets behind me." Cletis nodded.

"A beer for me and one for my pard," Cody yelled at Curly. "And put it on the settlement's tab."

"It ain't authorized," Curly said, holding the beers where he stood.

"I'm authorizing it," Cody said. "No, hell no, I'll pay for it. You're looking at the future of this place and I'm buying in."

⌒

Rain followed the creek until she reached the place where she had once gathered mustang grapes for jelly before they became Ruth's product in Iowa's store. She sat under the thick vines and the trees they grew in and listened to the creek hoping to hear the grandmothers speak, her thoughts entangled like a buck with its antlers caught in the brush and a hunter nearby. The more she thrashed the more entrapped she became. She wanted Jade to be the sacred stone in her medicine bag, the father of her children. But to marry Jade she had to give up what she had been. Why didn't he defy them? Why didn't he fight for her?

He would want their children to be white, for her to forget her Indian ways. Skull Cap was gone. She had mourned him for 15 days and then at sunrise and sunset until the leaves fell from the trees. Now she would allow his memory to die.

How could she forget Brave Little Bear? Fetching his father's horse while Skull Cap painted his face, dusted his body with dirt from a gopher hole, and rubbed buffalo tallow on his hair because Rangers were near? Forget the way Little Bear sat the horse he had taken from soldiers? How proud he was when he brought her meat and a buffalo hide?

She wanted to tell her children of Brave Little Bear as they played on the buffalo hide that she made into a robe and used as a rug. How he had been the brave who protected her after Skull Cap was killed. After Little Bear died, only the grandfathers remained to protect the village.

Rain understood that she could not return to the people or the traditions of her husband and son. She understood that any white man could have killed Little Bear who celebrated the ways of his people. It might not have been Jade who shot him, but could she become one with people who denied her memory of another life, another husband, a son? Indians had also killed boys. She had accepted that because they fought for their people, their culture, not to take someone else's land and to destroy their memory.

She knew she was born white. She remembered her mother and father and how she loved them before the Indians killed them. Her brother had almost spontaneously become an Indian. She had rejected Indians and their ways until her anger and hatred had been overcome by the love of her Indian mother. And then by the love of her Indian husband. When Little Bear was born she knew her heart would be Indian forever. But her heart loved Jade too and to marry him she would accept paleface ways. She chose to be Indian, she could choose to be white.

Rain returned to the settlement and went to the store to tell Ruth she wanted to be white. Ruth eyed her critically. "It's going to take more than clothes but we can start with that." Ruth picked out under-things and a dress that Rain could fit to herself with pleats, plackets and gores. On Sunday Rain had to ask Jade to help her dress. She dared not ask how he had acquired such skills. Sporting a bonnet to disguise the haircut Ruth had given her, Rain went inside the church house with Jade. She wobbled in high heels with cotton stockings although no one could see them beneath her long, ruffled dress.

Ruth was proud of her handwork. "She almost looks civilized," she whispered to Jade. Others looked at her as though she smelled bad.

⌒

Jubal went to the saloon for a beer. Four Augur hands standing at the bar began to talk about the smell. "Whooee," one of them said. "Smells like a black blue belly." They moved from the bar and sat at a table.

"Look at the way he struts in them blue pants. Hard to tell if it's a man or a woman."

"Look at the color of that jacket," another said. "Matches his gums."

"Ooo, ain't that a six-shooter he's carrying? Wonder if he's ever fired it.?"

"I've killed your kind before," Jubal said, "so make your play."

One man went for his gun but Jubal shot him before the gun cleared the table. By then the other three had stumbled from their chairs, pulled their guns and started shooting. Jubal wasn't trained to be the first to fire but he was steady, deliberate and deadly. Three Augur hands were dead. The other dropped his gun. Curly counted four bullet holes in the only wooden wall of the saloon. None had hit Jubal.

"They're trained to talk big, not to kill," Jubal explained to Jade.

"They were in the war, in the cavalry," Jade said.

"Yeah, but someone was giving them orders," Jubal said. "I wasn't facing four men, I faced one man four times."

⌒

Rain prepared an organized meal and invited Jubal

and Cody who were tired of their own cooking. Cody was used to chuck wagon grub and accepted whatever he found. Jubal was accustomed to army chow at the fort or campfire cooking when on patrol. He and other Buffalo soldiers used their meager pay to spice up their mess hall meals and an occasional rabbit, antelope or deer to sweeten campfire chow. Rain had stirred eggs from her guineas with diced jerky that she had soaked in beer and feared they could tell the difference between guinea eggs and hen eggs. She had tried to sell guinea eggs but only the lungers and the beaten bought them. White folks ate hen eggs.

Jubal and Cody either ate alone or took turns cooking but mostly it was biscuits, bacon and beans but rarely all three at the same time. They made no complaints at Rain's meal and she was relieved. Rain was determined to organize another and better meal and she would invite Hannah and Wilbur. Jade was pleased at how ordinary and white it seemed.

⌐

The settlement had progressed enough for a professional gambler with skills adequate for whiskey money but not enough to avoid getting shot. Cody killed the first one. When Jade heard the shot he went to the saloon with his shotgun and saw Cody faced off against three men who could be Tejano cowboys from Jefe's wagon or pistoleros looking for easier work. Jade studied their faces and hands.

"Is the dead man your compadre?" Jade asked. They shook their heads. They had drawn their guns because

Cody had drawn his. "Then holster your guns," he said holding the shotgun to his shoulder and aiming at the fastest looking one. Jubal parted the canvas curtain behind them and stepped in holding a rifle. The three holstered their guns, swearing in Spanish.

"If any of the money on the table belongs to you pick it up," Jade told them. They stared at him believing if they reached for the money they would be shot. "Cody give them what's theirs," Jade said.

Cody handed money to each of them. They pocketed it without looking at it. "In the settlement you'll be treated fair," Jade told them. "Break the law and the law will break you. Now vamoose. This fandango's over."

Jade explained to Jubal and Cody. "Gunfighters are never killed by someone in front of them, someone they can see," he said. "Sarge, Brine, Segundo aren't back-shooters but they're not going to back down either. Those in the card game were Tejanos. Good cowboys and loyal to Jefe. Treat them square and you'll have no problem with them. Watch out for the pistoleros, those just passing through, maybe eating at Jefe's second wagon where it's safer than sleeping in the open. Segundo ramrods the pistoleros. He won't allow them to cause trouble if he can help it but he can't trust them any more than you can. They can't trust each other. Keep them in front of you. And learn to tell pistoleros from Tejanos."

"How do we do that?" Cody asked.

"Get to know them," Jade said.

"I don't exactly savvy their lingo," Cody said.

"Study them. They don't all look alike and they don't all speak Spanish. A man who works with horses and cows has hands that are rough, calloused, cut, scraped and bruised. Gun work don't cause calluses. A Tejano's got a different complexion from a man who sits indoors and studies mischief. A man who's dodgy acts different than a man who ain't," Jade said.

"What does a man who's dodgy look like?" Cody asked.

"Like me," Jade said. "Always sleeping light, always looking over his shoulder. A shotgun is more effective than a six-gun close up or in a crowd so until you get yours you can use mine when you need it."

"Why does Jefe have a second wagon?" Jubal asked.

"So the pistoleros don't ride for the Augur," Jade said. "They'll ride, steal or kill for anybody. They don't belong to no brand, they don't make friends and they don't take chances."

"What we have here are plantations of the West," Jubal said. "You have the Tejanos who kill or die for the brand and the pistoleros who kill or die for the money. Kind of like the Confederacy. Hard to know which is most dangerous."

"My pa died for the Confederacy," Cody said.

"How many slaves did he own?" Jubal said.

"None."

"What did he die for?" Jubal asked.

"For what was right," Cody said.

"That's the most dangerous kind," Jubal said.

⌒

Wilbur searched the law the way he had been searching the Bible. He said there had to be an inquest regarding the gambler's death. Cody testified that the gambler was armed and was cheating at cards so Cody shot him.

"How much money did you lose because he cheated?" the parson asked.

"Forty-one cents," Cody said, still mad enough to spit blood.

"You killed a man for forty-one cents?" asked Wilbur who had seen men in pine paneled boardrooms steal millions of acres of land from Indians, tens of thousands of dollars from unwary consumers, hundreds of thousands of dollars from taxpayers.

"Damn yes," Cody said. "I caught him cheating."

"The gambler was armed so it was self-defense," Jade testified.

Wilbur so ruled but afterwards appealed to Jade. "A man's life is worth more than forty-one cents," he complained.

"That was before cat's had whiskers," Jade said. "If Cody hadn't killed him he would probably go right on cheating."

⌒

Jade had Smitty make Cody a wagon-bow stirrup so that Cody could get his misshapen foot in it and gave him a horse so he had freedom to ride but Cody disappeared for a few days at a time without telling Jade. "Putting you back on a horse may have been a bad move," Jade said.

Both Jade and Jubal had looked for Cody during his disappearances fearing he had been killed or had shucked his star to work as a gun with one of the cow outfits. "You work for me," Jade said, "And you will report to me when and why you leave the settlement. If you've been cold-ironing someone's cattle I'll lynch you myself."

"Hell, I have to have some time to myself, see my pards," Cody said. "I don't have no money to loaf here. And I ain't stealing no damn cattle."

There was no office for the law so Jade and his deputies took turns in the saloon. Trouble festered around the saloon and the shack behind, especially when pistoleros, Augur Rebs and Rat's Ass scrubs were rubbing elbows. Dutch, a German immigrant, had fought with the Union and that stain clung to his cowboys. A careless slight or imagined insult converted into gunplay.

Jubal had seen a half-box in a saloon in Mexico where a guard sat overlooking the patrons. Curly was prospering and he ordered a real bar to replace the boards over sawhorses, and lumber to enclose the saloon. Jade told him to order thick planks for the half-box and iron plates to cover the inside of it. "And you're paying for it," Jade said.

When built, with a loophole on each side if the gunfire was aimed at the box, Jade or one of the deputies armed with a shotgun stood in a chair and stepped over the half-wall and into the raised box when traffic got heavy or voices were raised. Curly and his axe handle were in charge of fights. The shotgun was in charge when guns were pulled and the law took no sides, aiming at whoever held one. When the saloon was enclosed by wooden walls no one standing outside could draw a bead on the man in the box.

～

The settlement watched Rain's attempts to be white with amusement. "Squaw woman pretending to be white," they whispered when Jade was not around. Jade and Rain asked the parson to marry them secretly believing the settlement would accept them living together as long as they didn't threaten the taboo about mixed marriage.

"My authority to marry you comes from the congregation, the ones from whom I will have to hide what I have done," Wilbur explained. It was dangerous for him because some day what he had done would become known. Nevertheless, he married them in his home with Hannah and Jubal as witnesses. It was the right thing to do.

Their first evening together they spent in Rain's house, and then Jade's shack fearing knowledge that they were cohabiting. Before daylight Jade returned her to her house to wash clothes and tend her garden, pigs, guineas, plow horse and cow, skirting the settlement and watching to be certain no one was skulking in the darkness. The excited dog told everyone they were coming. Nevertheless, they kept the dog because after Rain had started her washing it was up to the dog, the guineas and the wild kids to warn her of danger.

They switched houses frequently and irregularly under cover of darkness to make it difficult for night riders to shoot them where they slept. In Jade's shack they could drop into the hole in the dirt floor if there was shooting. In Rain's house the creaking of the floor told tales of Jade's future.

Rain wondered if this was what their life together would be. Always half-hidden from others. Maybe if she had ridden away with Jade they could have lived a life without violence. Where would they have gone to find it? By encouraging him to return to the settlement she had doomed him to the kind of life he had--preventing violence by being more violent than anyone else. Once he had turned to violence there seemed no way out.

She did not like the name Jade but others liked it for the reason she didn't; Jade meant paleface with hell in his neck. When they were alone she had called him Riley. Now, in public she avoided speaking his name whenever possible and remembered to call him Jade until she thought of him as Jade.

She did not love Jade as wildly as she had loved Skull Cap. Jade did not love her as achingly as Skull Cap had. That was to be expected. But there was something practiced about Jade. Skilled, but also planned. The fine edge of love dulled by meaningless sex in casual encounters with prostitutes and other loose women. He had lost the wound of love as he had lost the soul of death. Killing was no longer its own terrible and everlasting hell, dulled rather than heightened by replication.

⤸

One night when they were in Jade's shack beside the hole he had dug in the dirt floor Jade heard a horse running toward the shack. Jubal had his shotgun so Jade picked up the Winchester. The rider shot a hole in the roof. Jade ran outside with the Winchester and knocked the shooter off his horse.

Jade approached the man cautiously but when he turned the body over he saw that it was one of Dutch's greeners and he was dying. The kid caught Jade's hand

and held it tightly until he could hold it no more. "Mama," he said. "Hold me, Mama." It was worse than the first Indian Jade had killed.

At the inquest Curly and others who had been in the saloon testified that Doby had gotten drunk, spent a few minutes with Girl and was riding back to the wagon with his tail up.

Jubal testified that there was a bullet hole in the shack that hadn't been there before. "Likely the kid didn't intend no harm but a man has to protect his home," Jubal said.

"Hell, Doby, or maybe Dopy, was the best kid I had," Dutch said. "A serious kid who loved being on a horse rain or shine. Took pleasure in doing a good job. He came to town on a lark, tasted some fruit he'd never tasted before, got drunk and shot at the shack out of exuberance at the new world he had discovered. Shot at the shack because it was there with no thought of who it belonged to. I wish it hadn't happened but there's nothing can be done."

"Could you have just shot at him as a warning?" Wilbur asked Jade. Wilbur was troubled that the secret marriage had caused a man's death and by memories of a Yankee soldier who never went home, whose wife and child never knew what had happened to him, killed by a boy.

"There've been a lot of threats," Jade said. "I can't permit shooting in town, particularly when someone shoots at my house. I would never be able to sleep safely."

"Could you have shot him in a less lethal way?" Wilbur asked.

"It was dark, he was riding away, I shot at body. That's the shot I had. I'd have been happy to hit the horse."

When Jade and Dutch were alone, Jade said, "I'd like

to do something for Doby's ma. At least tell her what happened."

"He drifted in, ate at the wagon, stayed on to work," Dutch said. "He called himself Doby, Dopy. I don't know whether that's a first, last or nickname. I don't where his folks live."

Rain also grieved Doby's death, remembering squaws who never knew what happened to their sons or husbands, sometimes their daughters, who never came home; squaws who never gave up hope that they would see them again. "I'm not sleeping in the shack anymore," she said. "I don't want to live like this in fear. We live in our house and if we die we die in our house."

Jade appraised the idea. He had lived in fear a long time. And alone, always prepared to kill for fear of others. It would take time to change but he would try. "Jubal and Cody can use the shack for a bunkhouse," he said.

❧

When Pancho's family made an infrequent trip to the store, Jubal went inside with them to see there was no trouble. He bought some of Ruth's cookies for Pancho's boys, mounted them on his horse and gave them a ride through the settlement. The wild kids followed, begging for rides but Jubal took Pancho's boys back to the store, ignoring them. After Pancho's family left, Jubal told the wild kids, "They behave. If you behave you might get a ride."

❧

The wild kids who heard and saw everything that happened in the settlement told Rain that someone had been dry-gulching cowboys as they rode back to the range. One of them rode for the general and his cowboys were going to raid the settlement in retaliation.

Jade doubted the story. Spud and Reese had ridden for opposite brands in an earlier range war but now both rode for the Augur. They agreed the feud was past but each surveyed the other with suspicion. Each wanted the other to move on but feared that the one who left first would be regarded as a coward.

Jade believed that was behind Spud's death. Cletis was in school in Waco and Jade had no way to send a message to the general until he saw an Augur cowboy in the saloon holding a drink in his shooting hand. The cowboy shot holes in Jade's theory. Spud and Reese had ridden to town together and left with three others from the same brand. Spud stopped to relieve himself and was shot by someone from the settlement. When his riding mates went back to look for him, his body and his horse were gone.

Jade didn't think anyone in the settlement was brazen enough to start trouble with the cow outfits, but the days of the back-shooting seemed to be roughly the times when Cody disappeared for a few days. Jade talked to his deputies.

Cody confessed a nasty habit of watching for wanted men, following them when they left the settlement and bushwhacking them. To claim the reward he took the bodies to Fort Clark, Fort Concho, Menardville, the settlement at abandoned Fort Chadbourne, whichever trail was likely to show the fewest of their compadres.

"You followed two pistoleros outside the settlement and ambushed them?" Jade asked Cody.

"There were four of them," Cody said. "I knew they would head straight for the wagon so I left ahead of them and waited. I got two of them, the other two split up and fogged it."

"And Spud?"

"He was with his brand mates. I followed them hoping to catch him alone and I did. I shot him, tied his body on his horse and rode for Fort Concho. If the others came back looking for me I was long gone."

"What did you do with the horses?" Jade asked.

"I brought them back and turned them loose with the bridle hanging from the saddle horn figuring they'd be picked up by someone. Two of them showed up in Smitty's trap. I don't know how he explained them."

Jubal was more discriminating. He had shot only one man who was in the settlement and Jubal gave him a chance to surrender.

"The settlement gets half of any reward for those killed in the settlement," Jade said. "They get all the reward for those killed outside the settlement."

"That ain't fair," Cody said. "You said I could keep reward money."

"I thought you was smart enough to not go outside the settlement and start a fracas you can't stop," Jade said. "Now it's coming to the settlement. You are going to be in the saloon when they come. When you hear their horses, get outside in the dark."

The saloon's finished but unpainted wooden walls cut down on the amount of information the wild kids gathered but Jade believed the night riders would come on a moonless night, have a couple of drinks, leave, wait for the settlement to close down, then come back. When six Augur hands rode into the settlement on a stormy night and left after a couple of drinks, Jade believed they would return.

"I'll put Rain in the shack behind Curly's saloon with her shotgun," Jade explained. He didn't think anyone would shoot Girl and it was a safer place than Rain's house. "Jubal, I want you outside the store. I'll take Rain's house.

"They may just shoot up the sky as a warning. They may shoot up the buildings as a stronger warning. Don't shoot unless you have to. If they go in Curly's saloon we all converge on the saloon. The first one there runs off the horses. That should be you, Cody. There's not but one way in so we ain't going in because there's only one way out. If they come out shooting then shoot to kill. If they want to talk, I'm their man."

It was long after midnight and the saloon had closed early. The only one inside was Curly who was in the box. Cody waited outside. The cowboys rode through yelling and shooting up the sky. When Rain's yapping dog chased the horses one of the cowboys shot it. Then they rode around Jade's shack and came back. When one of them fired a shot at the store, Jubal dropped his horse. The cowboys rode out of town with two of them riding double. No one was hurt.

Iowa complained about the hole in the store that also punctured some airtights that splattered a bag of flour. Curly complained about the dead horse close to the saloon and believed Iowa should have to dispose of it. Iowa said he was the victim and the riders had earlier patronized

Curly's bar. Curly paid Smitty to drag the dead horse out of the settlement and charged it to the settlement. Jade confiscated the saddle.

⌒

When Rain had opened the door to the shack behind the saloon a man yelled, "Occupied." She had to roust him out with the shotgun. He got up with a grunt, pulled on his hat and drawers and with his pants, shirt, coat and boots in his hand backed out into the storm with Rain's shotgun in his belly.

"I'll pay," he begged. "Just let me stay. I don't want to ride back to the wagon in this wind and rain."

"Put on your slicker," she said and closed the door.

Rain had seen Girl wash Curly's clothes and her own in the creek regardless of the weather. She hadn't tried to befriend her because being Mattie's friend had put Rain in the same tepee as Mattie and she was trying to convince everyone that she was white. But in Girl she saw herself--alien.

'What's your name?" Rain asked.

Girl trembled in fear of the wild woman with the shotgun.

"Where are you from?" Rain asked. "Do you want to leave this place?Where would you like to go?"

Rain was convinced Girl had the mind of a child unable to understand what had happened to her. Perhaps that was a blessing. Not knowing what else to do, Rain lay beside Girl and held her like a mother would. She wondered if there was a way to deliver Girl and others like her from life as an animal for the gratification of men. She could think of nothing.

When Girl turned toward her and tried to snuggle in her arms, Rain realized Girl was pregnant and must be terrified not knowing what was happening to her. "Pregnant," Rain said. "You are pregnant." Girl showed no understanding. "Baby," Rain said, patting Girl's belly. "You are going to be a mama."

"Ma-ma?" Girl asked, making a smile for the first time. "Ma-ma?" Rain believed Girl thought Rain was her mother.

⌒

Rain and Jade talked to Wilbur and Hannah about Girl's pregnancy and how to get her out of her situation. Wilbur knew no way except sending her to an asylum for the insane. None of them wanted that. And none of them knew how to talk Curly out of his property. When Wilbur asked Curly to set Girl free Curly's best offer was for the church to buy her.

Rain and Hannah told Curly that Girl needed to stop work before she or the fetus was injured. Curly agreed to stop selling her when it was necessary, meaning when cowboys, soldiers and freighters found her pregnancy inconvenient or unattractive. At that time he would remove her from the shack but only if they took her in.

***

Pearl, a wild girl Rain had treated for ringworm, told Rain that the cowboy who shot her dog was in the saloon. "Are you sure it's the right man?" Rain asked.

"His horse knocked me down when he rode away," Pearl said. She was shoeless, wore a thin dress with long sleeves and shivered from the cold. Rain drew her in the house and put moccasins on her. Rain had store bought shoes for church but preferred moccasins for home and the washing she did for coins. Rain placed the buffalo robe over Pearl's shoulders. "It's warm," Pearl said.

"It's too big and heavy for you," Rain said. It was all she had of Little Bear that she could hold in her hands.

"When I grow up I want one just like yours."

"When you grow up there won't be any buffalo," Rain said. "What were you doing at my house after dark?"

"I'm scared of thunder and lightning," Pearl said. "There wasn't no one at home so I came to sleep with Pooch."

"In the rain?"

"We were on the porch until the shooting started and we heard horses coming this way. We hid behind a bush but Pooch ran out to bark at the horse that jumped over the bush and I saw the man who shot Pooch."

"Show him to me," Rain said.

It was cold but bright and sunny and the door of the windowless saloon was open. "Squat down like I'm tying your moccasin," Rain said, and Pearl squatted. "Take a look-see in the saloon and describe him to me. Don't point and don't stare."

"Damn squaw is going to have ever nit in the settlement wearing moccasins," someone said loud enough for Rain to hear.

"She damn sure won't have to teach the little devils how to steal," another said to laughter.

Rain took a quick look inside the saloon to identify the man who kept his pants up with belt and suspenders and sported a blue bandana around his neck and a

Montana high crown hat with a pinch. They all wore flannel shirts, leather vests and mackinaws except the dog killer who wore a buffalo calf coat. "Let's stand," Rain said, leading Pearl to the store.

Rain bought Pearl a cookie but made her take it outside to eat it. Soon Pearl was surrounded by other wild kids. Rain bought a cookie for each of them, took the cookies outside and handed them out one by one as they walked past the saloon. When the cookies and the kids were gone, she walked back to her house and picked up her army Colt revolver rather than the shotgun Jade had given her. She walked back to the saloon and pointed the six-shooter at the cowboy. He slowly stood, his arms away from his sides. "Show me your horse," she demanded.

They went outside and the cowboy pointed out his horse. Rain shot it in the head where it stood and then pointed the Colt at the cowboy who had his own gun half-way out of the holster. "That's the penalty for shooting a dog," she said.

"How am I going to get back to the wagon?" the cowboy asked.

"The same way I'm going to get a new dog, I reckon."

"Whose brand was it?" Jade asked when he learned of the incident.

"Augur," Rain replied.

"That will cause trouble for the whole settlement. And they're going to fault you," said Jade, who also faulted her.

"Why didn't you tell me Pearl was at the house?" Rain asked.

"Because I was afraid something like this would happen. Why didn't you come to me? They're never going to accept you as a white woman now. Shooting a cowboy's horse is like stealing it."

"If they'll never accept our marriage then there's no reason to keep it a secret," Rain said.

They planned a church wedding. Wilbur agreed with relief.

***

Rain made herself a simple rose-colored dress with a rolled collar and fitted waist tied with a bow in the back. She washed and ironed Jade's best coat and trousers, a new white shirt and a blue bandana for his neck. The wedding and reception were in the church house. Hannah made punch with powdered ginger, water, sugar syrup, yeast and lemon extract. Rain bought a cake from Ruth for the adults and made molasses taffy for the wild kids.

Not many came for the wedding. Pancho and Mick and their families, Curly who needed protection from Jade and tolerance from Wilbur. The general's and the dutchman's families came to the wedding out of respect but left before the reception to indicate their independence. The wild kids were there because of Rain and for the refreshments that they took outside and waited for the others to leave. Hannah gave them what was left of the cake and punch and thanked them for being respectable.

Some stood outside the church house to register their disapproval of the wedding. Cowboys, Iowa and Ruth, drifters who had no interest in the settlement talked about mongrelization of the white race. Most of the men were armed but Cody and Jubal stood outside the church house with shotguns.

Jade had rented Iowa's sidebar buggy runabout, Rain and Hannah had decorated it with ribbons tied into bows, and Jade and Rain rode to Rain's house with Jubal and Cody as mounted escorts. Inside they waited for the shivaree.

Rain studied the difference between the public marriage and the secret one, different because she understood better what was required of him and of her. Jade needed her to soften his wounds, dull his appetite for death. He needed her womb to immunize the savage poisons of his genitals. Skull Cap had wanted those things too. But Jade wanted more. He wanted her to deny who she had been. That she could not do. Rain wanted to be the heart of his life, to bear his children. But there had been no children. She prayed they would come soon.

Metal spoons banged on pots and pans, men sang ribald songs off-key. Jade invited everyone in, except the wild kids. Some who had stood outside the church house came inside Rain's house. Rain offered them Hannah's punch, with dark rum or without, cookies she bought from Ruth, and pies she had made. Jade watched them warily. So did Cody who was in the house and Jubal who was outside it "because he was harder to spy in the dark," Cody said.

Rain took the taffy outside for the wild kids and after the adults left Rain gave left over cookies to the kids and told them to take them home to their families. Rain allowed Pearl to lick the dishes for reclusive sugar. Then she and Jade slipped out of her house and rode to Jade's shack.

Unknown to Jade, separately Jubal and Cody decided to watch for night riders outside of Jade's shack. There was shooting but no one shot at the shack and Cody and Jubal remained there all night. The door, window and the corner around the bed in Rain's house showed bullet holes, her wash pot was dented, a buffalo horn cup and a china cup were shattered. Some who had accepted Rain and Jade living together were unable to accept them living together as husband and wife.

⤳

Jade rode his morning scout through the settlement. Rain had delayed building a fire under her wash pot until the snow stopped. When she looked outside she saw a small band of Indians at the springs. Mostly squaws with a few old men and fewer scrawny, shivering children, the buzzard-bait horses their commissary. The wild kids saw them almost as soon as Rain and ran to tell everyone.

When Jade heard the wild kids and saw citizens hurrying to the roundhouse with guns, he raced his horse through them to Rain's house. He saw her with the Indians. They showed no weapons but huddled together to share the little warmth provided by their frail bodies held together by parasites. Their freedom gone, they were trying to get to Indian Territory where they would be allowed to live. Victims of the subtle torture of the palefaces.

The Indians told Rain that buffalo soldiers and palefaces had burned their villages, killed their husbands and sons, killed their horses and dogs, took their sisters and daughters. Only a few old men, women, girls and boys who had hidden or run away had survived and they were freezing. "Build a fire. I'm going to make biscuits, hoecakes, gravy and anything else I can find."

Instead of doing as Rain instructed, Jade stationed

himself between the Indians and the whites in the roundhouse to prevent shooting between them. When the wild kids reappeared, Jade set them to gathering wood and starting a fire. Some of the Indian children joined them in picking up wood but avoided being within hitting or throwing distance.

When Wilbur heard of the Indians' plight he thought his time had come. Many times he had mentally preached to Congress, to presidents, to throngs, reciting the wrongs the nation had done and pleading the cause of the Indians. He had prayed for a platform from which to aid the Indians, a larger church, a place in the Legislature or Congress. Then he had remembered Jesus' prayer, "lead us not into temptation." That platform, that power could be the temptation that led him to destruction.

Perhaps the arrival of the Indians was the reason he had been sent to this place, to reconcile the Indians and citizens and find accommodation that could be a model for the nation. He went to the roundhouse and asked those there to contribute food. "Jesus asked us to feed the hungry, to care for the sick--"

"Jesus didn't mean savages," Ruth said. None of the Christians wanted to feed Indians. "We don't want them here," Ruth said.

"If we give them food we'll never be rid of them," Iowa said.

"They're going to Indian Territory but they can't get there on empty stomachs," Wilbur explained.

"That's blackmail," Curly said. "We can't go back to our homes until they leave and they won't leave until we feed them."

"They already attacked us once, tried to burn down

the settlement," Smitty said. "Get the cowboys here. What more reason do we need to kill them all?"

"You'll have to kill Jade first," Wilbur warned.

"Why is he protecting savages when we pay him to protect us?" Curly asked.

"Because he married one," Ruth replied. "In the church house and you did it," she said pointing a finger at Wilbur.

Wilbur rode back to Jade to report. "I bought what flour, cornmeal, lard and milk I could from Iowa," he said, leaving unsaid that only the lure of money persuaded Iowa to sell food for Indians. "I started Hannah making biscuits."

Jade dug into his pockets and gave Wilbur the money he had. "If you see my deputies, tell them to report to Rain and bring their shotguns."

When the saloon closed Cody had spent the rest of the night with Girl. Jubal had slept in Jade's shack. Curly spent a cold night in soogans behind the bar.

Jubal reported first and Rain told him to butcher one of her pigs. Rain fried the meat as fast as Jubal cut it up. When Cody came she told him to take the liver and heart to the Indians knowing they preferred it raw. Cody was squeamish about handling warm, raw and slippery organs until Rain shamed him into it.

"A calf would be better," Rain told Jubal, but not even the law dared kill a branded calf.

After Cody had delivered his cargo to the Indians, Jade sent him to get Pancho and Mick. Mick brought another pig and eggs. Pancho offered a mutton and more eggs. Both came with pails of milk.

By midmorning the Indians had milk, cornbread,

biscuits, gravy, eggs and fried pork, and an audience of a few men who had come to the fire fully armed and the wild kids who watched hungrily as the redskins filled their bellies. By noon most of the settlement was in the audience to gawk at the savages up close and talk about their smell, the sorry condition of the three horses they had, how dirty they were. "Beggars," the palefaces complained. "Why don't they work like we do?" they asked.

A few cowboys came to see the red devils. "Look at them now," they crowed. "Look at that horse. They've gone to stealing the poorest horses they can find." One of them yelled at the children. "Hey kid, where's your pa? I think I planted him at Buckhorn Draw." "It was me and it was in Dark Canyon," another said. Others called out to the squaws. "Where are all your men? You so ugly they all left?" "You looking for a man? I got what you want right here." "Take squaw woman with you," some yelled when Jade wasn't watching them. The taunting became so savage that the store keepers looked for someone to do something. Most of their wives left.

A former muleskinner gimped his way to the springs, aided by two former soldiers whose lives had also been altered by arrows. All three winced at every step and sometimes gasped through their teeth in pain but savored one last triumph over the subjugated savages. A couple of lungers also staggered to the fire with the female relatives whose duty it was to care for them.

"I hope you red devils die," the muleskinner yelled. "I hope ever last one of you rots in hell for what you done to me."

Jubal had ridden back to Jade's shack, put on his blue

belly uniform except for the insignia and rode between the Indians and the cowboys. The cowboys turned their taunts to him. Cody wanted to get in the fight but Jade stopped him. Jubal turned his horse toward the cowboys and at an angle slowly pushed his horse toward them until they backed up. One by one they left. Jade believed Cody had learned a lesson in crowd management.

Rain started another fire to smoke meat that hadn't been cooked. Hannah and Wilbur gave left-over prepared food to the wild kids.

The audience remained as Wilbur talked to the Indians with help from Rain. He promised to start a school for them. He told them about Moses who freed the Hebrews from slavery in Egypt, and Jesus who freed men from their sins.

"Was Moses Egyptian?" they asked.

"No, he was from the Hebrew tribe."

"Was Jesus a paleface?"

"No, like Moses he was a Jew."

"Then we must find an Indian Moses or Jesus to free us," the grandfathers said.

The audience grumbled threats and one by one left the meeting, the entertainment over, replaced by politics. Jade stayed.

"An Indian could not set Indians free," Wilbur warned. "That chief would likely be killed."

"Was Moses killed?"

"No," the parson said. "But Jesus was. He died for your sins."

"Then we should seek the God of Moses."

"It's the same God. God protected Moses."

"Why didn't God protect Jesus?"

Wilbur looked at Rain for help. It was so simple. Yet, there was so much to explain. "God sent Jesus to be killed for our sins, yours and ours."

"Can Jesus save us from the soldiers, from the Rangers?"

"Not at this time," Wilbur confessed. "The Hebrews were in Egypt for many moons before Moses saved them from the Egyptians. Many moons before God turned Pharaoh's heart."

"Can Jesus turn palefaces' heart?"

"Yes," Wilbur said. "Already he has turned some white men's hearts but they are far, far from here."

"Will we find such white men in Indian territory?"

"You will find a few," Wilbur said. "You will find more white men who have turned their hearts to trinkets that glitter, like coins." He turned to see if the store keepers were listening but they had all left.

Wilbur and the Indians powwowed for a long time, the Indians telling of the Great Spirit and Wilbur explaining that the Great Spirit was the God of Jesus. "Perhaps white men have come so that you may know the Great Spirit of Jesus."

"Before white men came we were free to worship the Great Spirit as we wished," the Indians argued. "Now we learn of the Great Spirit of Jesus but we must worship as palefaces worship."

Both Cody and Jubal came to see if Jade wanted one of them to take his place but Jade refused to leave. The outcome was too uncertain.

Wilbur prayed for the words to explain. "There are false gods that do not free people but enslave them," he said. "The land, the sky, the water, the buffalo are not gods. They are things made by God."

"Why do white people who have been freed by Jesus kill for the land, for the water? Do they kill buffalo because buffalo are false gods?"

"White people do not worship the land and water. They covet the land and water for themselves. That is a sin. It is a sin to take what belongs to someone else. It is a sin to destroy for profit what others need for survival. Jesus forgives us of those sins and Jesus will forgive you for killing people to preserve your way of life." Wilbur knew he was getting confused and again looked at Rain for help.

Rather than giving him words, Rain asked a question. "Are guns false gods?"

"Guns, arrows, spears, clubs, knives, rocks that one relies on for safety are false gods. There is no safety in this life for whites or Indians. The only safety we have is our faith in God."

"Didn't Jesus believe in God?" the Indians asked.

"Yes," Wilber said. "Jesus believed in God. Jesus was the Son of God. Jesus gave up his security in order to give new life to men."

"Where is this new life?" they asked. "Where can we find it?"

"You have to find it in your heart. You can't find it in this world until Jesus' followers act like Jesus."

"Will you be our Moses and deliver us?" they asked.

"I will start with my people to teach them love and justice," Wilbur promised. He rode over the trail again and again but the Indians' faces were clouded with doubt when he and Rain left. Wilbur had prayed so long for a chance to preach to the Indians but the meeting was a disaster.

"I didn't know what to tell them," Wilbur told Rain, Jade and Hannah. "God must first set Christians free from greed and vengeance. Until we see the harm we are doing to others made in God's image there will be no peace."

Wilbur saw no way that he could lead the Indians to freedom and equality through the Gospel. When he talked to the ranchers, preached in the settlement they stopped their ears and hardened their hearts. He would have to go farther from the Indians, farther from settlers who demanded free land as the Indians did. As far as Washington, D.C.? Not as a parson but as a representative of white people who tried to represent all people?

That was the temptation to personal glory and public power that could lead to his destruction.

"Have you lost faith in your message?" Jade asked.

"The message of grace is clear and certain. But forgiveness is far from these people," he said of those in the Devils country. "The Hebrews were in Egypt for 400 years before Moses delivered them. There was slavery in America for generations before God could turn men's hearts. The Indians are being starved out and driven out because that's what people want. I don't know how long it will take."

"Would it have been better for everyone if we had killed them all?" Jade asked.

"Forgiveness is hard for them, too," Wilbur said. "But if they can't forgive us they will be a beaten people, forever at the mercy of white Christians."

"And if they do forgive us?" Rain asked forgetting

which people she belonged to.

"They have a chance," Wilbur said.

Cody was ready to kill the Indians the way Jade had. Follow them, pick them off with the Sharps. Hurt them enough that they didn't return.

Jubal said he had killed hostiles for the white man but he wouldn't do it again. Jubal feared and respected Indians. He swore he would never allow himself to be captured by Indians, whimpering out his life like the lieutenant who sent men to death to cover his own cowardice. Yet Jubal had killed Indians for those who treated him as they treated the Indians, as their creation to preserve or destroy according to their pleasure. "They were tough," he said. "If they had what we had, the battalions, the bullets, the cannons, Gatling guns, or maybe just the buffalo, I don't know if we could have ever beaten them."

Late that night Rain took the buffalo robe she had made from the hide Little Bear had given her and placed it on the shoulders of the oldest grandmother who gathered it to herself like a vestment. She looked up at Rain with eyes the color of clouds trying to see the Indian in her.

The Indians spent the night in the snow and by first light they were gone, leaving nothing but filth in the snow and something to talk about for weeks afterwards.

It was the last chapter of their story. Jade saw in their future a glimpse of his own.

Chapter Two

Organizing the Devils Country

With the Indian menace gone, the cow outfits built houses on the range to get their families out of the settlement and into the country where it was cleaner and safer for women and children.

When the general moved his family to his ranch headquarters, in addition to a house he built a ranch store, invited a blacksmith shop and a lumberyard, allowed a saloon and a church. A settlement called Rebel Town sprang up like the early settlement at the springs. And Caroline had a new house with columns like the one the Yankees had burned.

The disfigured gold and silver that Caroline had saved by fire, and the loss of the troops' own heritage kept them together as they rounded up every stray cow and horse they could find until they reached the Devils River country, sometimes having to defend their claim with their guns. Three men, former Rebels like themselves, and one woman died trying to hold on to whatever the Yankees hadn't stolen or destroyed.

"Get your chins off your saddle," Sarge told the other riders on the long ride to Texas. "I don't want no hangdog soldiers."

"Tell them, Sarge," the general commanded.

"We ain't defeated. We didn't surrender. We didn't quit. We didn't give up our guns."

"We're going to Texas to fight in a different way," the general said.

The soldiers yelled hurrah. Some had families and hoped to rejoin them someday but for now they followed the general as they had done during the war. Some vowed to follow him to their death. Newer hands moved on. The older ones stuck together in a knot that grew tighter as they aged.

⁓

The Rebel Town church had a preacher from the general's own heart. Brother Gabriel believed abolition was a foreign notion grafted to a war for dominion. He was a tall, parched man who walked with his head down, his neck thrust forward on the warpath against evil forever before him. He had never married or had need to. The sins of the flesh were never as tempting or fulfilling as the pleasures of righteousness.

Those who had called the general the Big Augur because he didn't "augur" with anyone but made pronouncements like they were writ, began calling Brother Gabe the Augur because he would augur with a tumbleweed and run alongside it to get in the last word for there could be no compromise with evil.

"A cowboy is self-reliant," Brother Gabe preached. "He don't need or want help from nobody, especially some gov'ment." Augur top hands were paid less than Jefe's or

Dutch's. "A cowboy is resolute, he is resourceful, above all he is loyal." Brother Gabe had been a Confederate chaplain urging the boys in gray to give their lives for the noble and virtuous South. Now he called on Augur cowboys to give up better wages and chances for families because cowboys were loyal to the brand, whether it be a cross or an auger.

Few cowboys had families. That was especially true of Augur hands. Some had been too young to marry before the war. Some had lost families during or after the war. Sarge's wife said she had found her own life while he was fighting the war and had no intention of giving it up. That was the problem with women; they had opinions and the war gave them options.

Gabriel was not the name Brother Gabe was born with. He named himself after the Angel Gabriel who would sound the last trump. Gabe aimed to prepare people to hear that trump. He had first blown that trump for the Confederacy calling down God's wrath on the godless Yankees. According to some Brother Gabe had drawn his sword and dispatched wounded Yankees with a prayer for their godless souls.

"How do I know the Bible is true? Because Jesus' disciples deserted when he died. They didn't believe Jesus would be resurrected. The same is true of some who fought for the holy cause. They have surrendered to the Yankee class warfare that will make us brothers to black slaves and other inferior races and deny us the wealth that we had before Lincoln stole it. They have surrendered because they don't believe the South will be resurrected and they have gone astray their own way. Well, God bless them now because they will not be blessed when they discover the truth. The South Will Live Again."

The few Augur hands who left for better wages were called "turn coats," "deserters," and "gray pretenders." Whenever they met Augur hands, there were slurs, auguring, fist fights and one suspected murder. Swede, a former Augur Rebel, became a top hand for Dutch and disappeared. Dutch was subject of custom-made contempt because slavery was repugnant to him and he fought for the Union. When Jade asked Augur cowboys if they knew what happened to Swede they said he went to Washington to become a politician. That always provoked laughter from Augur hands.

Dutch also had a small settlement around his headquarters. Some of his cowboys had married wild girls and built houses for them near headquarters. Dutch opened a store and saloon and encouraged his cowboys to do their shopping and drinking there to avoid scrapes in the settlement that had already gotten some of his boys killed. Dutch scoffed at Brother Gabe's notion of the "God-favored South" chastised for its lack of unyielding duty and devotion to itself.

But the divine South appealed to Dutch's hands who were too young to fight in the war but gravitated toward Brother Gabe because they too believed in cowboy virtues, especially that cowboys were knights of the range and noble heads of their families.

Jefe did not move his family to the range. His wagon and rag house were always on the move between the grass and the water holes claimed by the general and those claimed by Dutch. Besides, he tried to keep his Tejanos apart from Segundo's pistoleros. The pistoleros gravitated to the settlement for fun and Jefe encouraged his Tejanos to go to Rebel Town. They weren't accepted by the unreconstructed Augur hands but they were tolerated as long as they stayed together and didn't get in the way of Augur cowboys. When the Tejanos played cards they played only with each other.

Chuy, a pistolero, found a wife and the general permitted him to open his own saloon in Rebel Town for the Tejanos. His wife, Lupe, had worked for the Rebel Town saloon but she was wanted less when she moved her business to her husband's saloon. There were no gunfights over her.

Others came to the settlement at the springs, merchants and those who bowed their heads over a plow. Bethel Mannen, a weak but pleasant man, opened a clean, modern store with glass windows, lamps on the wall and a coal burning stove. He sold both green and roasted coffee, dry and prepared mustard, clarified and crushed sugar, and salt, pepper, cinnamon, ginger, cloves, cream of tartar and baking powder by the packet rather than the pound. And such things as the settlement had never seen before--raisins, prunes, evaporated apples, canned pears, canned oysters, salted fish, white floating laundry soap, buttermilk glycerin soap by the box, loufah flesh brushes, and real human hair switches.

Sideboards with drawers, dressers and commodes, divans with matching chairs, overstuffed sofas and shoo fly rockers. And toys. Mannen sold store-bought dolls, stick horses with horse heads, hobby horses, toy wagons, tool chests, spinning tops. Children begged their parents to visit Mannen's store where they could see the penny saver where every penny dropped into a slot caused a cowboy to raise his pistol and an Indian to fall dead. Children cried for store-bought jumping ropes, when they had hand-made dolls, stick horses, tools and all lengths of rope at home.

Mannen's wife had divorced, deserted, disappeared or died, depending on the teller. He had not remarried. His eyes were always open for his next wife but there were no good prospects in the Devils country. He helped women purchase dresses, admired the way they looked when wearing his merchandise. He allowed children to play gently with the toys while their mothers shopped. He teased the wild girls when they were in his store and sometimes gave the girls scarves, gloves, cotton-stuffed, felt-covered toy animals but in public he was circumspect.

The Widow Waller, a squat woman with close cropped hair and big hands, opened a saloon with a plank floor, lamps on the walls, and a piano. A small room behind the bar had no windows but a plank floor, lamp, candle stick, mirror and a new, clean brass bed.

There was another blacksmith shop, a barber, a lumberyard, a drilling crew that drilled small bore holes and erected windmills above them so folks didn't have to go to the springs for water. They could have water in their backyard, in the country, enough water for their horses and pets. Elvin, a flamboyant wagon seller who affected colored shirts and galluses, sold "anything that moved on wheels except a locomotive." Elvin assembled the parts and sold tools to repair the wagons.

The newcomers built stores, the old timers expanded. No longer the only store within a couple of days of hard riding, Iowa faced competition for the first time. Iowa's sad-eyes and drooping mustache denoted the injustice of it, a look that made customers feel sorry for him having to sell them food so that he and his wife could eat better than customers ever would. Furtively, mothers brought their children, especially their daughters, to see Ruth's pocked face to warn them of what would happen if they scratched at sores.

Iowa added a porch to his board and batten store but inside it remained as airless and fly-ridden as ever. Ruth kept clean cloths over her baked goods but had to lift the cloths to tempt shoppers. Others found Rain's mustang grapes but Ruth tried to claim them and made jelly to sell in the store. Jade told Rain not to go there alone after a shooting over the grapes.

Ruth expanded her kitchen into a small cafe where one could buy bacon, eggs, ham, steak, stew, biscuits, tortillas, and pies by the slice. She bought a milk cow, raised chickens and pigs; beef was always available. Mannen usually had one meal a day prepared by Ruth's hands and she hovered over him as closely as she did customers in the store, following them for fear they would run a wet finger over a sugar cone or hide a needle under their skin when they couldn't pay for it. Occasionally cowboys and teamsters paid for a meal but some days no one came.

Ruth also built a room attached to the house where a decent person could stay. Few needed a bed for the night, except for lungers and she turned them away. Once a lunger slept in a bed no one else wanted it for fear of consumption. During a skin-scouring sand storm three teamsters shared the room and she charged each of them full price for the use of it. A busted up cowboy stayed for a few days until his money played out and he crawled back on his horse and rode off with no place to go.

Ruth allowed the room to be a hospital when Hannah and Rain nursed a plow lover who was kicked by a mule. And again when a cowboy was shot, accidentally he said. They stopped the bleeding with salt and ran a silk cloth through the wound to clean it, both bought from Iowa's store. Patched up, the cowboy rode for San Felipe del Rio where there was rumored to be a Christ doctor who cured gunshot wounds with holy water, prayers and chants.

Smitty opened a livery beside his blacksmith shop to provide shelter, water and stalls for horses. Feeding, grooming and cleaning the stall was the responsibility of the horse owner . "I ain't nursemaid to no horse," he told customers. He also repaired harness and rented or sold the snipe-gutted horses he pastured in a trap behind the blacksmith shop.

There was enough wheat, corn, barley and oats grown in the Devils country for a miller. The new settlers brought dogs with them, and children, chickens, stool and bucket cows, vegetable gardens, cabbage patches. They also brought complaints from those who got there first. Mick and Pancho complained that the newcomers used the creek for a toilet. Others complained that they dumped their trash in Barefoot Street, their dogs ran loose, their cows got in someone else's garden. Jade went to the newcomers, told them of the complaints and warned them that if he returned it would be to collect for a fine and that the Council used fines to feed the treasury.

Some newcomers ate mutton, others gave pet lambs to their children for Easter. Wilbur and Hannah opened a school, first in their home and then in the church house. Rain didn't want another dog, although there were free pups. She helped Hannah with the children. The first generation of wild kids had done little to better the Devils country. Wilbur, Hannah and Rain believed the school children would determine the future.

There were frequent fights between the wild kids and the newcomers. Pancho's and Mick's children fought beside the wild kids.

The new inhabitants were blamed for rising taxes and a crime wave by those who blazed the trail.

⤳

Wilbur, Hannah and Rain worked at the school for free, but Wilbur asked the settlement to provide books, slates, chalk for the children. That request split the settlement like an earthquake, dividing those who arrived first from those who came later, those who had grown children from those whose children were young, those who thought all children should be educated from those who were willing to buy books for their children but not for Pancho's. Some included Mick's children as well.

Brother Gabe declared himself the voice of the people outside the settlement and Brother Gabe said the government had no right to tax what one man earned to support another man's wishes. Those who wanted schools for their children should pay for them. Those who wanted to ride down fancy streets should pay for the streets. Cowboys would provide their own. They wanted nothing from government and they weren't paying to be governed. Being governed meant they were slaves to the government, and slavery was something that the buggy bosses in Washington said was so bad they killed men, raped women and burned cities to stop.

"If citizens have to pay taxes for children to be educated, then citizens will decide what they learn," Brother Gabe said.

Wilbur believed children should learn reading, writing, arithmetic, and the history of their country. Brother Gabe believed children should know the story of the South and how the North had made war on the South to steal land and other private property. Others believed that children were happier not knowing all that political foolishness. Mannen said that learning to read the Bible was all anyone needed.

If Mannen hoped to curry favor with Brother Gabe, he failed. Brother Gabe said that reading the Bible was not required; the children could be taught what the Bible said about the children of Ham, that they were to be hewers of wood and bearers of water. That's all those people were good for. There was no reason to educate them. "As for the rest of the Bible, they're better off not knowing about all that meanness."

Brother Gabe didn't want to pay for books for the girls because all girls needed to know was what the Bible said about women bringing sin into the world, and bearing children in pain, and serving men. The majority agreed that children should be taught that the founding fathers created a Christian nation where white male landowners governed the country, blacks were three-fifths of a person, and states had a right to enslave others if they wanted to.

Since Wilbur and Hannah were the only ones in the settlement qualified to teach, the citizens agreed to pay taxes to support the school but Brother Gabe warned he would be watching. After the meeting Wilbur asked to speak privately with Brother Gabe, who regarded Wilbur with suspicion if not hostility. Wilbur concluded that Brother Gabe could not read or could not read well and recognized the danger of Gabe self-righteously demonizing those who disagreed with his shallow understanding of the Bible. Wilbur offered to privately teach Gabe to read the Bible.

"No sir," Brother Gabe said. "I have heard sons of Satan who claim they can read the Bible when all they do is take words and sentences apart, pervert the meaning, and handle Holy Writ until there is no life in it. And then say they understand it. I pray for hours reciting the words that I have memorized and their meaning comes to me and that's what I preach. What has all your learning got you? The Bible says you are not to be unequally yoked together and you married a white man and a savage. I don't care what color she claims to be that woman is a savage. The Bible says that black folks are to be servants of all, not a law above all. And you permit one of them in your church? You are an abomination."

Like Rain and Mattie before him, Jubal stood at a church window and listened to the services. He had been taught Jesus by the white folks he served and he had been baptized in a river. Wilbur invited him inside. When Jubal went inside he sensed the resentment of those present. He pretended to be checking the meeting for disturbances and left. Afterwards, when he came to meeting Jubal sat at the back of the building with a shotgun and pretended to be protecting them.

Wilbur discovered that Jubal had a magnificent voice

and invited him to sing to the church. Jubal sang, "I am a poor wayfaring stranger." Gabe thought it was a slave song, a begging song and that begging was evil. Jubal also sang to the school. "Ain't no grave can hold my body down." Gabe believed it was a song calling black people to rise up and slay their masters.

"We must teach children that for one man to own another is monstrous," Wilbur said.

"We are the property of God just as slaves are the property of white men. And a man can own his wife," Gabe retorted. "The Bible says so. If you don't own your wife, you're a heretic. If you do own her you're a hypocrite, believing one thing and saying another."

"Husbands don't own wives," Wilbur said. "Hannah cares for me the way a slave might but she does it out of love and a sense of duty. I have no right to require it of her."

"Heretic. There are no natural rights, only the rights that God gave us. The strong always exploit the weak, the smart exploit the ignorant, the rich exploit the poor, the old exploit the young until their time comes. That's God's will. God gave us the right to freedom and the right to deny it to others. He gave us the right to the land and not to the savages. There will always be need for a mudsill race like Indians and Negroes. God made them inferior for reasons best known to Him. That's why the Chinks and Micks are here."

Wilbur had seen it in the North, immigrants forced into difficult and dangerous jobs, paid subsistence wages that did not permit them a means of escape. Some companies required workers to buy necessities at the company store making them indentured servants. If they were injured, too sick or too old to work they were no loss; they were interchangeable parts and discarded like rubbish.

Wilbur had been taught the Southern arguments for slavery: slaves had to be cared for like other valued property. Slaves had a home, food every day, care when they were sick or too old to work. They had families; they had children who were also cared for, they had security and contentment.

Wilbur had seen enough of slavery and the aftermath of slavery to recognize the idealized portrait, but where had Gabe learned of the mudsill theory? The general? Gabe couldn't read but he had combined that idea with the false notion that Noah's condemnation of the children of Ham applied to all people of color forever.

"There's always been a battle between education and indoctrination," Wilbur told Hannah and Rain. "In the short term indoctrination wins but slowly facts slip out and indoctrination retreats to the next no-more-truth position."

⌐

The wild kids had less time to prowl because of school and homework and it took longer to get news. Jade had to abandon his practice of riding through the town. He left his horse at Curly's saloon, a central location, and walked from building to building receiving complaints. He learned to judge the temperature of the town, what unsettled the citizens, who was suspected of using rigged scales, who lied about the quality of goods. Curly complained that Jade's horse in front of the saloon was restraint of trade.

Pancho and Mick had long complained that Iowa cheated them and reported that Mannen gave them better weight and count on their produce.

Iowa complained that Smitty wasn't a trained gunsmith. Most of Iowa's gunsmithing was cleaning, minor repairs and modifications for faster drawing- -lighter trigger pull, removal of front sight and front of the trigger guard. Iowa used proper tools for such modifications but Smitty used a hammer, chisel and grind stone. Jade explained that the settlement had no requirement for licenses.

"Mannen would steal the knot from a suicide's noose," Iowa bellyached.

"Iowa won't sell me milk, butter or chicken eggs wholesale," Mannen protested. "I don't have nothing against guinea eggs but my customers don't want them. And Ruth keeps her hens in wire pens so foxes, hawks, eagles or some kid doesn't get them. That's not natural. The hens need to be running around eating grasshoppers and worms or the eggs won't taste right."

Jade had Smitty make him three sets of weights weighing exactly one ounce. At random Jade and his deputies checked the scales. The merchants agreed that the law had no right to interfere with business. If a merchant cheated after a while customers would catch on and no longer trade at that store. Business took care of itself.

A card mechanic was attracted to the growing settlement. After a few complaints, Jubal and Cody sat at a table with him and put their guns and coins on the table. The other players left the table. Jubal turned out to be the biggest winner of a small pot. They were back the next night and Cody won a small pot. One or both of them appeared every night winning fifty cents or more a night until the sharpie followed a freight wagon train to a more hospitable climate.

Men selling phony water-testing equipment showed folks a drop of well water through a microscope. Some couldn't see anything but those who could saw strange creatures with spindly legs that moved like oars on viking ships. No one wanted to swallow that.

The testers told grim tales of those who drank water contaminated by beavers, buffalo, lobos, dogs, cows, horses, and Indians. However, they had pills guaranteed to purify water. Jubal told them to move on and when they cited their rights, Cody broke their equipment including the microscope, and punched one who protested.

Jade and his deputies disarmed and removed drunks from saloons. They broke up after-school fights and arrested a man who walked into the parson's home where Hannah was teaching and removed his clothing. Hannah screamed and Rain seized a kitchen knife, forced the man out of the house and threw his clothes after him. Jade made him put on his clothes and placed him under arrest. The man explained to Jade and Wilbur that he was looking for a place to start a colony where men and women could live as God had made them. Naked and unashamed.

The idea that nudity was natural excited the town more than anything since Mattie's lynching. Wilber tried to calm folks down, explaining to them that the man harmed no one. The nudist was perhaps touched in the head to believe that naked people could live in a sun-baked land where everything dead or alive wore barbs. While Jade watched, Wilbur talked to the mob and Cody escorted the man out of the settlement where he left as quietly as he had come.

Someone stole one of Ruth's pigs. Pancho was the first suspect and Ruth had citizens in a lather. A crime wave was sweeping the settlement and citizens had better do something about it fast or no one would be safe. Jade left Jubal and Cody to keep mob fever hobbled while he checked things out.

Jade found the pig's head with a well rope around it near Pancho's house. Pancho didn't have a well, drawing water directly from the creek behind his house. Jade placed Pancho under arrest and told him he had found the pig's head on Pancho's property. Pancho asked if the head was any good. No, the blow flies had gotten to it.

Pancho yelled at his wife and told her that Jade had found a pig's head.

"Dig a pit," Aurora said.

"Tell Jade what you will do," Pancho told her.

"Pancho will dig a pit, build a fire in it, and peel the head. When the fire has burned down he will line it with maguey, put the pig's head on top of it, cover the pig's head with more maguey, build a fire on top of it, then when it burns down he will cover the pit with dirt. Mañana he will open the pit, remove the pig's head and I will make barbacoa."

By then the boys had come and the whole family was salivating. Jade knew Pancho would not have discarded a pig's head. Nevertheless, he was the suspect and Jade took him to the settlement, latched him in the roundhouse and put Jubal in the suicide hole.

Jade rode around the settlement until he found a smokehouse in brush behind the wagon seller's barn. When he opened the door he saw pork hanging inside. When he talked to Elvin, Elvin offered him cracklin's fresh from the fire.

A crowd had gathered at the roundhouse and Jade told them there would be a hearing at the church house and if they wanted a seat they had better get there before the prisoner. Then he, Jubal and Cody escorted Pancho to the church house, the three of them riding with shotguns between the accused and the crowd.

Ruth told her story of the crime wave and how what had started with pilfering by the wild kids and the new ones had turned into outright theft in broad daylight, although no one had seen the pig taken because it had been at night. "And the thief is sitting right there," she cried, pointing at Pancho who turned white. His wife and children were crying.

Some of those in attendance shouted, "String him up." Ruth screamed, "Let's clean out the whole mess so this can be a good place the way it once was." Others also embraced the doctrine that hanging a man or two could bring reform if not salvation.

Wilbur called for silence and when it didn't come, he began to pray. Prayer usually quieted the most excitable. When order was restored he asked for Jade's testimony. Jade asked Aurora for her recipe for barbacoa. She described how Pancho dug the pit and cooked the pig's head between the coals from two fires. Then she described pulling the tender meat from the head, chopping it up and wrapping it in tortillas.

"Have you made barbacoa?" he asked.

"No," Aurora said. "There is no pig's head."

"Would Pancho throw away a pig's head and keep the rest of the pig?"

She said he would not. Jade described the pig's head as he had found it with a new well rope around its neck. He asked Mannen if he had recently sold well rope. Mannen had not. Jade asked Iowa and Iowa said that Elvin had recently purchased well rope. Jade showed Iowa the well rope he had taken from the pig's head and asked if it was similar to that Iowa had sold Elvin, the wagon seller.

"Well rope looks pretty much the same," Iowa said. "I couldn't say for sure."

The audience had grown quiet and were now paying attention, trying to figure out what Jade was doing.

Jade asked Elvin if he had a smoke house. Elvin did. Jade said if those in attendance were to look in the smoke house what they would find.

"Pork," he said.

"And when I spoke to you about an hour or two ago, what did you offer me?" Jade asked.

"Cracklin's," Elvin said. "Look, I took the pig. And I'm willing to pay for it. I tried to buy one from Ruth but I wanted to butcher and smoke it my way rather than buying it a piece at a time. Name your price," Elvin said to Iowa.

Iowa looked at Ruth. She had built this knot and now he was going to have to untie it. "I don't want to see no one hanged," he said. 'Not for a pig. Elvin, let's me and you talk in private and work out a deal."

Elvin knew that privately Iowa would want the price of three or four premium pigs. "Let's settle it here so that everyone knows that we're square."

"We'll work it out at the store," Ruth said, not wanting to reveal markup.

"I'll pay you for it cut by cut," Elvin said. "Each ham, each shoulder, every spare rib, even the hide. I didn't have no use for the head but I'll pay you for that too and give the money to Pancho for his trouble."

"That's square," Mannen said.

"More than square," Widow Waller said.

What had once been a mob became spectators at a business deal, learning how trade was done by professionals. It was subject of conversation for days. It bothered no one that a man who would steal a pig because he wanted to do things his way might steal in subtler ways.

Wilbur was dismayed that citizens were ready to lynch Pancho for stealing a pig but when they discovered it was a businessman who stole it, paying for the pig was punishment enough.

⌒

When Pearl reached puberty she went into business also. Pearl was special to Rain and Rain tried to dissuade her from whoring but Pearl had to help her mother provide for the younger children. Widow Waller took Pearl under her wing with hardly more than a few slaps and a promise of a new brass bed to get her off her back in a room with younger children in the other room or a blanket spread on the ground.

Smitty, who had loved Girl, switched his affection to Pearl. Cody was also attracted to the lighter hues and he and Smitty exchanged snarls. Jade had to intervene to prevent gun play. Smitty was older but twice the size of Cody. Cody had to escalate to guns to win.

"Smitty doesn't have a six-shooter," Jade said. "He has a shotgun and no one is going to walk away in a duel with shotguns."

"Every time Smitty kisses her she gets tobacco juice from his mustache or his mouth. I told him to stop kissing her."

"If he pays for her he can do whatever he wants with her. You know that," Jade said.

Jade warned Smitty and Smitty fell in love with Girl again. But a cowboy named Eph also loved Pearl.

"He wants to marry her," Cody said.

"Do you want to marry her?" Jade asked.

"She's a whore."

"Marry or be a whore, those are her choices," Jade said. "And the longer she's a whore the slimmer the trail to something better."

"If I married her I'd have to shoot anyone who insults her or beats her," Cody said.

"I think one or two would be all it would take. Word gets around."

"I'd never know why they were smiling, what they were saying behind my back," Cody said.

"If you think of her as your wife, that's how they'll think of her."

"What if...what if she wants to go back to whoring?"

"Either you trust her or you don't. You have that problem with any wife."

"You and Rain ever talk about her life before you?" Cody asked.

"When we first met. She loved her husband. She was proud of her life. Still is."

"Did you have problems with that?" Cody asked.

"Still do," Jade said. It gnawed at his brain until his desire for her swept it aside.

"You have a woman but I don't," Cody said. He wanted Pearl but he didn't want to marry her. He warned Eph to leave her alone.

⤳

The general allowed that his son, Cletis, was not made for the hard work, bed on the ground, grub when found of the cowboy. It was a disappointment the way a drought or low prices for cattle was a disappointment, but when one trail closed you took another. And it was one for which Cletis was well suited.

Cletis went to school with two changes of clothes and a greasy sack of food. He traveled with wagoners, then by stage, then train afraid to be alone, especially at night. Cletis returned home with a horse and surrey, a lady-broke horse, a good suit, money in his wallet, and a wife. His wife came from Tehuacana. The money came from selling lightning rods that weren't grounded and a fake gold nugget that he used to peddle stock in South American gold mines. That training and his law studies allowed Cletis to assist the powerful by finding ways to do the unethical without violating the law so they could prey on those with no one to protect them.

Cletis also came home with a plan that had ruffles. With his father's spread and power and Cletis's education and political skill they could run the Devils country, maybe even the state. First, they had to form a county and move the county seat to Rebel Town. Then get Cody elected county sheriff and Cletis elected county judge to assist his father in taking over the other cow outfits. With the county in their grip, he could be elected to state, perhaps federal office.

All that stood in the way was Jade and Parson Wilbur. Jade could be voted out of office and Cody could accuse him of murdering Indians and lynching suspected rustlers, and start rumors about his scandalous marriage until Jade drifted. For Wilbur they would have to unsettle his congregation with doubts about his allegiance to popular opinion. Make preachers like Wilbur the outsiders and with Gabe's kind subvert the nation. God willed it.

Cletis and his wife moved into the house his mother had left vacant when she moved to Augur headquarters. When Cletis announced himself a lawyer, for the first time citizens knew the general's real name, Alvin Tezel. Alvin Tezel was not a heroic name. The general believed his name was the only reason he never achieved the rank. He coveted a name like Stonewall Jackson. Robert E. Lee. Even Ulysses S. Grant was better than Alvin Tezel. His soldiers and later his cowhands understood and called him general.

Folks also understood why he insisted his brand was T over Z, not Augur. Those who rode for the Skillet called it the Thumb Screw. After Brother Gabe arrived and helped Tezel hold down cowboy wages Skillet and Rat's Ass riders called it the Screw.

Cletis set about organizing the county and was named Justice of the Peace. The committee became an elected Council but they were the same people except for Ruth who was not permitted to serve or to vote at

Brother Gabe's insistence. Ruth believed the county was organized to exclude her.

The next order of business was a name for the town and a post office. Cletis recommended that the town be named Augurville as the Augur made smooth the way for the first stores and houses in the settlement. Brother Gabe wanted to honor Quantrill, "A great patriot and son of the Old South."

"Why not Bloody Bill Anderson?" Iowa snorted. Iowa had procured whiskey and whores for Union soldiers. "Or Jesse James. He was a killer and betrayed his country just like they did."

Brother Gabe pulled his six-shooter. "You will not call those who rebelled against a tyrannical government traitors. Not while I'm standing."

Jade had to step it to prevent a shoot out to decide whether Rebels were traitors or patriots.

"Why not call this place 'Gun Powder?'" Smitty suggested without irony.

"My father was the first man to build a home here," Cletis said.

"You want to name it Tezelville?" Ruth said.

Brother Gabe objected that Ruth was not a member of the Council and had no right to speak. Ruth noted that Brother Gabe was not a member of the Council either.

Ruth's womanhood stopped Gabe from pulling his gun again. "I represent the county outside the settlement," Brother Gabe declared.

Cletis warned that calling the town Tezelville around Augur hands would mean a fight.

Iowa said he was the first man to live in the settlement and he wanted the town to be called Iowa City. Curly and Iowa opened stores at the same time but Smitty worked for the Augur until he opened his blacksmith shop in the settlement, therefore the settlement could be named after him.

"What's your name?" Ruth asked.

"Tobias Porter," Smitty said.

"Tobias Town?" Curly asked with ridicule.

"As good as Curlyville," Smitty said.

Wilbur wanted something inspirational, a name that would challenge citizens to be their best. "Philadelphia," he suggested. "Brotherly Love." Seeing their dismissal of the name he proposed Hope Springs. "Hope is as heartening, as constant, as refreshing as the spring," he said.

Curly was vexed by competition from the Widow Waller saloon. Some claimed competition was good, two whores kept prices low enough for dirt farmers and cowboys. With Pearl in the back room the Widow Waller drew much of the cowboy trade to her saloon. Curly hoped when the newness wore off they would return to his saloon but a new name might help, especially if it contained the name of the new town. Brotherly Love Saloon was not it.

Pancho suggested the town should be called Jadeville. Pancho was not on the Council and he and his idea were ignored until Curly threw in with him. Jadeville Saloon would be okay. Wilbur didn't think a town should be named for someone associated with killing. Iowa and Curly noted that many towns, even counties had been named for men known for killing. Washington, Houston, Travis, Bowie. After long and pointless discussion the name chosen was Jade Town because it was everyone's second choice.

Jade Town needed a post office and both Iowa and Mannen wanted it in their store. Mannen explained to Cletis that soon the pilgrims would outnumber the pioneers and Cletis understood the math. The post office went to Mannen's store, partly for revenge because Iowa did not support Augurville.

When Iowa complained, Cletis suggested that Iowa open a bank in his store. Iowa had been unofficial banker for the ranchers, and loaned money and ran tabs for Smitty and Curly. Cletis suggested that Iowa could perhaps someday be treasurer for the town, maybe the county. Iowa ordered a bigger safe and opened a bank in his store.

There was still no jail but only one prisoner escaped the roundhouse. Leon, an Augur cowboy, got drunk, had an argument with a teamster, pulled his weapon and shot at the teamster but missed him twice before Jade and Jubal disarmed him and put him in the roundhouse. Leon escaped when someone unknown unlocked the lock and unlatched the latch. The key that was kept in Cletis's house was still in the lock. Leon stole a horse from Smitty and raced for the Augur.

Smitty's calf-legged horse wore out less than ten miles from town. Cody caught up with Leon and brought him back with a rope around his neck, threatening to lynch him. Jade placed Leon in the roundhouse and assigned Cody to keep him there. Then he talked to Cletis who was surprised that the key was gone. Someone must have stolen it.

Cletis thought the charge of drunk and disorderly should cover all Leon's offenses, including the theft of a horse. Wilbur disagreed, and if the parson had not been the only spokesman in the territory opposed to violence there would have been a fist-fight that the parson would have won.

There were no Augur cowboys on the jury that Cletis appointed but they were in the church house and outside it when the trial was held. Although Jade offered the jury protection he and they knew he couldn't protect all of them all the time and they weren't leaving the church house after finding Leon guilty of assault, attempted murder, and theft of a horse. They found him guilty of drunk and disorderly after Cletis pointed out that Leon escaped jail to return to work and Smitty's horse came home on its own.

Alvin Tezel paid Leon's fine and paid Smitty for the use of his horse. Wilbur decried the injustice to both the church and the Council but to no avail.

Someone coyoting around stampeded Augur cows and a cowboy was killed. "He didn't try to steal them, just chased them for meanness," Tezel complained to Jade. "If we catch him we'll decorate a tree with him," Tezel swore.

⌐

A bronc stomper's glory days ended with broken bones including ribs and pelvis when a horse piled him into a tree and stepped on him a few times. It took five days in a wagon to get Buck to the settlement because every bump caused him agony and every time he fainted from pain they stopped the wagon. Six men carried Buck into his mother-in-law's shack and delivered him into the care of Hephsibeth, his young, wild-kid "wife." His screams were heard in every house on Barefoot Street.

Hannah took biscuits, honey and the only pain relievers she could find--Mexican Headache Cure from Iowa's store and French Cure for Rheumatism from Mannen's store--to the cowboy. She discovered Hephsibeth wearing Buck's clothes and that Buck had been buried without ceremony or notice. Hephsibeth and her mother were memorializing his death with a feast of roasted potatoes, lamb, airtights of tomatoes and peaches. Hannah wished she had not seen it but she knew she had to tell Wilbur. Wilbur wished he had not heard it but knew he had to tell Jade, who had to tell Cletis.

Hephsibeth's mother cleaned, washed, sewed, stitched and pilfered food from houses where she worked or delivered her products. When she became too ill and too undernourished to clean and wash she continued sewing but it was never enough to feed Hephsibeth and herself. Jade discovered that Hephsibeth and her mother had nothing to eat for two days when Buck returned with broken bones and empty pockets. He died and was buried naked within an hour.

Hephsibeth had gone to Iowa's store and slipped airtights of peaches and tomatoes into her clothing while her mother haggled with Ruth over the value of Buck's chaps, boots, spurs and gun. Hephsibeth left the store first, put on Buck's clothes and under cover of darkness dug up some of Pancho's potatoes. A pet lamb followed her home, she said.

The only remedy Wilbur knew was to beg the plaintiffs for mercy. Jade didn't want to arrest Hephsibeth, a widow at sixteen. That would mean she would be in the filthy roundhouse and her mother without care. Cletis insisted that she violated the law and had to be punished like any other thief.

Wilbur persuaded Iowa to overlook the theft. Pancho pointed out that what Iowa lost was to be sold for profit. What Pancho lost was food for his family. Wilbur paid for the lamb and worked out an agreement where Hephsibeth planted, watered, weeded corn and then helped Pancho gather it to feed his family and his mules. Pancho gave Hephsibeth two rows of corn for her and her mother.

"You're auctioning off justice," Cletis complained to Wilbur. "You have given thieves license to steal."

"Had you rather Hephsibeth be in jail?" Wilbur asked. "Only God can give justice. All the rest of us can do is give mercy."

Cletis grumbled that coddling small thieves made big thieves.

꩜

Iowa's safe was scarcely installed when four desperados entered just before closing time. They gagged Ruth, stuck a gun in Iowa's face and ordered him to open the safe. Iowa refused. One of the robbers hit him in the head with his six-shooter knocking Iowa down but still he refused. Then another bandit forced Ruth's hand flat on the wooden counter, took a stolen knife from the store, thrust it in Ruth's face and locking his eyes on hers, plunged the knife into the counter. Ruth fainted and Iowa agreed to open the safe.

Because of the newness of the safe and the blow to the head, Iowa couldn't remember the combination. He did remember where he had written the combination in pencil on the underside of one of the shelves. A gunman held a lantern and Iowa read off the numbers.

After gagging and tying both Ruth and Iowa, the desperados locked the door, mounted up and rode out of town. It was almost morning when Jubal heard pounding and falling cans from the store. He dismounted to investigate but the door was locked. "Is that you, Iowa?" Jubal asked. There was more pounding on the floor.

"If that's you knock one for no, two for yes." There were two knocks. "The door is locked. Do you want me to open it?" Again there were two knocks.

Jubal dared not shoot the lock off because he didn't know where Iowa and Ruth were. He tried to break in by kicking and hitting the door with his shoulder but the door was designed to prevent such break-ins. Everything he needed to open the door was inside.

Then he remembered the side door. It was not locked. He fumbled in the darkness until he felt Ruth's belly under his hand. Ruth jumped when he touched her and he knew that could be trouble so he crawled around until he found Iowa, cut the rope and removed the gag. Iowa knew where to find the lantern and matches and he freed Ruth while Jubal rode to get Jade.

Jubal picked up the trail while Jade woke Cody, who was in Hephsibeth's bed, and told him he would be in charge in town until Jade and Jubal returned, and to gather a posse. And do it quietly. All three ranchers had money that was stolen in the robbery. The gang was likely from one of the brands and cowboys the gang encountered were likely to lynch them or allow them to escape, according to the brand. Jade wanted to keep the robbery quiet until he, Jubal and the posse had a head start.

Jade went to the store, got a description of the robbers and gathered up enough food for three days. Then he left the town to Cody and led the posse in pursuit.

It had been a long time since Jade and Jubal had been on the trail and with the anxiety there was joy in the creak of saddle leather, the jangle of the trappings, the rhythm of the hoof beats. Jade knew that if the robbers were cowboys the posse was in for hard riding through thorny cactus, octillio. catclaw, mesquite, prickly pear, Spanish dagger. Men like Curly and Mannen weren't accustomed to it and none of them were wearing chaps.

Curly had been the most anxious to see the thieves hanged because his gold and silver had been in Iowa's safe, most of it. A portion was kept buried in the cotton pad on the bed in the shack in the back where most of it was earned. By midday Curly had pressing business at the saloon. He turned back and Elvin went with him.

Mannen's store had been closed all day while curiosity seekers filled Iowa's store to hear Ruth's story and gawk at the knife hole in the counter and the open and empty safe. Mannen turned back at nightfall. The second day the wind had teeth in it. And sand. "How can I be so cold when I'm covered in sand," Jubal asked. By noon Jade and Jubal were alone but moving faster than before.

At dusk they came upon a small patch of Texas frog fruit. Too cold for the bees that made the flowers dangerous to ride through in spring and summer it was a good place to bed down in a freezing rain. Difficult for anyone to slip up on them through the icy turkey tangle, the name Indians gave to the small flowers. Jade threw his soogans under a Spanish dagger and Jubal bedded down in a small barren spot in a thicket of prickly pear. They staked their horses separately but nearby.

The freezing rain fell all night, covering the hills, prickly pear, mesquite, dagger with ice. In the rising sun the country looked lacquered. Jubal and Jade shook the ice off their canvas-covered soogans, shook out stiff joints and Jubal rustled up enough wood for a small fire to make coffee. Jade saddled the horses, rolled up their bedding, tied it to the saddles, and hunkered with Jubal beside the fire trying to get warm. They chewed on jerky, gulped the steaming coffee and mounted for another long day in the saddle.

They stopped only for the horses to water at Red's water hole and washed down jerky with the chilled coffee. Near dark they saw a campfire and approached it slowly. Whoever it was made a dry camp.

Both Jade and Jubal were accustomed to fighting Indians and moved almost silently until they were close enough to see the bandits. Jade saw him first. Segundo. There were seven others with him. Jade and Jubal backed away until they were far enough to whisper without being heard at the campfire.

"Did you see a guard?" Jade asked.

"There weren't one," Jubal said. "That and a fire don't make sense unless they're not bandits."

"Or, unless they have enough guns they feel safe," Jade said.

"I could try to take one prisoner," Jubal said. "We could learn some stuff."

"If he spoke English," Jade said. "You stay under cover. I'm going to talk to Segundo. If they shoot me, hightail it out of here and spread the word. But shoot Segundo first, the others may scatter."

Jade called, "Hello the fire."

"Quien sabe?" someone answered and Jade could hear movement as they shifted away from the fire and into cover.

"Jade."

"You're not no high grass constable out here," Segundo said. "Who's with you?"

"I had a posse but they turned back, not used to hard riding," Jade said. "Can I come to the fire?'

"Bueno," Segundo said.

Jade was relieved that Segundo wasn't holding a gun but he was sure others were. "You who I'm looking for?" Jade asked. "Fellers that held up Iowa's store."

"We're the caballeros looking for the cabrons," Segundo said.

"Got your own posse?" Jade asked.

"The pendejos ate at the wagon but no good for work. I tell them drift. One of El Jefe's Tejanos heard them talking about robbing the store and told me he saw them riding to town. We have been after them since."

"You didn't come to town," Jade said.

"They are headed for the Rio Bravo. We cut them off mañana."

"You can ride with me," Jade said.

"This is El Jefe's posse," Segundo said. "Get your own. You are no law here."

"Mañana, then," Jade said.

Jade wondered if the other ranchers had posses out looking. He returned to Jubal who was already chewing jerky. Jade joined him. "We need to be up early and ride hard tomorrow," he said although Jubal already knew.

Jade and Jubal slept apart with their horses staked out separately, not knowing what Segundo's men might do if Jade and Jubal were caught asleep.

They were both up at first light the next day and when Jade looked at their horses, he wished for the days when he had extra ones. They rode to Segundo's camp separately and saw that Segundo's bunch had already left. Jubal said, "They're taking a different trail from the bandits."

"The rough trail. Maybe planning to head them off, maybe to join them for a trip to Mexico. They could be in cahoots," Jade warned.

"Should we each take a trail?"

Either way they were outnumbered and Jade didn't think splitting up was a good idea. "Let's follow the robbers. I don't know what Segundo is up to."

Jade and Jubal ate in the saddle, stopping only to water the horses that were beginning to stumble. By late afternoon Segundo's and the robbers' trails merged. Segundo had turned the robbers into Mud Creek and chased them down the Dry Devils to the steep walls that trapped them in the main Devils River with no way to ride out. Jade and Jubal heard shooting and spurred their horses into a cautious lope. Soon, they saw Segundo and his crew standing with extra horses. They slowed and approached cautiously.

"You can have them," Segundo said.

There were four dead men on the ground. "I hope these are the right ones," Jade said.

Segundo made a sweeping gesture at the dead men, indicating they belonged to Jade. Jade examined the men, found the knife stolen from the store and the money, including Iowa's gold and silver, still in the gunny sack they had put it in. As near as Jade could tell, it was all there. He also noticed that one man likely would have survived if he hadn't been shot while lying on the ground. "You'll have to come to town if there's a reward," Jade said.

"No reward," Segundo said. "Pleasure."

"Let's powwow," Jade said, walking away from the others. Segundo followed. "I intended to arrest those men," Jade said. "Why did you shoot them?"

"They do not ride for El Jefe," Segundo said. "Everyone know they do not ride for El Jefe. We give justice."

"You ever think about being a deputy?" Jade asked. "You couldn't shoot people without justification but you'd make a good lawman."

"I ride for El Jefe," Segundo said proudly, walking back to his men, the conversation over. "Those horses belong to El Jefe."

Jade doubted that but didn't argue. The cowboys mounted up and rode away, leaving Jade and Jubal with two tired horses and four dead men.

⤚

On the second day without food and water riders from Jade Town led by Cody found them and gave them food and water. Jade gave Cody the responsibility of the dead men. An Augur cowboy rode back to town for a shovel and they buried the desperados where Jade and Jubal had left them out of the river bed. On their fed and rested horses, Cody's posse almost made it back to town before Jade and Jubal.

Jade went home and washed in Rain's wash pot. Jubal washed in Curly's barrel and went to the new barber shop for a shave and a haircut. Like Mannen's store, the barber shop had a window that faced the trail. Jade Town was becoming Glass City.

"Not hiring," Haskell said. Haskell had cut hair for the Union and followed soldiers to the South and then the West looking for a place where his poor skills had no competition.

"Need a haircut," Jubal said.

"Not here you don't."

"Ain't this a barbershop?"

"Not for your kind. Get a sheep shearer," Haskell said.

"You got something against law officers?" Jubal asked, his hand on his gun.

The barber allowed Jubal in the chair but soon Jubal said, "Pull my hair one more time and you and me are going to face-off with guns, scissors or razors, your choice."

"These hand clippers won't cut hair as thick and curly as yours," Haskell said.

"The army barber never had no trouble cutting it." Jubal said.

Haskell used comb and scissors but the result didn't please either of them and neither of them wanted Haskell to give Jubal a shave. Jubal paid Haskell but with a look that said he expected better next time. A couple of Augur hands wanting shaves had looked in, seen Jubal and walked across Broad Street to the other side, motioning other Augur hands to join them.

In retaliation for dismissing Augurville as the name for the settlement, Rebel Town had changed its name to Augurville. With two saloons in Augurville Augur hands had little reason to be in Jade Town except for diversion and diversity usually meant confrontation. "Any guns in your shop?" Jubal asked Haskell. Haskell shook his head no. "When I go outside there's likely to be trouble. Unless you want part of it go sit in a corner."

When Jubal opened the door he saw Cody who had just returned to town, studying the congregation of Augur hands. When Cody saw Jubal he understood the situation. Cody got off his horse, joined Jubal and they walked to the other side of Broad Street, their hands on the butts of their guns. "If you want trouble stay where you are," Cody said. The cowhands drifted.

"Some people hate you for the star you wear," Jade told them. "But there's a flicker of consideration before they draw on you and that gives you control of the situation. Back-shooters don't want to face the star."

⌒

Haskell complained to Cletis and the Council that Jubal was hurting his business. "No one wants to sit in a chair after a darkie sat in it, or be shaved with the same razor. If I have to provide service to people like that then I'll have to move some place more hospitable to business." Iowa and Curly said the town had to consider profits before passing regulations. Mannen and Widow Waller said new businesses wouldn't come if Jade Town weren't business-friendly. Cletis asked Jade if Jubal could go to the barber shop after the white clients had left and the shop was closed.

"If he wants to," Jade said. "If this town ain't hospitable to the law then the law will have to find some place law-friendly."

Cletis said the Council would discuss the matter in an executive meeting where only Council members were present.

Jade went to the barber shop and asked for a shave. Before sitting in the chair he pulled his gun and placed it in his lap. The barber placed Jade where he faced the window and could see anyone coming in the door.

"Things are getting quiet in Jade Town," Haskell said.

"Not quiet enough," Jade said. "But I expect this to be a quiet shop."

"Yes sir, sheriff," Haskell said.

"If anyone shoots through that window, ever, at anybody, I will shut this place down."

"I can't work and watch the window," Haskell said.

"It will be real unfortunate if you have to shave someone by candlelight after dark and someone hiding in the dark shoots someone sitting in the chair."

"I don't have a gun," Haskell said.

"I do," Jade said. "Who do you reckon is safer?"

"Me?" the barber asked.

"If you don't plan on using a gun, don't keep it around for someone else to use."

Haskell turned to Cletis, the Justice of the Peace, for protection from the law. Rain shaved and cut the hair of the lawmen but Jade thought she should not do it again. "From now on at least two of us will go to the barber with one standing in the door with a shotgun."

"No one is going to go inside with one of us standing in the door," Cody said.

"Right," Jade replied.

"For how long?"

"Until every store in Jade Town ensures our safety."

Jade also ordered Smitty to make lead slugs to replace the buckshot in the shotgun shells for man-killing. Instead of two dozen pellets, the shotguns would fire one solid slug that would mushroom when it made contact.

⌐

Eph opened the door to Pearl's room at the back of the Widow Waller saloon and saw Cody in bed with Pearl. Eph pulled his six-shooter and Cody grabbed his gun under the pillow. Both shot and missed. Eph ducked behind the wall, fired three shots through the wall at the bed where he last saw Cody, then ran through the saloon and outside. Cody was on his feet pulling on his trousers and the bullets shattered a lamp, broke the mirror and hit Pearl who was sitting up in the bed. Pearl screamed and Cody dashed through the saloon and into the street. Cody and Eph exchanged shots both missing, but leaving Eph with no bullets. He turned and ran up Broad Street. Cody shot him in the back and Eph fell. Eph got up and stumbled a few more steps and fell again.

"I'm done," Eph said, throwing his useless pistol away. "I give up."

Cody continued to advance, shot Eph again, then standing over Eph shot him in the face. "Pearl won't think you're so pretty now," he said.

⌐

Despite her wishes Rain had no more children. She wished Pearl were her daughter and believed that Pearl and Eph could become a respectable family with a place in the community and that she would be grandmother to their children. When she learned that Pearl had been killed and Eph had been shot in the face after he was on the ground she thought it was worse than what cowboys and Indians did to each other. Rain insisted something be done about Pearl's death. So did newcomers who expected such things kept outside the town.

"It was a fair fight," Jade said. "Both men were armed."

"Pearl was murdered."

"Eph was the one who shot her and he's dead."

"Eph was executed," Rain insisted. "Cody didn't have to kill him, shoot him in the face."

"Cody didn't violate any laws," Jade said.

Justice of the Peace Cletis agreed. "Nothing I can prosecute him for," he said.

"What about the boy?" Rain asked. A wild kid had been hit by a stray bullet. It was some hours before anyone discovered the boy who bled to death unseen. No adults claimed him and the other kids said they had not seen him before. He was buried in an unmarked grave beside Eph and Pearl.

"No one knows which man shot him," Jade explained.

⸜⸝

Curly hoped that the shooting at the Widow Waller Saloon and the loss of her whore would scare some of the widow's trade his way. Instead, men who had never been to either saloon went to the widow's bar because of curiosity over the shooting.

The widow, who as far as anyone knew had never been married, procured another widow, Hephsibeth, although she was not yet seventeen. Hephsibeth was tall and thin, pretty in a long-faced, long-haired boyish way. As a wild girl she had challenged boys in running and climbing the trees around the spring, fighting them over insults or scraps of food. Everyone had been surprised when Hephsibeth married Buck, although without ceremony or signing. After Buck died, Hephsibeth had no other way to support herself and her ailing mother. She was ambitious, uninterested in men except for wages and seemed more than a daughter to Waller. The widow shot a man who slapped Hephsibeth and explained to Jade that she was protecting her property. Hephsibeth claimed the man threatened to kill her if she didn't do something that not even dirt farmers and lamb lickers did.

᠆

Rain and Hannah told Curly it was time for Girl to quit work. They knew it was a good time to ask because Hephsibeth was drawing much of Girl's trade but didn't mention it; Curly already knew and they didn't want him to free her for commercial reasons. Rain said she would take Girl into her house but there was only one bed. There were two bedrooms in the parson's house and Belle was in one of them. Hannah and Rain agreed to put Girl in Ruth's rent room and to both watch over her.

Hannah and Belle walked to Ruth's rent room to visit Girl and Hannah left Belle with Girl. Hannah wanted to look in Iowa's store for a suitable school and church dress for Belle without Belle begging to shop in Mannen's store where there was fashion. A younger Belle had cried for factory made dolls, a luxury that Wilbur could never afford or permit. Hannah shopped in Iowa's store because she and Rain needed Ruth's and Iowa's accommodation. When Hannah returned to Girl she discovered that Girl and Belle were talking. Girl was not stupid. She had no education, no one to talk to, little vocabulary except for ugly words that she knew demeaned her, and even less knowledge of life outside a whorehouse.

Girl was born in a border town bordello. Her mother died in the same place and event. The madam was unwilling to throw her in the Rio as some did. There was no place to send her. Few families wanted to adopt a whore's daughter so Girl grew up in the bawdy house with the indulgence of the temporary and permanent residents and no one to play with and no one to talk to. The madam would not permit her to talk to the men and the girls talked about things she knew nothing about. The madam told her that her mother had intended to name her Beneficia but Girl had not been baptized. She did not know whether that was her name or not and had never told her name before.

Even before Beneficia bled a sporting man bought her for pleasure, his and others. He lost her in a poker game and she was misused by men of varied professions, wages, languages, colors and predilections. Beneficia didn't know how old she was but Hannah believed she was thirteen or fourteen when she arrived in the settlement. Belle taught Beneficia to write her name and Hannah helped her with numbers and English.

When Beneficia's time came, Ruth would not permit her to give birth on the bed. Rain brought the tarp Jade used to wrap his soogans in and Jesus was born on that. Rain carried off the afterbirth. Hannah suggested that

Rain bury it under the mustang grape vines, but Rain did not wish Beneficia to be clingy or fruitful. She buried the afterbirth in Mattie's grave and washed the tarp in the creek. It had been a hard birth so when Rain returned she lifted Beneficia by the heels and held her upside down to put things back in their rightful place.

Hannah explained that Hay-sous would be misunderstood and mispronounced in Jade Town and likely a problem for Jesus when he began school. Beneficia insisted his name was Jesus. Some of the bordello bouquet had told her that was the name of her father.

Beneficia slept in Belle's room and attended school taught by Rain and Hannah. Rain offered to take Beneficia's baby but Beneficia refused. Jesus was the first thing that had ever belonged to her. Even Beneficia's clothes were costumes given to her by others for their entertainment.

Curly insisted that Girl return to work and no amount of pleading by Hannah or Wilbur could change his mind. Girl owed him the money that he paid the teamsters who brought her to his place. Rain kept the baby close enough for feeding when Beneficia worked, sometimes sitting in the saloon with Jesus squalling to be nursed until some man was finished with Beneficia. While Beneficia was nursing Jesus, Rain taught her the multiplication table.

Since Beneficia's pregnancy became known there had been joking, blaming and boasting in the saloons regarding the father. Jade, Jubal and Cody had to break up fights. Some wondered out-loud what color the baby would be, usually when Jubal was around. Fewer wondered what would become of the boy.

When gossip blew news of Jesus' harelip across the

Devils country everyone believed it was Smitty's child and he was butt of the blame and laughter. Smitty punched two or three jokesters but after a few days Smitty decided he was, by God, a man and he was proud of what he had done. He promised Beneficia she would never work as a whore again and asked her to marry him.

↝

Pearl and then Hephsibeth were more spirited, more imaginative than Girl who had always been a warm corpse, and now she quit. Curly had borrowed money from Iowa to buy a real bar and put walls around his saloon. He couldn't afford to put in a floor and lamps around the walls. But without improvements, his saloon would fail. Not knowing where else to go, Curly went to Cletis for help.

Cletis almost gasped at the opportunity Curly provided. Cletis understood that victory, after a moment of ecstasy, was forgotten except for brief recalls at anniversaries and reunions that had less meaning every year. Defeat lingered and infected anniversaries and reunions that festered every year like a boil that erupted poisoning the body politic. "You need to make it more like a club," Cletis told him.

"A club," said an incredulous Curly. He couldn't even afford a floor.

"Yes," Cletis insisted. "An informal club. There are folks in these parts that don't like the way Jade runs things. Cody is with us but hiring Jubal was a mistake. What's he doing here anyway? This is not his place. I hear Hephsibeth pays Jubal to be her personal protector, if you know what I mean. Remember when Eph was shot in the face? Pearl was paying Cody the same way. But Cody is as white as you or me."

"I never did take to Jubal," Curly said. "Coming in here like he was a white man."

"And these newcomers?" Cletis said. "The widow was never married, she was a Yankee whore. That's how she got the money for her saloon. We ought to run people like that out of the country, out of the state. Pancho and Mick? Do they ever come here?"

"They buy liquor at the store and drink it at home," Curly complained. "Too good to drink with us."

"They got no right to be in this country," Cletis continued. "Where were they when we were fighting savages? The sooner we get shed of people like that, the better off we'll be. And you can start the movement right here in this saloon."

"How?" Curly asked.

"First, no membership rolls, no dues, but everyone knows who belongs and belongers have privileges," Cletis suggested. "Keep their own bottle here. Girl or the next whore free for special members. Second, say who you are. My pa kept a Confederate battle flag after the war. Put it on your wood wall, you ain't got nothing else on them. Get some pictures of heroes like Nathan Bedford Forrest, William Quantrill, Bloody Bill Anderson. Put up some signs, 'no Yankees, freedmen, Spics, Micks or Wops allowed.'"

"That would include Jade," Curly objected.

"You don't have to enforce it. Just let people know where you stand. And you can keep the dirt floor, the dim lights. Keep it homey."

Curly had never been troubled by political or religious opinions. Gold was pure good, entire, unsullied by questions of morals or ethics. Any way you could get gold was good and war had been the easiest way. He had bought his way out of the Union army and had procured alcohol and whores for troops, charging officers more than enlisted men because the officers had more money. What would be the advantage of a club?

"In a club you know who your friends are. You can make plans, share secrets. You can be an insider."

After Cletis, and Haskell the barber, Curly was the third Brother Gabe apostle telling customers that Brother Gabe said the government was giving ignorant, illegally freed slaves authority over white people, including white women. It was an abomination and the Bible said so. If Negroes were free they were free to go back where they came from.

Some from Jade Town went to Augurville to hear Brother Gabe dispute what Wilbur said. "The county has a God-given responsibility to take care of the weakest and neediest among us," Wilbur said, quoting scriptures and the Constitution.

"Every person has a God-given responsibility to take care of hisself without being pampered for laziness and promiscuity and charging us taxes to pay for it," Brother Gabe thundered in the voice he had perfected yelling over cannon fire. "The Good Book says that God made people to work and those who are too good or too worthless to work deserve whatever lot they receive. Drive them out of town. Let them live where folks have no regard for God or his laws. Citizens may have to rise up and enforce the law theirselves."

Wilbur refused to let people forget the lynching of Mattie. "That 'poor woman' was a whore who killed her own baby," Brother Gabe said. "Hanging her was justified even if it took citizens to do it because law officials failed their duty. And now we have another whore who has a deformed baby that will be a sodomite as stupid and filthy as she is. A baby named after our Savior. Some who condone that kind of behavior want honest, hard-working citizens to take care of both of them."

Iowa and Ruth got up early one Sunday morning and took Iowa's piano style runabout to hear Gabe. They liked what they heard so much that they encouraged him to preach in Jade Town. Desperate for trade, Curly offered Brother Gabe the use of his Jade Town Club in the morning when business was slow. Those present had hangovers, guilt, depression from a night spent drinking and whoring and weren't going to face the bright sunlight to avoid the shouting of a preacher.

Brother Gabe harangued from the box in Curly's saloon. God's law was greater than man's law and God's law said whores were to be stoned because they enticed young men into sin and ruin the way Eve tempted Adam into sin, ruin and death."

Curly had no whore and basked in his righteousness. Religion was a good seller, especially when mixed with politics because that's where the money was. The drunks woke up to soothe their heads with another drink. The depressed lifted their spirits, the guilty mitigated their offense, and the religious argued the rightness of their opinion with the clarity of demon rum.

Those who had a part in the lynching of Mattie, those who had done nothing to prevent it had drawn closer to

Wilbur because of unconfessed guilt. Ruth had cried in prayer and in church many times remembering Mattie and what had happened to her. Brother Gabe said that lynching Mattie had been a biblical deed. Breathing a sigh of relief they shrugged off stories of Mattie being stripped naked, of cowboys raping her while she was dying, while the wild kids cheered. They were tired of being uncomfortable in church; Brother Gabe offered them security in their goodness.

Ruth deplored the alcohol and the shack behind the meeting place, although it was empty, and was distressed when Brother Gabe said infidels were trying to make childbirth less painful, opposing God's curse that women would bear children in pain because Eve caused Adam to sin. Ruth had never borne a child, cursed with marrying the wrong man, but she had been midwife to Hannah with Rain's assistance. She believed that a less painful childbirth would be a blessing but it was a small heresy and by keeping her mouth shut she could hold it without fault.

Iowa had a more inquiring mind. Why did all female animals find birth painful, even deadly sometimes? He dwelled on that. Man was cursed to earn bread by the sweat of his brow but women also had to sweat for bread. Only draft animals and those ridden by men had the same curse as man. The other male animals were hunters or prey like men. Iowa took those thoughts to Brother Gabe. "If you believe the Bible you don't have questions," Gabe said. "The Bible has all the answers you will ever need."

The Jade Town Club was not a place for fancy dust-free shoes or work-free clothes but Cletis knew religion was men's way of keeping women in control. He took

Rowena to Curly's club to hear Gabe preach about a woman's duty to her husband. Sometimes he needed the Lord's help with her.

Other men found Brother Gabe equally useful. Gabe had never known human love, preferring the kind that God gave him and denied to his opponents. But Gabe knew women. They were weak-willed spawn of Satan who lured men from everything that was strong, manly and holy; they were the creation of God to torment weaklings.

Newcomers, some of them Yankee veterans, some of them from foreign shores, outnumbered those who remembered the Indian raid. Disabled Rebels, busted up bronc busters and freighters, the wild kids who had become cowboys and farmers, became the sullen but dangerous minority that rejected new ideas, new methods, new structures, new laws. They came to Curly's Jade Town Club to nurse a grudge against the present, feed a fear about the future, and invent the dream of a glorious and heroic past that never was.

↬

Cletis insisted that because of the growth of Augurville there needed to be an election to decide the county seat for a proper courthouse and jail. Cletis also ruled that Jefe's hands could not vote unless they could prove their citizenship. Few in the county could prove citizenship. Family records kept in Bibles were the only resource most had. Few Tejanos carried Bibles in their bedrolls. Dutch feared that Augur votes would make Augurville county seat. He told his hands to vote for Jade Town. Tezel spread a rumor by his Augur hands that Jade would require cowboys to turn in their guns when they come to town if Jade Town was elected county seat. The spark failed to ignite.

The election took place in Jade Town and Jade, Cody and Jubal kept order with help from volunteers. Brother Gabe, who wore a pistol, checked voters for feminine characteristics and overly brown skin. Widow Waller offered a free drink to everyone who voted for Jade Town and the news spread like mange on a dog.

Iowa and Mannen ran sales to lure voters to their store where they could find bargains and hear reasons why Jade Town should remain county seat. Smitty offered discount horse-shoeing and Elvin decorated a wagon and a buggy to attract viewers. Haskell announced shaves and haircuts at half-price and warned customers that Jade Town was not going to be friendly to outsiders.

The lungers and cripples on Barefoot Street couldn't make it to the polls and their wives couldn't vote. The votes by Dutch's cowboys won the election for Jade Town but nurtured a grudge against them. Cletis plotted for a rail line to Augurville to starve out Jade Town. Stores would move to the tracks leaving a virtual ghost town. He contacted a railroad company but there was nothing he could do because his father claimed Yankees owned the railroads and would have nothing to do with them.

⌯

Smitty asked Brother Gabe to marry him and Beneficia. Brother Gabe refused. She was a whore, he did not believe that her name was Beneficia, and she was not a member of the white race. Such a marriage would be illegal and obscene. The notion so outraged Brother Gabe that Smitty left with Gabe yelling curses and imprecatory prayers after him.

Wilbur agreed to the marriage and he and Smitty agreed the best place for it would be at the spring. It was a drought year and the small springs that seeped or bubbled during wet years had dried up. Only the big spring continued to flow and the trees around the springs provided shade.

The news of the wedding brought hilarity to the whole country. Cowboys and farmers had married whores before as there were few other women in the Devils country but there seemed to be something peculiarly comic about a hare-lipped blacksmith marrying a whore of an inappropriate color with a hare-lipped baby Jesus.

The ceremony took place under the trees with the spring in the background. Rain had loaned Beneficia her simple rose dress with rolled collar and fitted waist tied with a bow in the back. Rain had backslidden to her former manner of dress. Mannen came to the wedding because it was the right thing to do. Curly came to remind Girl that she belonged to him because he had paid for her transportation, more than he had paid for hauling the real bar. Iowa and Ruth were there because they, and Smitty, represented the old businessmen and they had to stick together against the carpetbaggers who came to take advantage of what others had built. But they were scandalized. "She's just a child," Ruth said.

"An old child," Mannen said. "We should hope for the best."

Cowboys and other curiosity seekers were separated from the wedding party by Jubal and Cody. Jade, best man, wore his badge and pistol and kept his eyes on the unofficial guests. Rain stood close enough to him to be considered another impediment. Hannah was matron of honor. Wilbur used Smitty's legal name, Tobias Porter, and some snickered.

After the ceremony Rain invited everyone to her house for a celebration. She had baked a cake and bought cookies from Ruth. Ruth ignored the cake and ate the cookies she had made. Some of the curious came also but stood outside the house. Rain carried cookies and punch to them.

Afterwards Beneficia and Smitty walked to his blacksmith shop that offered one dark room that smelled of coal smoke with a bed and nails on which to hang clothes. Smitty had done his cooking on the coals from the forge, and he had seen no need for improvement when he married. It was a good bed and there was a wooden window that could be opened for a breeze, and it was the best home Beneficia had known.

Jubal and Cody stood outside the shop to see that the shivaree stayed outdoors. There were the usual catcalls, whistles, songs, no fights. When Curly asked Beneficia when she would return to work, she clung to Smitty.

"Beneficia will never whore again, not as long as I'm alive," Smitty said.

Curly recruited the wife of a Rebel who had lost one arm, one eye, was deaf and had a crippled leg. Ellie was a rancher-size woman with permanently chapped face, hands scalded with harsh soap, worn by lariats, reins and horns, nails broken and ragged, but good for get that could fork a horse before they were weaned. She cleaned houses, clothes, barns, stables to feed her husband and three sickly children. Beaten down by sickness, futility, a hopeless future she agreed to work in the shack when her husband could watch the children.

Brother Gabe prayed that Curly would end that shameful business and publicly condemned him. "Who's going to feed her children?" Curly protested. "Who is going to buy medicine for her husband?" He received no response, not even from Brother Gabe. "You criticize me but I'm the one who keeps her family together, who keeps them alive."

Nevertheless, Ellie was shunned by the community, her children were harassed in school, and when her husband died few went to his funeral--Wilbur, Hannah and Belle, Jade and Rain. Not even Curly was there. Ellie and the children left with the next freight wagon train.

Chapter Three

Breakup of the Ranches

It began as a lark. The wild kids discovered a band of mustangs at the springs. Wild horses had not been seen for years. As soon as cowboys painting their noses in the saloons heard it they mounted up, shaking out their lariats. The news quickly spread down the lariat line and other cowboys joined the chase, first trying to get the horses between them to contain them while roping. The race that began at the springs moved to the range and then through Jade Town as the mustangs ran down Broad Street the cowboys after them. By dusk enough cowboys had arrived to roundup the mustangs into a tighter band to hold. Some cowboys left to buy tortillas or biscuits, canned sardines or meat that was advertised as ham, washing them down with beer. By daylight, every cowboy present had shaken a loop in his lariat and the fun began with the cowboys going after the mustang they coveted. Sometimes two or three cowboys chose the same mustang.

Folks from the town came to see the action as cowboys got their strings on the mustangs, sometimes two or three strings at a time. Some of the mustangs jerked the lariats free of the saddle horns. Some horses were pulled down, two with broken legs, and had to be shot. One mustang broke free and ran down Broad Street trailing ropes. The ropes tangled in Curly's iron hitching posts, jerking the horse down. It choked to death while two cowboys fought over who it belonged to. Another mustang was shot to settle the dispute regarding its owner.

In time there was more auguring and fighting than roping. Jade, Jubal and Cody, holding shotguns, kept up with the action riding their horses between the contenders. Already there were two broken arms, a broken leg, broken wrists, numerous broken ribs and assorted bumps and bruises, some of them spectacular.

Jade declared that the one who stayed on the horse got to keep it and the flip of a coin decided who rode it first. That gave the advantage to the first rider if he could stay on and the advantage to the second if he rode a worn down horse. Sometimes it was the third or fourth rider who got to claim a horse. Some horses were never claimed.

Dutch's scrub kids had become real cowhands but were still regarded as thumb suckers by the older men. They used their youth and their ability to absorb punishment to advantage. The Tejanos and rebels had the advantage of experience when they got the second ride or later.

It was high fun until it turned nasty. Cowboys from each of the three cow outfits took part in the competition to claim the most horses. The first losers were those either still drunk or grinding out hangovers after a night in a saloon. Those who hadn't gotten a rope on a mustang, those who hadn't successfully ridden one, and those who were injured retired to the Jade Town Club to repair bodies and spirits. Jade sent Jubal to take Rain her shotgun, get the women and children in the church house, and to tell Rain to guard it. He sent Cody to sit in the box in Curly's club, and distributed the slugs to those with shotguns.

Jade believed the cowboys would not threaten the homes of the range bosses nor burn the shacks on Barefoot Street. They were interested only in each other. He warned the storekeepers there was likely to be trouble. They could stay and guard their stores, lock them up and go home, or leave them open and go home. Those who tried to protect their stores were likely to face guns, those who locked their stores were likely to have the doors and windows kicked in. Their choice. Most left their stores unlocked and went home. Widow Waller sat in the door of her saloon, her shotgun in her lap, and warned riders that the saloon was closed until further notice. Most cowboys preferred Curly's club anyway.

Before getting in the box at the Jade Town Club Cody warned Cletis to go home where he lived with Rowena in his father's town house. Then he identified an Augur hand in the saloon and sent him to protect Cletis. Things were already at the edge of control when Cody got in the box. Arguments between the brands became fist fights. No one knew who fired the first shot.

Jade and Jubal raced their horses to the saloon and Jubal pulled down both horses for cover. They lay behind the horses and Jade told Jubal to shoot anyone who shot at them. Cowboys spilled out of the saloon to escape the gunfire inside. Two shot at Jade and Jubal and both were killed. The others raced to cover in other buildings separating into brands as they ran.

Cody came out of the saloon for air and Jade went inside. It was still hard to see because of the gun smoke in the always dim saloon. There were three dead, two on the floor dying, those with minor wounds ran. "I shot at gun flashes," Cody said. "That's all I could see."

Jade told Curly to get in the box with his shotgun. He stationed Cody outside the saloon to keep cowboys inside as there was no way to prevent them from leaving town, getting more weapons and returning to the fight.

Jade and Jubal rode to the deputies bunk house at the edge of town, dismounted, checked to see the shack was empty, and with one taking each side, they walked down Broad Street keeping their horses between them and the buildings. At each building they called for those inside to come out with their hands up, put down their weapons and go to Curly's club.

At the church house Jade asked Rain to come out to be certain no shooters were inside and the children were safe. At Mannen's store a pistolero came out shooting and Jade shot him dead. "What happens if we come out?" another asked.

"After you put down your guns you will go to Curly's where you will be safe. You can pick up your guns when you leave town. And take your dead with you."

Slowly Jade and Jubal worked their way down main street from one building to the next forcing the fighters to retreat. Tezel had come to town to see the mustangs but when the arguments and fights erupted he went to Cletis's house. Sarge led the Augur hands there, stationing them inside and outside the house.

Jefe's men retreated to the roundhouse and Jefe placed a man in the suicide hole. Segundo, who had been leading the Skillet cowboys, didn't see them ducking into the roundhouse and was caught in the open between the roundhouse and Augur cowboys in Cletis' house. Segundo fell to the ground taking what cover he could. Seeing him trapped, Jefe ran to his assistance, shooting as he came, and went down in a hail of bullets. Segundo holstered his pistol and stood up. The shooting stopped. He picked up Jefe's dead body and carried him to the roundhouse.

With the lull in fighting, Jade left Jubal and rode to Curly's club. Most of those inside were Dutch's men. He cut out the others and put them beside the box for Curly to watch. Then he told Dutch's crew to get their guns, pick up their dead and get out of town. If they were seen in town before tomorrow they would be shot on sight. "What about the mustangs?" they asked.

"They have done been turned loose," Jade said. "I don't know where or how far they have gone but they will not be chased today and they will not be caught in town."

Dutch, who had taken no part in the shooting, told his boys he would meet them at the edge of town and they would ride back together. Jade and Cody stood outside to be sure they left.

Jade returned to the roundhouse and explained the situation to Segundo. "We want to bury El Jefe first," Segundo said. "In the graveyard."

Jade agreed. The pistoleros could stay in the roundhouse if Segundo stayed with them. Jubal would be in the suicide hole. There was to be no shooting while he talked to Tezel. Jubal climbed into the suicide hole with Jade's big fifty, and Jade called, "Tezel, come out."

Tezel went out the front door and came around the

side of the house where Jade could see him. Tezel came closer as Jade approached leading his horse for cover. "If you try to arrest me my boys have orders to kill you," Tezel said.

"Jubal is in the suicide hole with the Sharps and it's aimed at you. So let's talk like two enemies surrounded by Indians. We both live or we both die."

Tezel asked about the mustangs and was given the same answer. He agreed to pick up his dead cowboys and lead his hands back to Augurville.

"I guess the brand is yours now," Jade said to Segundo, after the Augur outfit was gone.

"El Jefe don't own nothing but horses, cows and wagons," Segundo said. "We're going to drift west where everyone's not so near and there's freedom for everybody. We don't have no place here."

"What about Jefe's family?"

"El Jefe owes all of us back wages. The Tejanos will stick with me and buy in to the outfit and that money will go to the family. The others will ride for the Rio. They don't like fights where everyone's their enemy. They'll donate their wages to the family. If that's not enough we'll sell some cows to Dutch."

"How long will it take you to get moving?" Jade asked.

"A few weeks to get the cattle bunched and on the trail," Segundo said.

"Bring the cattle down Broad Street," Jade said. There was no way that he and two deputies could control cowboys from three outfits who were likely to disagree over brands. "Dutch,Tezel and two hands each can be here to cut out any of their cows. Me and Jubal will ride with you for one day out of the settlement and ride night guard with you one night to be sure there's no trouble and then you're free."

"I talk to the vaqueros," Segundo said.

The roundhouse had become a foul and fetid place from keeping prisoners there. The Skillet cowboys were glad to be free of it. One by one they came out of the roundhouse, placed their guns on Jade's tarp that Cody had fetched from Rain's house, and went to their horses. Cody and Jubal took the guns to the club for them to reclaim.

Segundo picked up Jefe's body and with the mounted Tejanos following him, carried him to the graveyard. Most of the pistoleros had grabbed their horses and vamoosed. While the Tejanos dug a hole, Segundo went to fetch Jefe's family and his buffalo robe. Wilbur came with them. Wilbur read a scripture, the Tejanos sang a song, shouted "El Jefe" three times and threw a handful of dirt on the buffalo robe spread over Jefe's body.

Jade rode to Cletis's house and explained to Cletis that Segundo was going to round up Skillet cattle and head west toward the territories. The cattle would take the trail through town. Tezel and two hands could observe Segundo's strung out herd to look for his brand. Any disputes over ownership would be decided by Parson Wilbur.

"What about Brother Gabe?"

"Wilbur lives in Jade Town." And Wilbur called Brother Gabe a company man. Wilbur had seen it in the East, men who put loyalty to an abstract organization above church, state, employees, investors, customers, sometimes their own families.

Jade and his deputies clapped each other on the

shoulder and laughed after the town was cleared. No residents had been killed, they had kept the gun smoke away from the houses and there was only minor damage to the buildings in which the combatants had sought cover. Jade was prouder of his actions and decisions than he had been since he had asked Rain to marry him.

⤶

Rain kept the children safe in the church although she feared Jade and Jubal would be killed trying to stop the gunfight that had spread over most of the town. The children went home, Jade and his deputies rode around the settlement to be certain no cowboys returned. Under cover of darkness Rain dug up Jefe's body and took the buffalo robe that had covered him. She had no fear of the night. Darkness was the Indian's ally. It was at sunrise or later when paleface killers attacked villages.

Rain reburied Jefe, carried the robe to the creek, beat the dirt out of it, washed it in the creek and hid it in bushes to dry in a secluded place. She left it for several days for the sun and wind to clean. One day when Jade returned home he stopped when he saw the robe on the floor beside the bed. He picked up a corner, examined it, sniffed it and almost said something but never did.

⤶

When he learned of the judging of the cattle brands, Brother Gabe demanded to be in on the deciding. Jade refused. It would be a religious fight with one impartial judge and one who would side with Tezel on every cow.

It was a political mistake to reject Gabe, but Jade knew he had to do it.

"The storekeepers aren't going to like bringing the cattle through town," Cletis warned. "Think of the mess, the smell, the flies. This is not a place on the trail any more. This is a town. You have to respect that."

"And I'm the law," Jade said. "You have to respect that."

Things quieted down in Jade Town with Segundo's hands rounding up cattle and Dutch and Tezel moving their cattle out of the way. Then Cody spied four men wanted for train robbery and told Jade and Jubal. They captured the four without a fight in Widow Waller's saloon. Jade feared they were with a cow outfit or a larger gang that might try to rescue them. They should be moved to the place with the strongest jail. That meant Fort Clark but three law officers couldn't take four criminals to Fort Clark and leave the town defenseless.

Jade was the sheriff and shouldn't be escorting suspects. Even with a star Jubal would likely be the suspect if they encountered others and Jubal would not be welcome at Fort Clark where he had been discharged. That left Cody.

Jade and Jubal gave Cody advice. They would keep the prisoners in the roundhouse and see they didn't sleep much so that Cody was rested and could ride hard the first day to tire them. Jade told Cody at night to tie the prisoners' handcuffs to their feet and their feet to their saddles and separate them to discourage them from trying to untie each other. Jubal told Cody to hobble only the front legs of the horses and tie the prisoners to the back legs so the prisoners didn't sleep much for fear of getting kicked by the horse.

"No fire," Jade said. "Sleep where they don't know where you are or whether you're sleeping. Rain will fix up grub that you can eat without cooking."

"And bring the reward money back with you," Jubal said

When Cody returned three days later Jade knew he hadn't gotten the prisoners to Fort Clark. "What happened?" he asked Cody.

"They tried to escape and I had to shoot them," Cody said.

"All four of them?"

"Yeah."

"You shot them dead?"

"Yeah," Cody said. "I had to shoot one of them twice. I brought the cuffs back."

"Did you bury them?"

"I didn't have no shovel. I dragged them into the brush."

"Get a crew and go bury them," Jade said.

"I figure the lobos and buzzards have cleaned them up by now."

"When did you shoot them?" Jade asked.

"First night."

"You took your time coming back."

"Well, I studied taking them to Fort Clark and collecting the reward," Cody explained.

"For two days you studied on it?"

"Their horses ran off and I couldn't find them. I had

to have their horses to take them to the hoosegow. I tried dragging all four of them on a rope but by the time I got them to Fort Clark no one would recognize them. If I got the reward half of it would go to the town Council and I'd have to split the other half with you and Jubal so I just left them in the brush."

"Close together."

"Yeah," Cody said. "I was dragging all four on the same rope. I'm going to the bunkhouse to get some sleep."

"I don't like it," Jubal said. "Do you think he collected the reward?"

"Yeah. And sold their horses."

"I shot some captured Indians but I didn't like that none either. Too close to what happened to folks back where I come from," Jubal said.

⌐

Segundo and his Tejanos drove Jefe's cattle slowly through the town under the watchful eyes of Dutch, Tezel and their two cowboys each and Iowa and Ruth who surveyed the cattle the way they followed customers in their store, determined to keep the cows off their porch.

Jade and one of the deputies minded the cutting out of suspect cows. The deputies took turns riding around the town to turn back cowboys who weren't needed and would be a worry. Cody returned from a round with Brother Gabe who insisted as a preacher of the gospel he had a right to be anywhere God needed him to be. Jade reluctantly agreed that Gabe could stay.

Fifteen yearlings with no or disputed brands were cut from the herd. Three of them appeared to have been cold branded, just enough to burn off the hair so that they looked branded. When the hair grew back they could be marked with a real brand. The other yearlings appeared to have escaped branding.

Wilbur was unable to decide the rightful owner or owners but Brother Gabe had no problem discerning the truth. Jade suggested that Segundo, Dutch and Tezel play cards to determine the winner. Each would start with five beeves, and bets would be limited to five beeves.

Gabe opposed vice being used to determine truth. He had been trying to wean cowboys from drinking and gambling because they paved the way to theft, murder and fornication. Jade ignored him.

The three cowmen retired to Curly's club, each with two cowboys to back his play. Brother Gabe who sometimes preached in the club refused to be a silent witness. Jade put Cody in the box with a shotgun; he and Jubal stood on either side of the table and warned that they would shoot anyone who touched a gun. "Keep your hands in your pockets or your armpits," Jade told them.

As Jade hoped, Segundo lost all his calves in two deals. He and his two Tejanos returned to the herd that was already past the town. Tezel won three of Segundo's calves and one of Dutch's, leaving Tezel with nine and Dutch with six. Dutch won the next pot giving him nine and Tezel six. Dutch lost the following hand betting on an inside straight and he was down to two. Dutch threw in the next hand when he didn't have a pair. As the loser, Dutch and his cowboys left town first. After Tezel and his hands returned to headquarters, Jade and Jubal switched from shotguns to rifles and joined Segundo's crew moving west.

Segundo had driven the cattle hard once they were free of Jade Town, not just to put distance between the cattle and the town but to tire them so they were not so eager for freedom. He planned to drive the cattle hard for the first three days and then ease up after they reached good water so the cattle could graze. The first night was uneventful.

After Segundo had the cows on the trail the next morning Jade and Jubal returned to town. To learn that Widow Waller had been murdered and Hephsibeth was running the saloon.

No one had seen anything. At the time of the killing, the saloon was closed and Hephsibeth was in her room. When Jade questioned her Hephsibeth said she was with a man when she heard the gunshot. Hephsibeth refused to name the man because he was married and it would destroy his family. Breaking up a family was deemed a worse crime than murdering a calico queen.

Hephsibeth would no longer work the back room because she was pregnant. She hired Salvie, a sullen girl who hated her father and would not speak to her mother. Her mother would not leave her husband because she had no place to go and no way but whoring to feed Salvie if she left him.

Salvie was young, plump and for hire. That's all anyone cared to know about her. But when she smiled she clenched her teeth and lowered her eyebrows so that she seemed in the throes of pleasure or pain and that excited some men.

⌒

A drought savaged the Devils country. With El Jefe's cowboys no longer between them, both Dutch's and Tezel's cowboys rode hard to get their cattle to the scant grass and shrinking water holes. There was trouble when the herds arrived at the same time and there were rumors of a scalawag herd coming to the country to winter. Both ranchers complained to Cletis and Jade that those cattle would suck up more of the precious water and the law had to do something; the water holes belonged to those who were there first. Even Cletis confessed there was nothing the law could do. "I don't need no law to take care of things I can set right myself," Tezel swore.

Pancho had expanded his flocks and added goats wearing bells to keep the flocks together. While shepherding he and his sons hunted and trapped lobos, coyotes, foxes, bobcats, raccoons, skunks, anything with fur. He had found a market for wool and fur in San Angelo and there were promises that with a railroad a couple of years away the market would expand. But there was no market for mutton and Pancho had more sheep than he could water.

There had already been trouble between Dutch and Tezel over the water holes and with only his boys to help with the sheep, Pancho dared not get in the ranchers' way. He brought the sheep to water at the springs upsetting everyone. "If he pollutes the spring it will poison the town and the water holes," Iowa complained. "No one knows how long sheep poison will last," Ruth added. Pancho moved his flock although he feared doom.

Pancho persuaded Mick to partner him in a butcher shop after the first freeze to sell lamb, mutton, chickens, pork, and to butcher beeves for others, but only if it wore the customer's brand. Mick persuaded Pancho to buy yearlings from shirttail ranchers, keep deliberate records and save the hides to avoid lynching. They took turns working in the shop so that the other could tend his own business. If there was enough meat ready for sale, their wives manned the shop while the men and boys tended their farms.

Dutch had his young hands pile up rocks in the rock-strewn land. His wagons transported the rocks and Dutch hired Mexicans to build stone walls without mortar starting around the water holes. The Mexicans had skills Dutch's cowboys didn't have and didn't want to learn. When bawling cattle gathered around the walls trying to get to water part of the wall was taken down and the cattle were let in. Sometimes those carrying an Augur brand were driven away. Some unbranded calves may have gotten inside the wall and their mamas driven away. At least Augur hands said so.

Unknown to Dutch, a teamster told Iowa of a wire with barbs that could stop longhorns. Iowa didn't believe any wire could stop longhorns but he told Cletis hoping to regain some of Tezel's trade. Cletis swore Iowa to secrecy and informed his father who ordered the wire for his feed store.

Dutch's hands avoided the Augurville Saloon that was unfriendly, even dangerous. Chuy's Tejano saloon, having lost the pistoleros and Tejanos had to cut prices and welcome Dutch's cowboys to have clients. Chuy's wife had left with the Tejanos.

Tezel's barbed wire escaped the attention of Dutch. All Augur hands filed claims for the best grass and water and Tezel bought the land from them with a dollar of credit at his store. When off duty, Cody accompanied surveyors laying out Augur property lines, riding the horse that Jade had loaned him for law work.

Cody explained that he needed the extra money to get married and the surveyors wouldn't work without him or Sarge escorting them because someone had shot at them. Cody and Sarge agreed that the shooter wanted to scare rather than harm the surveyors but to the surveyors the gunman's intention made no difference.

"When you work for Tezel you ride Tezel's horses," Jade told him.

"You can have the horse you gave me," Cody said. "I never did like that crockhead."

"Who are you marrying?" Jade asked. He figured it was Hephsibeth since she was the only eligible woman Jade knew who was older than twelve or thirteen.

"You'll see," Cody said.

Cody returned Jade's horse and rode one wearing an Augur brand but wouldn't say whether or not he paid for it. The horse Cody returned to Jade had forgotten its learning, was shy when Jade approached, and had barbed wire scars on its legs.

⤳

A hard winter, cold but only a light frosting of snow for moisture and wind that not even slickers could break threatened the range. Cowboys not building fences carried axes to break ice so cattle could drink from the few water holes. They turned back brands that had no right to be there, but couldn't turn them all away. Cattle and sheep carcasses covered dry water holes. Some sheep were shot, some bell goats roped and led away, pied pipers leading sheep to deaths in ravines.

 With wire shredding his dreams, the boss of the scalawag herd headed them toward the Alsatian village of D'Hanis, for shipping to market. But the railroad missed the town by a mile and the inhabitants of Old D'Hanis were moving to the tracks.

Removal of the scalawag bunch relieved pressure on the water and grass but spurred fencing as sheep herders drifted in. Some of Tezel's surveyed lines paralleled or intersected stone walls Dutch's Mexicans had laid out, especially near the water holes. Augur hands were busy digging post holes and stringing wire, sometimes scattering Dutch's walls.

Dutch grumbled to Jade that it took him twice as long to get deeds recorded as it did Tezel but there was nothing Jade could do but talk to Cletis. Cletis said Dutch should talk to the government in Austin.

Tezel complained that Dutch's crews built fences with rocks from Augur land. Wires were cut, fence posts were lassoed and pulled down, there were words, threats, fist fights and some shooting but no one had been seriously injured. Then a prairie fire destroyed pastures and burned a mile of Augur fence posts leaving the wires hanging, an opening to grass and water that the general was trying to conserve for his own cattle. Dutch and nomadic shepherds were blamed for starting the fire but there was no proof that they were involved or that it wasn't an accident. Nevertheless, a sheep puncher was shot dead by an unknown person and the others moved on.

Jade and his deputies could not patrol the water holes or control the property disputes. Jade asked Cletis to write to the governor and request Texas Rangers to prevent violence but Cletis maintained that it was all talk. No violence had taken place.

⤸

Cletis informed the Council of an upcoming county election. "Yes," Cletis repeated. The county seat had been decided but next year there would be an election for county judge and county sheriff.

"Why can't the parson be declared county judge and Jade county sheriff?" Iowa asked.

"The law requires a lawful election," Cletis said.

"If that's what the law requires, that's what we will do," Wilbur said, hoping that Gabe's followers would agree with laws that were not in direct contradiction of the partial Bible that Gabe had memorized.

The Council members implored Wilbur to run for county judge. Wilbur found religion and politics like guns and gunpowder; the closer they were the more dangerous to everyone. When he served the town as parson he alienated some citizens and when he worked as justice of the peace he alienated others, but until Cletis returned there had been no one to replace him.

"I will not campaign for judge or any other political office," Wilbur said. "That would become a battle between churches, ours and Brother Gabe's."

"It wouldn't have to be a battle between churches," Hannah said.

"It wouldn't have to be but it would be," Wilbur said.

"That means Cletis will become judge," Jade argued. Even Hannah said it. "Cletis will favor his father and

Augurville."

"And if I win or lose I will no longer be a parson trying to speak for God but a judge trying to speak justice to those who will oppose me. The church and justice must never be in conflict."

"True justice," Hannah corrected him.

Rain also wanted Wilbur to run but not Jade. Jade had earned the town's respect and she had benefited from it, still an outsider but most forgot about her Indian past until she did something that reminded them. They found it difficult to look at hare-lipped Jesus that Rain brought to church but they admired her for helping Beneficia. Twice Beneficia had come with Rain but others avoided seeing her. Whether or not Jade won the election, he would be tarnished by the campaign and so would she. Jade Town wasn't the home she had dreamed of but she and Jade had made it a better place and they would continue to do so. But if Jade were elected county sheriff Jade Town would be less a home and more an office for both of them.

To her dismay, Jade said he was going to run for county sheriff. "For the same reason Dutch couldn't keep Cody or let him go. Cody is a scissorbill at deciding right or wrong. He can't get the grasshopper in his mouth and he can't swallow it. Some people are going to get hurt."

"Can you stop it?" Rain asked.

"I can try," Jade said.

"Will trying make you one of the people who is going to get hurt?"

"Likely," Jade said. He did not look forward to a long campaign.

⌒

Chuy did not leave with Segundo and the Skillet but his wife Lupe did. Chuy abandoned his Tejano Saloon in Augurville and moved to Jade Town where he wore California drag rowels on his spurs, silver conchos on his black vest, and a smile around women. With no visible means of support he was suspected of a stage holdup but Jade had no proof.

In the Widow Waller saloon Chuy fluttered around Hephsibeth and threw the drunk and disorderly into the street. During the day he occupied a chair from the saloon placed outside the door. When Cletis' wife, Rowena, walked by on either side of Broad Street Chuy stood, took off his hat and bowed. When she walked by carrying a package from Mannen's store or baked goods from Ruth's kitchen he stood, bowed and offered his assistance. She always refused but with a smile.

Rowena was small with delicate features and long hair as dark as Cletis's dreams. She was fifteen when Cletis saw her in Waco where she accompanied her father who studied a new plow while she shopped for a month's groceries. She wore a worn, too-big gingham dress and a bonnet with ruffles at the back that had once been her mother's.

Cletis was entranced. Shy around women, as an older college man he took courage in her youth and offered to place her bags in the wagon. Uneducated, uncultured, she also was shy, especially around an older, college man who could rescue her from marriage to a farmer and a life like that of her mother. They scarcely spoke as he carried her goods to the wagon. He lingered until her father returned and followed them on foot until dark.

On their next visit to Waco to pick up goods at the

train depot Cletis followed their slow-moving wagon on a lady-broke horse until they took the road that ended at her house. As a farmer, Rowena's father had to have a good eye for land, domestic animals and men. He warned his daughter about men like Cletis who needed power over others to prove themselves men.

A few days later Cletis returned, this time with a two-seat cut-under surrey. Her father would not permit her to ride in it but did permit her to sit on the porch and visit with Cletis.

Rowena scarcely spoke but she listened attentively as Cletis told her about his father's house in the settlement and his ranch with thousands of cattle and hundreds of horses. She was frightened when he told her about the Indian raid but he assured her that he and his mother and grandfather had been safe and the Indians were unlikely to return. If they did, she would be secure in the roundhouse with the other women and children.

Rowena was suspicious of those she believed knew more of life than she did. That qualm did not encourage her to learn but to fear them and the worldly prowess they might have. Cletis's clumsiness appealed to her and made her less apprehensive. When he proposed to her she quickly said yes and promised to implore her father to say the same.

Rowena's father was as wary of education as she was. He required Cletis to tell him what he intended to do with all that learning he had. Perhaps he would like to teach in the college in Tehuacana. Cletis told of his father's loyalty and that of his troops during the war. Their loyalty led them to serve Tezel as he moved west and became a rancher, rich in livestock and faithful hands but poor in land and money. As a lawyer, perhaps a politician, Cletis intended to change that.

With some misgiving Rowena's father watched her marry a licensed lawyer in the country church they attended where the pastor, like Brother Gabe, could neither read nor write but had memorized all the scriptures it was necessary to know. For the rest, the pastor trusted God to give him the holy words.

Rowena was fascinated by the chivalry of Chuy, dark skinned, dark clothed but with silver outlines. Although she did not speak, she did give him a sideward glance and could not hold back a smile. One day he gently took from her a package she carried and escorted her home. She was entranced by the stories he told of the places he had been. Promenades. Dancing. Sunrise on mountain tops. Rivers that fell into the sea. It was her most exciting day in the settlement.

Cletis told Cody he wanted Chuy's attentiveness to Rowena stopped. When Jade shot him in the foot Cody had lost faith in his reputation and his quick draw. Eph had gotten the drop on him and that was enough to convince him not to take on Chuy face to face.

Cody waited until Jade was visible on the street then went to Chuy outside Widow Waller's saloon and told Chuy he was to stay away from Rowena. That meant no standing, bowing or carrying packages for her. He was to avoid her presence. "You'll be safe as long as you stay inside a saloon," Cody sneered.

⌒

Jade walked along the street, looking into stores.

When he looked into the barber shop he saw a cowboy in every chair, four of them including the barber chair where Brother Gabe was perched. When Jade opened the door, Gabe stopped preaching and everyone looked at Jade. The cowboys had their hands on the butts of their six-shooters. Gabe appeared to have a gun under the barber's cloth.

"Boys, it looks like the good Lord has placed the enemy in our hands," Gabe said.

Jade pulled his six-shooter, pointed it at Brother Gabe and said, "Drop your gun belts or the Brother dies."

The cowboys unbuckled their gunbelts. Gabe's gun fell to the floor. Jade left.

Jade told Jubal and Cody to keep an eye on Haskell as he seemed to be part of Brother Gabe's gang of secessionists. Rain cut his and Jubal's hair. Cody campaigned from the barber chair as Haskell cut his hair.

⌒

Dutch's stone walls were ineffective, expensive in time and reputation. Augur horses could jump over Dutch's stone walls for water and Augur cowboys could scatter Dutch's fences and cattle but Dutch's horses and cattle could not get to water unless his cowboys cut the wire.

Dutch had ordered wire through Iowa but Tezel stopped or delayed freighters carrying the wire. Tezel charged the freighters were trespassing on his land and had damaged his fences. That required the teamsters to find a way to cross the creek twice with heavy wagonloads of barbed wire and some day it would rain again. The battle moved to Jade Town.

An argument between Tezel's and Dutch's cowboys turned into a gunfight that raged for some minutes and caused a lot of smoke and some damage to Curly's saloon until stopped by Jade and Jubal. One of Dutch's hands was killed and one Augur cowboy was shot with the bullet breaking his arm. Jade believed the arm would have to be amputated but the cowboy's riding mates tied his arm to his chest, put him on his horse and they rode back to the Augur.

Cody arrived after the shooting was over.

⤚

When Hephsibeth became pregnant folks expected Cody to marry her. Cody spent a lot of time with Hephsibeth and he talked of marriage with the bride going unnamed. When Chuy was inside rather than outside the saloon Chuy was with Hephsibeth but Cody threatened anyone who said it was Chuy's baby.

Cody had long mocked Smitty for marrying a whore that every cowboy in the county knew better than Smitty did. "What kind of man has to marry a whore?" Cody asked.

"I'm a decent man and that's what a decent man does," Smitty said. "You poked a baby into Hephsibeth's wound but you're not man enough to marry her and be a father to your kid."

"Hell, you should have let the whore leave the harelip kid in a gully and forget where it was," Cody said.

Smitty knocked him down and Cody pulled his gun and shot Smitty who was unarmed. Jade took Cody's star and placed Cody under arrest but did not pen him in the roundhouse.

"He knocked me down and he would have stomped me to death," Cody said. "What else could I do? You weren't there to protect me."

Cletis agreed that it was self-defense and told others that the arrest was political. He refused to prosecute Cody and said he should continue his work as a deputy. Jade refused. Cody and Cletis appealed to the Town Council.

Smitty was an old-timer, a founder of the town. That he could be shot down by someone carrying a badge troubled those on the Council. They believed those who arrived first should receive special treatment. With the argument going against him, Cletis moved to a new subject. What should be done with Girl and her baby now that Smitty was dead? Some refused to accept Beneficia's name or that of her son.

Wilbur said the church and the town should care for them and quoted scriptures regarding widows and orphans. Certainly Beneficia and her baby qualified. Brother Gabe said sin should not be rewarded. "The whore is in the sorry shape she is because she chose to be a whore and that brought her the God-given child as punishment. The hare-lipped kid is the consequence of her sin and that of Smitty. It would be a sin for others to reward her for it. We'd all be better off if the Devils country were clean of her and her kind."

"You call that civilization?" Rain asked appalled at the malevolence toward Beneficia and Jesus. She was shouted down because women had no right to speak at the Council meeting. Wilbur said the Council and the county should consider the root cause of prostitution. "Mothers who have been deserted by the children's fathers cannot support themselves otherwise. Some fathers want families but are unable because of poor wages."

"God prospers the righteous," Brother Gabe said, "but the wages of sin is death."

Curly complained that driving whores out of town was restraint of trade. Iowa suggested that whores be taxed. Curly and Hephsibeth decried special taxes and interference with the economic development of the town. "Tax whiskey sold by the bottle from the stores and remedies for male weakness and female complaints," Hephsibeth said. Hephsibeth was ejected from the meeting.

Cletis recommended that Girl and Hephsibeth be arrested and fined on a regular and equal basis to aid the town's always troubled treasury. Ruth favored the plan and also wanted fines on those arrested for fighting and drunkenness. Like Rain she was shouted down and threatened with removal. Wilbur and Gabe agreed that taxing prostitution would be licensing it.

Agreement was reached that the whores would be fined. Those jailed for fighting and drunkenness would have to pay for their food while jailed. A further compromise was that Cody would continue as deputy but only until the election.

Gabe stopped Wilbur after the meeting to point out that moderation was a sin. "To pamper a whore is no different than being her pimp."

Wilbur pointed out that Jesus said that those who did not feed the hungry, clothe the naked or care for the least of the community were doomed for the same eternity as Satan and his angels.

"You can't trick me with your warped beliefs. That

was a judgment of the nations."

"Does that mean all Americans go to hell or just those who oppose feeding the hungry, clothing the naked, caring for the sick?"

"No sir. No. The Lord has spoke to my heart and you will not tempt me with your corrupt, satanic scriptures. Jesus told his followers to take up the sword that means against all those who think they can compromise with evil. No sir. Compromise is evil."

⌒

No one knew whether Smitty was just another client to Beneficia or whether she cared for him either before or after he married her. She refused to give up Jesus but had to return to Curly's shack. Rain sat with Jesus in a corner of Curly's club when the weather was unpleasantly hot, cold, windy or wet. That was almost every day. No one bothered Rain because they were afraid of Jade but sometimes she had to listen to Brother Gabe.

"That baby is not an orphan," Gabe shouted. "That is the evil produce of whoredom. You are assisting a whore to do her filthy work producing more whore-children that the good people of this place will be asked to care for, providing it with special attention."

Seeing Rain in the club, listening to Jesus cry, hearing Brother Gabe's denunciation lessened patrons' desire for Beneficia. Some chose morality, others switched allegiance to the more expensive Salvie.

Curly, tired of Gabe's condemnation and Ruth's moral superiority, agreed to tear down the shack. Beneficia was hardly worth her keep. As a compromise Gabe continued to hold meetings in Curly's club and Curly continued to sell alcohol. Beneficia substituted for Salvie during her monthlies. Curly no longer had a whore but he never got around to destroying the shack behind the club.

Skeet, one of Beneficia's clients asked to buy a horse from her. Beneficia didn't know she owned any horses. Skeet told her she owned whatever Smitty had owned, including Smitty's wind-broke whistlers. Beneficia sold him a horse. When Cletis learned that Beneficia was selling Smitty's property Cletis ordered Jade to stop it because Beneficia was of a different race and her marriage to Smitty illegal by state law. She had no claim to Smitty's property.

Since Smitty had left no will and since Smitty had no deeds for any of his property there would be a delay so that anyone having a claim on Smitty's property could make it. If there were none, Cletis would hold a public auction and the money would go to the county treasury. Jade allowed Beneficia to return to the living area of the blacksmith shop and she reopened the livery stable.

Cletis asked his father if he had any interest in the property. Tezel's only interest was that it go to someone who didn't know a horseshoe from a whore's shoe so that anyone needing a blacksmith would go to Augurville.

⌒

Chuy disappeared. Jade questioned Cody, fearing that Cody had bushwhacked him. Cody believed he had run Chuy out of town. Jade questioned cowboys who came to Jade Town. No one had seen him.

When Chuy returned he told Jade that Segundo had

been shot, the Skillet cattle stampeded, the horses stolen and the Tejanos set afoot before they reached the Texas border. Chuy believed the stampede was a dodge to kill Segundo and thought he knew who did it but wasn't ready to say so.

Several days later a horse with a Skillet brand showed up in what had been Smitty's corral behind his blacksmith shop. Skeet, an Augur cowboy best known as the author of memorable farts, had gotten too old for $40 and found. He moved to town and took over Smitty's blacksmith shop after buying it from Beneficia.

"I have a paper here with her mark on it," Skeet said.

"Skeet? Is that your name?"

"It's what the general called me," Skeet said.

"Did you write this paper?" Jade asked.

"Naw, I can't write. Cletis did it for me."

"How much did you pay her?"

"Twenty dollars. It's all I had. She kept the house part of the shop and the livery."

"You know that Beneficia can't read well and may not understand numbers?"

"I can't say that I do either. I asked Cletis about the price and he said it was okay so I give him the money. He said it was for legal fees."

"Where did you get the horse?"

"Cowboy sold it to me. He was riding one horse and leading three. This one's got a limp. I paid him two dollars for it. You think it's worth it?"

Within a month Skeet and Beneficia were married.

⤾

Rain's first son had come hard with agony and exhaustion. Her second son came easy. Hephzibeth didn't want him, didn't want to name him and didn't want to see him. A baby was a side effect of her trade, no more than that. Hephsibeth intended to have the baby at Ruth's rent room but Ruth refused. Wilbur took her into his home but limited the time that Belle could spend with her.

At first Hephsibeth refused to nurse the child until Wilbur reminded her of what happened to Mattie. "When these people are riled up, common sense or common law can't stop them," he said. She gave the boy to Rain.

Rain carried the baby to Hephsibeth at all hours of the day and night despite her fear that Hephsibeth's heart would stretch watching her baby suckle and she would demand his return. Sometimes Rain waited until Hephsibeth was through in the back room. Sometimes she watched Hephsibeth drinking beer or whiskey while feeding her son. Each time Hephsibeth returned the infant with something like disgust at his needs.

When the infant thrived on goat's milk, Rain bought a nanny from Pancho and named her son John Crying in the Wilderness.

"Do you want him to be an outsider the way you were?" Jade asked.

"We'll always be outsiders and that includes you." Nevertheless, Rain changed his name to Noble after her white family name, Knoebel.

Once when she took Noble to Hephsibeth for feeding, Chuy was outside the saloon and asked to see the baby. He examined Noble closely, nodded his head and returned to his station. Later, he told Jade that the baby was not his and that he did not yet know who had killed Segundo but he knew which outfit did it. He refused to say more but suggested he would take care of the matter himself.

Two days later Chuy was carrying packages for Rowena when Cody stepped behind Rowena and yelled, "Get away from her and draw," shooting Chuy with his gun that had already been drawn. Chuy had time to drop the packages but was already falling when he pulled his own six-shooter. His only shot broke the front window of Mannen's store and the arm of a plow boy's wife inside. Cody advanced shooting Chuy twice more.

Rowena was in shock, unable to stop screaming, staring at the apples that she had bought at Mannen's store as a treat lying in a pool of blood, not noticing that her dress was polka dotted with the same blood. Hephsibeth pulled her into the saloon. Jade took Cody's gun and marched him to Cletis.

"I want you out of the Devils country," Cletis said when he was alone with Cody. "You can leave on your own or you can stay as a permanent guest of my father with your own plot of land. You are not fit to be sheriff."

"I did what you told me," Cody said.

"I didn't tell you to kill Chuy in front of my wife. I didn't tell you to kill him in front of the whole town. You could have arrested him and shot him for trying to escape; you've done that before. You could have shot him outside of town or at night where no one would know who did it."

"I'll say he insulted your wife and I defended her honor."

"You are not to mention my wife in connection with him. Not in the same conversation. A lot of people have a reason to want him away from here but you shoot him in front of my wife. Protecting her? Like she needed protection from that beast? If she needed protecting I would have done it. And if you ever coyote around my wife the way you're doing with the parson's kid I'll kill you."

"You will kill me," Cody mocked, remembering Cletis cowering before him.

"I won't dirty my hands with you," Cletis said. "You won't know who to look out for, but when you die you will know I pulled the trigger."

"I'll tell everyone it was self-defense. He threatened to kill me and seeing him armed I shot him," Cody said, "although he was using your wife as a shield."

"Not in the same sentence," Cletis raged. "Not on the same subject. He threatened to kill you, he was a known shooter, and probably a criminal and you shot him in self-defense. That's the story."

"Got it," Cody said, relieved to have escaped flaying.

"And you're going to have to do something for me," Cletis said.

"Name it."

"I'll tell you when I'm ready. The best thing you can do now is ride out to see your old Rat's Ass mates. Remind them to vote. Promise them you will take care of them."

"I thought I was supposed to take care of you and the general."

"You are," Cletis said with venom. "Tell them you will take care of them. Reassure them. They'll be leaderless if something happens to that damn foreigner. You'll have to be their leader."

"And lead them to the general?"

"Shut your ignorant mouth. The less you say the smarter you seem. This will require some intelligence."

Cody nodded. "On your part," Cletis said.

⁀

Rowena shuddered when she saw Cletis. "Cody hid behind me," she said. "He used me for a shield. He shot Chuy for being courteous, something I would like from others."

"It was all pretense," Cletis said. "He was pretending to be courteous to take advantage of you."

"Of me? Is that what you think of me? You're the one who has taken advantage of me. You're justice of the peace. Couldn't you have spoken to Chuy, asked him to be less polite to women? Did you tell Cody to kill him? I want to know."

"Stay out of things you have no right to know about," Cletis said.

"Right to know? I'm your wife. What does that mean to you?"

"It means you do what I tell you. If anyone is to blame for Chuy's death, it's you."

⁀

Jade knew that nothing could be done without Cletis's support but whether Chuy was killed because he flirted with Rowena or because he knew too much about the death of Segundo was gristle in his teeth. Either way he was certain that Cody should not be sheriff.

Beneficia moved into the living quarters of the blacksmith shop with Skeet and reopened the livery, feeding horses and mucking out the stalls while Jesus played around the horses and slept in the hay. Flies buzzed around him but he cried only when bitten by horseflies. Rain warned Beneficia about bot flies laying eggs in Jesus' nose.

Scoot, a former wild kid who had married one of the girls and grabbed the blister end of a plow homesteading a farm along the creek, told Wilbur that he had heard Augur cowboys talking about Cletis helping his father buy the springs and maybe the creek. That could ruin Scoot's rain-prayer farm. Scoot was building fences for the Augur to feed his wife until a rain permitted him to plant a crop. When Wilbur asked Cletis about the springs, Cletis tried to mill around the question and then denied the story.

Rain discovered surveyors' markings around the springs. She and Wilbur destroyed them. The surveyors returned to re-mark. Rain secreted herself in the trees and bushes around the spring and fired shots to scare them away. Jade suspected Wilbur had destroyed the markings. He didn't know who fired the shots but he was bound that it wasn't Wilbur. Jade didn't know that it was Rain.

Cletis, unnerved by the discovery of his father's plot to control the water and Jade's inability to discover who shot at the surveyors, called a special Council meeting. The meeting crowded the church. Ranchers and farmers feared that during another drought like the present one Jade Town might use so much water that the big spring could not keep the water holes filled. Those with wells and windmills didn't want to pay for water for those too lazy to dig wells or erect a windmill. Although no one named them, everyone knew the reference was to the sick, crippled, widowed and poor on Barefoot Street.

"Jade has done nothing about fence-cutting or protecting surveyors," Tezel charged. "I followed the law and had my land surveyed before putting up fences."

"When horses and cattle die for lack of water no surveyors or property rights can prevent a range war," Dutch said. "My fences have been torn down; my cattle have been turned back--"

"You don't own the land you fenced," Tezel said. "A surveyor has never set foot on the land you claim."

"You won't let teamsters deliver wire to my headquarters. I have to pay them extra because of your interference."

"Not let them cross my property and cut my fences, I won't," Tezel said. "No sir. You come here because of what this country offers but where were you when the damn Yankees wanted to change our way of life? Not just slaves but our religion, society, values, traditions? Helping them. They still want to blur the white race, defile our women. And you want foreign freighters crossing my property? I'm not having it. My cowboys will shoot them on my property. First the mules and if that don't stop them, shoot whoever is behind the mules."

Cowboys grumbled and sided up. Jade and Jubal placed themselves between the two men and their hands to calm them and Wilbur changed the subject. He knew that after the election, Cletis, as county judge, would quietly allow Tezel to control the water. "Why don't you tell us about your desire to own the springs," he said, wanting to make Tezel's plan known.

The discussion raised voices and temperatures before Tezel confessed that he might be interested in owning the springs. But water did not concern the church, and

Wilbur should not be preaching politics. Wilbur said he was not involved in politics but in the welfare of the community.

With Sarge and Brine beside him, Tezel glowered at Wilbur. Some of his former Rebs placed hands on the butts of six-shooters. "The water from the spring is God-given," Brother Gabe said. "No man dug that spring, only God. Therefore, it belongs to everyone. Except Indians," he reassured citizens. "Anyone who wants me to pay taxes to buy water that belongs to everyone is a thief. There is no other word for it."

"The government has no right to control water when only those who live in Jade Town are members of the Council and the water is required by the entire county," Tezel said.

Some in the crowd nodded, even those who had fought to deny water to Indians. "Jade Town isn't trying to control the water, just to protect the springs so that the town has the water it needs," Mannen explained.

"Squatters are pumping water out of the creek," Dutch said. "If everybody does that no one will have water."

Cletis ruled that one must own both sides of the creek to own the water in the creek. Neither Mick nor Pancho had the money to buy land on both sides of the creek or to pay a lawyer to fight for their rights. No one wanted to pay taxes to buy water. They especially did not want to pay for the right of Pancho and the Mick to the water in the creek.

"What about the future?" Wilbur asked. "What if the town continues to grow?"

Tezel insisted there was no problem; he would allow the town as much water as they needed.

Mannen encouraged spending money now rather than leaving the burden for their children to pay, but it was hard to get citizens to care about a future problem. "What if Tezel decides we need less water than we think we need? What if someone else becomes owner of the property?" Everyone knew that was a veiled reference to Cletis inheriting the springs but Mannen was a newcomer and all his ideas were suspect.

Cletis charged that Wilbur and Mannen were beginning a whimper campaign. As long as he had water in his well, so would everyone else. If someday his well went dry then some arrangement could be made but there would be a lot more people to pay for it. They weren't passing the debt to their children to pay, they were requiring newcomers to pay for the security, advantages and prestige the town offered them.

Wilber hungered for theological discussion. Everyone in Jade Town either agreed with him without question or dismissed his ideas as "funny," as though the Bible were a set of rules rather than visions of God. After the meeting, Wilbur sought to discuss ways in which the church could protect universal needs such as clean water or seek justice for those unfairly taxed.

"The Bible is absolute," Gabe said. "Thou shalt not steal," is absolute."

"Actually, in his Sermon on the Mount, Jesus revised the Ten Commandments," Wilber reminded Gabe.

"Heretic," Gabe snarled. Paying taxes was part of the Bible Gabe had not memorized and taxes were not an issue where the Bible applied or that reason could win.

‿

Wilbur knew that some citizens would not pay taxes to protect their future and that of others. If water became expensive they would move farther west where it was free. He also knew that if it became a legal battle it needed to be won before Cletis took an oath as county judge.

Wilbur launched a private and secret subscription plan to buy the springs and the creek at least to the limits of the town. After they had secured water for the future they would offer it to the town at the price they paid with the threat that they could sell to outsiders at a profit or charge citizens for the use of it.

Mannen recognized the necessity and invested heavily. Iowa invested hoping for a profit. Beneficia gave money because Wilbur asked her to. Hephsibeth donated money to gain status in the community. Pancho and Mick gave the few dollars they could afford. Curly wasn't told because the investors feared he would join the ranchers in a bidding war. Wilbur carried the money to Austin to buy the springs and as much of the creek as the money would allow.

～

Jade and Rain were certain he would face no opposition for county sheriff; neither would Cletis face opposition as county judge. They were half-right. Cody announced he was running for county sheriff. Everyone knew Jade so it had not occurred to him that he needed to campaign and was caught off guard when both Cletis and Cody campaigned for office.

It began with malicious gossip. Jade was a desperado, believed to have killed several men not counting Mexicans and Indians. Horses and cattle disappeared wherever Jade went. He never stayed in one place for long, never lived in a house he owned, married a savage who carried a bastard into places a decent woman would never go. That story was not as useful as before and wobbled until Brother Gabe carried it to his pulpit. "Red birds and black birds don't mingle their blood," he shouted. "Doves and hawks don't nest together."

Gabe created a colorful and damaging story. Hephsibeth killed Widow Waller in a jealous rage over their unnatural relationship. Jade allowed Hephsibeth to remain free because she was carrying his baby. Rain adopted the baby as soon as it was born in an attempt to license a furtive marriage that had to be done in darkness to allow Jade to share a squaw's wigwam, with Parson Wilbur's approval, a marriage so vile, so abominable they could not confess it to honest people. When their foul, perfidious union became known Wilbur desecrated his own church house to publicly sanctify it.

Gabe denounced secret marriages and marriages to a person from an inferior race. Because of lust, a lust so savage that Jade must also defile Hephsibeth, a child. Gabe also declared Wilbur a heretic who perverted the Holy Scripture, giving Wilbur another reason to be pleased he wasn't running for office.

"Rain carried that baby into places where no decent person would go," Ruth said.

"Jade hasn't done anything about the murder of Widow Waller," Curly told customers, although he had hoped her murder would drive his competition out of business. "And the whore is running the widow's business like she owns it. What is the law going to do about that?"

In the story Hephsibeth was both victim and criminal, both innocent child and murderous harlot.

"Jade permitted a bunch of Mexican gunmen to drive their herd through the town, interfering with trade, leaving a mess for others to clean up and putting citizens in danger," Iowa said.

"Jade promised he wouldn't marry a savage and then he did. Secretly because it was so shameful," Ruth said.

Jade Town had no newspaper and no means for Jade to respond or explain except to one or two people at a time while rumors spread like wildfire. He had to wait for the fires to burn themselves out.

~

Tezel hired his own newspaper to represent his interests. Hoot Jordan, a printer, brought his press to Augurville to replace the wild kid network and promoted himself to publisher, editor and reporter of the Advantage Advertiser. Hoot loved curious and clever but hollow news, entertainment and information. His first story was about a half-mad prostitute who was lynched by a mob. "Her blood still cries out for justice," he wrote "but her murder has never been investigated and no charges have ever been filed by the sheriff." The story never got to its feet as too many people were involved in the crime.

Tezel aimed Hoot at the right target. Jade intended to disarm the Devils country so that only he and his deputies could carry guns and citizens would be helpless under his reign of terror.

"Only in the business section of Jade Town," Jade explained to Hoot. "Those who live here can leave their guns at home. Those visiting can turn in their guns at the livery stable and pick them up when they leave."

Hoot quoted Curly. "That law will raise taxes and cut profits when cowboys take their business elsewhere." And deputy Cody. "We'll spend all our time disarming honest citizens who don't want to harm anyone but do want to keep outlaws and Indians out of the town. We should enforce the laws we already have."

Hoot reported the battle between the churches. "In some Northern cities men are not allowed to carry guns to defend their wives and children," Brother Gabe preached, "Because they have no need to," Wilbur countered. "That's the purpose of law."

"Whose law?" Gabe demanded. "God's or man's. Guns are a God-given right.

"A God-given gift to killers and cowards," Wilbur said. "No one else needs one."

"Why does Jade wear one?" Hoot asked.

"Because I represent the law," Jade said. "If no one carries a gun in town then I won't carry one either," he pledged.

That made folks skittish. Citizens had more faith in guns than in God or law. Neither had ever stopped an Indian attack, a lynching or a government that wanted to disarm citizens.

"Maybe Jade Town has become so dangerous that Jade is afraid to go to the barbershop alone, but I'm not," Cletis boasted.

"If there is violence in Jade Town, why hasn't Jade done something about it besides shooting a cowboy in the back?" Sarge asked Hoot.

"I'm trying to," Jade responded, "by getting the

Council to pass this ordnance."

"I'm spokesman for the good, honest people of the Devils country who have no voice," Gabe said. "But we have a vote. We come to town and we know that we are going to be cheated because that's the business of towns and stores. That's what they do. They don't raise cattle, they don't raise crops. The only thing they raise is their prices. They are no better than warbles or screw flies. Our only protection from the parasites is a good rifle and a steady hand."

Tezel persuaded Hoot to edit Gabe's statement to: "I'm spokesman for the good, honest people of the county who have no voice. But we have a vote. Our only protection for our vote is a good rifle and a steady hand."

Wilbur tried to reason with Hoot, but who had the right to control water, land and guns was not an issue that morality or reason could win.

⤸

Dutch was discovered shot dead beside a barbed wire fence. Nearby were wire cutters. Jade, Jubal and Cody investigated. It was clear to Cody that Dutch had been shot while cutting an Augur fence. Jade and Jubal had doubts. Dutch's horse was nearby, there was blood on the saddle, no wire was cut, the wire cutters leaned against a post on the Augur side of the fence, and horse tracks suggested that someone on Augur land had baited Dutch to the fence where he was shot. The murderer threw the fence cutters at Dutch's body but they landed against a post.

Jade questioned Skeet who could sharpen knives,

scissors and plow points. He was trying to learn new skills and expand his business. The Augurville blacksmith readily confessed to Jubal that he had made the wire cutters for the Augur. "They use a lot of them working wire," he said.

Dutch's death shocked the Devils country. Everyone believed it was the handwork of Tezel. Tezel's newspaper said the killing was justified because Dutch was caught cutting Augur wire. Wilbur said that protecting property could not justify the taking of human life. Gabe likened killing to protect private property to killing to protect a man's wife. Jade believed Tezel had approved the murder of Dutch and that Cody, Sarge or Brine had done it but knew no way he could prove it to Cletis's satisfaction. Dutch's cowboys believed that if Dutch could be killed they too were vulnerable.

Dutch's wife and mother, both now widows, moved to San Antonio to join their children, taking clothing and a few personal items. The rest they abandoned. Dutch's cowboys divided among themselves the horses, cows, and the land that Dutch had secured. Some swore vengeance. Some sold their parcel of land to Tezel and moved on. Two cowboys were lynched for successfully starting with no cows and growing a herd of steers. There was a gunfight over one wild girl and when the boy she favored was killed she hanged herself to punish the killer.

Dutch's hands that stayed put their trust in Cody. He had been one of them and he said that if he were elected county sheriff he would protect them. Dutch had taught them loyalty worked both ways.

As Election Day bulged on the horizon Tezel's newspaper carried the story of Cody's courage. Cody had killed a pistolero who sat on the street daring anyone to arrest him. Dutch's murder proved that Jade could not stop a range war or prevent it from coming to Jade Town. Cody would arrest those that Jade refused to arrest. Cletis promised to be a hanging judge.

Dutch's and Tezel's cowboys knew Cody was a killer and thought violence was required for law and order. Jade was also a killer but cowhands from both brands believed Cody was loyal to them. The Tejanos who remained, the plow pushers, the counter jumpers believed they were safer with Jade.

On Election Day Tezel's hands publicized themselves, so did Dutch's. They filled the saloons and rode through Jade Town with guns. Some residents stayed home fearing violence. Jubal stayed in the bunkhouse knowing that like women he would not be permitted to vote no matter what the Fifteenth Amendment said, fearing his presence would cause violence. Voters forgot that Jade kept the town safe during the big fight between cow outfits and remembered the noise, the flies, the mess of the cattle being driven through town.

The election altered the balance of power. The crown shifted from Jade and Wilber to Tezel, Cletis, Cody and Brother Gabe. With Dutch dead and his cow outfit splintered, Tezel intended to extend his grip on the land and Cletis's grasp of the law into a cattle empire. He would fence the water holes and buy them when he could, Cletis would take care of the paper work, Sarge would guard the fences. That empire would propel Cletis to political power with license to give or withhold as suited his purpose.

Sarge would ramrod the ranch while Tezel sought and passed favors in Austin.

Cletis wanted Cody to hire Sarge as deputy to remove Sarge as Augur range boss. Sarge laughed in Cody's face. "You want me to do your killing for you? I work for the general and we got a cattle spread to look after. Brine, Buckshot Bob are good with a gun. You might ask them." Buckshot also rejected the offer. Brine said, "I work for Sarge. When Sarge becomes sheriff I'll be his deputy." Cody didn't like the veiled threat that Sarge might become sheriff and told Cletis.

Cletis mulled the idea. "Hire Jubal as deputy," Cletis said. "He could balance Sarge. Maybe the two will kill each other. It would be cause for celebration if either of them was killed."

Jubal sneered at Cody's offer. "Jade Town hired Jade as town marshal," Jubal said. "I'm Jade's deputy."

"He was a slave wasn't he?" Cletis asked. "Offer him more money than Jade Town can. I'll make up the difference." Jubal didn't bother to respond.

Cody's first arrest was Dewey who had been one of Dutch's top hands before the ranch was split up. Cletis charged Dewey with adultery. He had been seen cohabiting with Salvie who was believed to be underage. His second arrest was Hephsibeth.

Hephsibeth had moved into Widow Waller's house next to the saloon where she lived and accommodated special clients. Mannen, Sarge whose wife had found a better life for herself, Cletis occasionally because Rowena had set ideas about what Christians didn't do, and Cody. Cody didn't pay her or Salvie. That was the price of protection. When Salvie's father tried to forcibly remove Salvie from the saloon Hephsibeth stopped him with a gun.

Dewey was placed in the roundhouse to await trial. Hephsibeth was allowed to return to the saloon as there was no one else to run it. Salvie returned to the back room of the saloon because she was the only whore in town for most folks. Jubal stood guard in the suicide hole of the roundhouse and exchanged shots at some angry person believed to be a woman. Keeping Dewey in the roundhouse was expensive in time and reputation. His imprisonment was the subject of jokes about "the hanging judge." Cletis fined Dewey and released him to the fury of his wife's mercy.

Tezel was not pleased. Cletis had allowed a private group to buy the springs and the creek to the edge of town. Not knowing about it was no excuse. Cletis was in the position his father had put him in to know those things and to stop them if they stood in Tezel's way. And all Cletis's talk about being a hanging judge was talk. Tezel wanted someone charged with Dutch's murder to stop rumors that he had done it or ordered one of his hands to do it. "I want someone hanged and it had better not be an Augur cowboy," Tezel said.

Cletis assumed his father was behind Dutch's murder and wanted to charge Sarge but his father would not permit it. Cletis told Cody to arrest Skeet. Skeet wasn't the brightest concho on the saddle and he didn't represent any brand. One man standing alone was an easy target and with Hoot's help Cletis could quickly separate him from any would be saviors. "Take some Augur wire cutters with you and find out where he keeps a gun."

"What's his motive?" Cody asked. Cody wasn't

concerned but curious.

Cletis plotted the story. "Dutch caught him cutting Augur wire and Skeet shot him to cover the crime."

"Why would Skeet cut Augur wire?" Skeet was dumb but Jade wasn't, and neither was the rest of Jade Town.

"He owes the Augurville store a lot of money." Cody looked doubtful. "Skeet borrowed money from the store to buy the blacksmith shop. He planned to rustle Augur cattle to pay for it. I'll set it up," Cletis said. "You do your part. If you have to shoot him that will be easier for everyone."

Hoot reported suspicion that Skeet had been interrupted cutting Augur wire to steal Augur cattle because of a large debt. No one believed it.

Cody arrested Skeet who was docile and unarmed, and Cletis explained why Skeet was the suspect. No one believed him either. Worse, Tezel was angry that Cletis involved the Augur with the Augurville store and the wire cutters. "What were you thinking?" he demanded. "But you weren't thinking." He slapped Cletis on the head. "I want you to take care of this mess and take care of it now. And don't involve the T over Z."

Jade, Jubal and Cody took turns guarding Skeet in the roundhouse. When Cody was elected sheriff, Jade knew that he and Cody would come face to face some day and he needed to know what he would do when that happened. The picture of two lawmen shooting each other in the middle of town troubled him but he made certain Cody was in front of him.

Beneficia brought food and Jesus to Skeet every day. She wanted Jesus to know a father. Jade talked to cowhands. No one remembered Skeet being angry or quarrelsome. Jade believed Skeet's story that he bought the shop with his own $20. Cletis feared even his appointed jury would not convict Skeet making his father look even guiltier. But Cletis couldn't release Skeet without looking weak.

Hoot reported that a county resident working as a gandy dancer, or maybe rail dog, had been beaten to death by his crew and thrown into the brush along the railroad track. Cletis ordered Jubal to investigate it. The state had carved the Devils country into more than one county. Jubal had no authority outside Jade Town and the track was now outside the county.

Jade knew that both town and county officials wanted to be rid of Jubal and feared they were trying to force Jubal into insubordination or the gun sights of unreconstructed riders who would aim at the star. He accompanied Jubal to the site. They talked to the crew bosses and to the rail dog's team. One of the rail dogs had tripped over a crosstie and another man tripped over him, the heavy rail fell crushing the head of the fallen man. The tampers confirmed the story.

A Texas Ranger appeared, wanted to know what they were doing on the site and asked them to stick around. He wasn't there to investigate the accident. The railroad had gone bankrupt and was in receivership. He was there to protect the section boss and prevent the workers from destroying equipment when they learned they weren't going to be paid.

When Jade and Jubal returned they discovered that masked men had disarmed Cody and forced Cletis to unlock the roundhouse. They placed Cletis and Cody in the roundhouse, dragged Skeet to his blacksmith shop and hanged him from the cross that Wilbur would not permit on the church house. Cody swore he had seen Rat's Ass horses and that the lynchers were Dutch's cowboys seeking revenge.

Rowena had gone to the roundhouse, saw that Cletis and Cody were inside and went to Rain's house to fetch Jade. Since Jade and Jubal were gone, Rain and Rowena returned to the roundhouse and found the key to the door dropped on the opposite side of the roundhouse. They freed Cletis and Cody and Cody saddled up and pursued the lynchers. They split up but they had definitely raced for Rat's Ass territory.

Hoot reported Cletis's story of revenge by Dutch's cowboys but others crowed, "Jade Town has become a hanging town without a hanging judge." Both hangings in the town had been by vigilantes.

With Cletis as judge and Cody as sheriff, there was no way to discover who the lynchers were. Tezel thought it smelled bilious but Hoot had suppressed the Augur connection to Dutch's death. "Next time I need something done I'll tell Sarge to do it," Tezel told Cletis and Cody.

Wilbur had believed Jade Town had outgrown its past, he preached, but it was still mired in violence, vengeance and the inability to love and live at peace with one another. Brother Gabe preached that the wages of sin was death, and death had rightly come to a murderer. Hoot editorialized that until justice provided a timely and appropriate punishment those who dispensed justice in an opportune manner were blameless.

Rowena dropped a letter in the post office while pretending to shop in Mannen's store. A few weeks later Rowena's father arrived in a wagon and stopped at Jade's house as his daughter had instructed. Rain joined him in the wagon with her shotgun and they went to fetch Jade so that everyone in town saw them. Jade stood in the wagon behind Rain as they rode to Cletis's big house that Tezel had built. Word of the visit had spread through the town and Cody walked out of the house beside an unarmed Cletis to meet them. "He's come to get his daughter," Jade said.

"She ain't going," Cody said. "He can turn around and go right back where he come from."

"I ain't leaving without Rowena," the father said.

"You're leaving," Cody said. "We ain't decided yet whether your toes will be pointed out or up."

"We represent the law," Cletis said.

"And we represent the family," Jade said, jumping down from the wagon for a better draw. He didn't know what the mules might do at the first shot. Rain and the father held shotguns. "I guess Rowena will have to decide which she's partial to."

"She ain't coming out," Cody said but without his usual bluster. Cody wasn't going to draw on three guns, two of them shotguns, one maybe loaded with slugs.

"She's coming out or we're going in," Jade said.

"Rowena, get out here," Cletis called.

Rowena came outside with a single bag. Her eye was bruised and her mouth cut. Cletis and Cody were between Rowena and her father but no one aimed a gun. Jade asked Rowena if she was ready to go. Rowena tried to walk between the two men but bumped Cletis with the bag. "Pardon me," she said politely. She walked down the steps and her father dismounted to place her bag in the wagon.

"Is that all you're taking?" her father asked.

"It's all I want," she said.

Rowena was helped into the wagon by her father who then drove away leaving Jade facing Cletis and Cody. First Cletis went inside the house and then Cody. Jubal rode up behind Jade leading Jade's horse. Jade followed the wagon for a day to prevent interference from Augur cowboys.

⤳

Tezel awoke to the tinkling of a bell. It was too early to get up so he tried to go back to sleep. As he was drifting off again he heard the bell. Where the hell was it coming from? That question prevented him from falling asleep again. The bell had to be on Pancho's goat that led his sheep. Or that of another lamb licker. Or some sod buster's milk cow. While he fretted he heard the bell again and it seemed to come from his wife's garden.

Tezel put on his hat, pulled on his boots, grabbed his shotgun, and went outside in his nightshirt intending to shoot the bell-bearer and leave the bell at the Augurville saloon. He peered into the dark trying to spot the critter when the first shot hit him, followed by two more. Sarge and his crew spent the night and much of the next day looking for the shooter. They found the bell and spent cartridges but the "goat" had disappeared.

Cody told Jade the details but did not invite Jade to see for himself. Jade went early the next morning but the scene was trampled.

Chapter Four

The Railroad Changes the Landscape

After Skeet's lynching, auctioning Beneficia's property for the benefit of the county was forgotten by mutual consent. Beneficia was unable to hire another blacksmith as qualified ones worked for a railroad. She and Jesus clung to the livery stable although there were rumors that she also took cowboys in the hay for pay. The ladies of Jade Town wanted her to move on but Beneficia refused. She had not known love until Rain discovered Beneficia was pregnant. Now she had Rain, Hannah and Jesus. Rain taught her and Jesus to make buttons and water dippers out of gourds. Hannah taught her to make bonnets.

The school kids had seen Belle walking along the creek with Cody and told Wilbur. Wilbur and Hannah worried whether taking Beneficia and Hephsibeth into their home had created adult notions that Belle was not ready to understand. "We voiced our disapproval of what they did and the circumstances that drove them to it," Wilbur said.

"But we never condemned them," Hannah said. Hannah believed women should help each other overcome the circumstances that put them in brothels--abusive husbands or fathers, the illness or death of the father or husband, the lack of opportunity to learn or to work.

"To deny kindness to even the least of God's children is a denial of Christ," Wilbur said.

"If we had turned our back on them, where would they have gone?" Hannah asked. "I still think we could have done more for Mattie."

"We gave her hope," Wilbur said. "The mob took it from her but we gave her hope." Both pondered whether allowing Beneficia and Hephsibeth to play with Belle had somehow contaminated her.

"We knew it was a risk," Hannah said. "But what life would she have if we hid her from the world?"

Hannah told Belle of Cody's worldliness, but that was what attracted her to him. He knew so much about life and people and she knew so little. He had known killers, bandits, cowboys, teamsters, Indians. Cody had also known Beneficia and Hephsibeth, Hannah reminded her. Belle liked them and it disappointed her that Cody knew them in a shameful way, that he spoke ill of them, but she could abide that.

Belle had known only those with whom she went to school and church. Hannah told her, "Some of those in church are guilty of murder, revenge, cheating customers and employees, lying about products they sell."

Belle refused to believe it. They went to church meetings, they wore clean clothes, they were polite to her, they spoke well of God.

Wilbur warned Cody to stay away from his daughter; she was still a child. Cody knew that Belle was as old as Beneficia when she first came to the Devils country, that his desire for her despite his intimate knowledge of what women offered was flattering to her and awakened passions that she had not known before. Cody also knew that Wilbur was not likely to shoot him. Wilbur did ponder killing Cody to save Belle, but could killing ever save anything?

Hannah's and Wilbur's talks with Belle made Cody more attractive to her. They decided to send her to a boarding school in Belton where she could continue her education hoping she would return with a new vision of what her life could be.

Brother Gabe envied Wilbur's church house where women spread out, fanning themselves with palm leaves or faded and folded newspapers in the stifling heat, or huddled against husbands and hugged children when it was freezing. In Augurville Gabe had a brush arbor to preach in and in Jade Town Curly's club. Privately Gabe encouraged his followers to join Wilbur's church and when they gained the majority to call a vote to fire the parson and replace Wilbur with himself.

With his benefactor dead, Hoot Jordan saw no future in Augurville and surveyed other places to move his press, trade skills and voice. For his own amusement he wrote about the Southern Pacific Railroad claiming that the 14th Amendment forbidding states to deny any person equal protection under the law applied to them. It was an old story but news came slowly to the Devils country and it was a chin dropper. The California Supreme Court ruled that the intention of the amendment was to protect former slaves, recent immigrants, and other citizens from discrimination by the majority or by their own government and not to protect powerful corporations against state governments.

The S.P. had more friends in the U.S. Supreme Court and the justices declared the railroad was a person. Hoot ridiculed the silliness of the Supreme Jesters. In the Devils country it was cause for jocularity and comments about Yankee stupidity. Wilbur declared it was theft of human rights. No one heard him.

Cletis had seen enough of government to believe politicians could be bought, maybe easier than court fools. Cletis promised to continue the Augur's investment in the paper. He also promised that the railroad would come to Augurville and that Augurville would become county seat. Stores and new businesses would move there and they would need his newspaper to advertise their wares.

Brother Gabe wanted to buy space in the newspaper to publish his preachments. Hoot had Southern sympathies regarding the aristocracy of the righteous and with no wife, no family, like Gabe his needs were few. He could print the facts as he saw them, Gabe would preach the truth and together they could create a new reality for the Devils country. Free, virile, and sovereign.

⤳

After his father's death, Cletis had gone to Austin to meet railroad lobbyists and was given a crash course in railroad history. With former Democratic opponents serving the Confederacy Republicans subsidized railroads and paid by the mile with tracks laid over rough terrain receiving twice the pay as tracks laid across the plains. Rather than planning tracks to serve the nation the moguls laid the tracks to enrich themselves, choosing rough terrain and sometimes laying parallel tracks over the same terrain. They bought mines and sold coal to themselves, they bought forests and sold bridge timber and crossties to themselves at twice or more their normal price, they formed construction companies and contracted themselves to build the railroads.

Soldiers seized the lands and the rivers for commercial exploitation, removing the Indians, borders were thrown open for indentured servants to replace those that had been liberated. Workers died in mines and along railroad tracks leaving pregnant women and fatherless children across the nation. The moguls had no aim but to lay as many miles of track as they could as fast as they could to make as much money as they could for as few as they could. There was no way they could fail. It was a great success story and it was told in board rooms, Chamber of Commerce meetings and restricted social clubs.

Then the federal government had stopped railroad subsidies. Several railroad companies were in receivership and there were rumors the Reading Railroad would fail. Railroads needed states, counties and towns to take up subsidization. Texas was already trading sixteen square miles of land for every mile of track, cities were offering cash. One Texas railroad needed quick cash to place rails and plat towns. Because of the prolonged drought the land Texas had given them for tracks wasn't selling as quickly as expected and needed.

Cletis had been forced to sell cattle because of the scant grass and water. The cattle were cheap because everyone in the Devils country had to sell cattle, sheep and horses. Cletis gambled that the drought would end soon and the price of cattle and land would rise. He gave the railroad the cash that he had from the sale of cattle, money that he borrowed by mortgaging land, promised county money and more land for membership on the board.

With his father no longer stifling his ambition, Cletis intended to run the ranch and the county from the courthouse and he wanted that courthouse to be in Augurville. However, many people believed Augurville was too rough and dangerous for a commercial center. Augur riders believed Tezel was killed by one or more of Dutch's cowboys who believed Tezel was responsible for the murder of Dutch. There were three more killings, two of Dutch's cowboys and one of Tezel's, broken bones, fractured skulls, knife and gunshot wounds.

Jade and Jubal had kept the killing out of Jade Town by confiscating guns that weren't checked at the livery stable. There were a couple of gunfights but no locals were hit. The cowboy trade and trouble shifted to Augurville and Cody couldn't stop it.

The violence unsettled the Devils country. Cletis feared for his political career if he couldn't control the county as judge. Cletis wanted Jade and Jubal in Augurville. Jade argued that with three law officers in Augurville, the range war would come to Jade Town. Cletis ordered Jubal to Augurville to help Cody. Jubal refused. Jade suggested Cletis ask the governor to send Texas Rangers. Cletis refused because it would make him look ineffectual. He hired Brine and Buckshot Bob as temporary deputies.

∽

When Belle returned from school she went walking

along the creek with Cody. She came home in tears, her face bruised, her clothing torn and bloody. "I tried to stop him," she said. She showed Hannah her bruised thighs. "I thought he loved me but he only wanted to humiliate me, or you," she told her father.

"I told him to stay away from you," Wilbur said. "I told him."

"He took something that was of value to me and that meant nothing to him. Why would a person do something like that?"

"Some people can't create and can't delight in what others create so they try to deface or destroy it," Wilbur said. "Those who value nothing try to rule or ruin what others value."

"I tried to stop him, Daddy. I did."

"I know. The evil is his alone."

Wilbur gnawed at killing Cody with a borrowed gun. Even punching Cody in the face would give him some satisfaction but would do nothing for Belle and he could no longer preach peace and love. Could Jade arrest Cody? Could he be punished for what he had done?

"Not in this place," Jade said. "Belle would be the one on trial, and you and Hannah. It would be ugly and whatever happened to Cody, Belle would be found guilty. You said we must have faith in God's justice. Do you believe that?"

"I want to believe it," Wilbur said. He prayed until he could go to Cody, tell Cody that what he had done was despicable but that he would try to forgive Cody if Cody would ask God for forgiveness.

"If you got anything to say to me, bring a gun to say it," Cody told him.

Wilbur went home angrier than when he had left and he prayed that God would help his unbelief in justice.

When Belle's pregnancy became known to the town, Brother Gabe pointed Belle out as the result of permissive parenting and liberal theology that preached peace with one another rather than war on wrong, love of degenerates instead of obedience to God's absolutes, and the refusal to call sin a sin and punish the guilty. Cody was never mentioned as being the guilty.

↬

After Tezel's death, Sarge was lord of the range to cowboys, plow mongers and store queens, and Sarge straddled three ambitions. Brother Gabe had plans for running the county from Wilbur's church house, Hoot's newspaper and Cletis's court. Gabe's followers were already gaining control of Wilbur's church with tales, taunts and threats. Sarge believed that Gabe killed wounded soldiers with a prayer for their souls but sneered at Gabe's cowboy pretense and rejected Gabe's accounts of driving cattle to Newton. He intentionally spat tobacco juice on Gabe's boots to the amusement of everyone who saw it and the others who soon heard about it.

As High Sheriff Cody wanted to be the hired gun until he and Cletis moved to Austin. Sarge wasn't fast with a gun but he was deadly and when he fixed his eyes on a man the man was going to go. On his feet if he was smart or on a borrowed horse strapped crosswise over the saddle. Cody was unable to get the drop on Sarge and Sarge was too savvy to be ambushed. If Sarge were killed Cody would be the first suspect. If Jade didn't arrest him then Brine or some other former Rebel would back-shoot him.

Cletis planned to improve his cattle empire with less land and better quality cattle. Sarge wanted Cletis to buy land while it was cheap. Cletis traded land for blooded bulls and put up windmills. Sarge didn't want blooded bulls. Cows that couldn't walk to water holes weren't fit for eating. Longhorns were God's invention; they looked like cattle and Sarge didn't want no man-made Yankee perversion on his range. He would shoot any of them he saw and he would castrate the man they belonged to, Sarge told Cletis.

Sarge did not accept any ideas, methods or philosophy that came after Appomattox. Sarge's cowboys weren't fence builders, well-diggers or windmill mechanics. They would, by God, work on horseback, sleep in the bunkhouse or on the ground, whichever was handier, and they would eat from the chuck wagon and Sarge would, by God, hire the biscuit roller.

Cletis hired Cody as range boss, making Jubal acting sheriff but the cowboys ignored Cody's orders the way they ignored Cletis, a swivel chair buckaroo. Sarge refused to yield control of the seasoned hands and Cody didn't know enough about cowboying to teach the young ones.

When Cletis's blooded bulls died of cattle fever, Sarge's cowboys never missed a chance to snicker at Cletis to his face. "How much did you pay for them fancy bulls that had to be burned because they couldn't be eaten?"

"You may own the land and the brand but the horses and cattle are in our hands," Sarge told Cletis. "If I leave the top hands will leave with me and you and Cody are going to have to teach the greeners by yourselves."

⌣

As usual the drought was ended by a flood that swept away cattle, crops, roads, railroad tracks and a trestle. Cletis went to a board meeting to learn why the unfinished trestle hadn't been repaired. No one was interested in a trestle. The battle was over the route to Augurville--crossing the Devils which was a shorter and rougher route but would require a bridge or around the Devils that was farther, increasing the square miles the railroad would earn, and more opportunities to plat towns or to connect with towns that paid them to come.

After a day of numbers, designs, plans, proposals, maps, charts punctuated with quarrels and shouts the treasurer reminded them they were a small company without national ambition and had no money to begin either route. They were giving stock to gain the good will of officials who held the purse strings. "How much stock?" one board member asked.

Cletis gasped at the answer. Each share given decreased the value of the stock he had and they were giving bundles. Cletis could cut his losses and his dream of a railroad fortune or sell more land and cattle and buy more shares of increasingly worthless railroad stock to keep the company alive. The drought-breaking flood had been followed with full water holes and new grass and the price of cattle and land was up. Cletis clung to his dream.

Cletis lobbied county and town officials to bribe the railroad to come to the county. Jade Town believed the railroad was coming to Jade Town but Augurville merchants and property owners were assured the railroad was coming their way, increasing population, business, and property values. Hoot wrote glowing words about the county's future and the part the railroad would play, always implying that the railroad would come to Jade Town.

In his brush arbor in Augurville, Brother Gabe preached hard work for men, frugal and near-invisible living to women, and fealty to the head of the church and the head of the home. In Jade Town from the raised box in Curly's club he denounced the evil railroads for bringing undesirables to the country. Ruffians, hooligans, men from foreign races and religions who did not give women the honor, the nobility that God intended. Coarse, crude women would accompany them. Whores, divorcees, women who worked alongside men. Was that the future that Jade Town wanted? Never.

Hearers who weren't merchants obliged Gabe with hostility to a railroad depot in Jade Town.

When Cletis had contracts signed by railroad and county officials in his pocket, he turned to the next problem. Sarge believed Cletis was behind the lynching of Skeet, paid railroad riffraff to do it, and that Cody lied that the lynchers rode Dutch's brand. While dwelling on that, Sarge noticed that old loyal soldiers quietly faded from the ranks while those remaining tightened their cinches and renewed their oaths of loyalty. Cletis demanded the kind of loyalty they had given to his father and those who were abandoned rode off in silence their dignity intact.

Sarge was the first to discover the plan to bring the railroad to Augurville. When Slats, his best roper, disappeared, Sarge rode after him, finding him on a railroad surveying crew. Slats said the surveyors were laying out the trail to Augurville.

Cletis had told Slats that he was reducing the size of the ranch and herd and needed fewer hands. Cletis told Slats to pick up his bedroll and drift and to take his horse with him. Slats owed the general that much.

Sarge confronted Cletis. Cletis acknowledged plans to sell land, horses and cattle to invest in the railroad company. Sarge could be range boss of what was left or Cletis could get Sarge a job as section boss on the railroad. Sarge calculated killing Cletis where he sat and pulling for the Rio with pards who wanted to ride with him. Then he slowly turned and walked away. Cletis was glad that Sarge left without punching or spitting on him.

꙳

A herd of longhorns driven by cowboys attacked track layers, damaged the tracks, scared off the workers and injured two of them near the Devils River. Railroad surveyors were shot at and their tools stolen. Riders dressed as Indians burned crossties and warped rails. It cost Cletis more land, cattle and horses to persuade the railroad honchos not to drop plans for a track to Augurville and move to east Texas that was drought-free with good timber, fewer rock-bound hills, rock-strewn valleys and fewer rivers across deep gorges.

Everyone knew that Sarge was behind the obstruction and Cletis told Cody to get rid of Sarge before the delays caused the railroad to change their plans. Cody was afraid to face Sarge. If he did kill Sarge and lived he would lose the next election. Cody tried again to deputize Jubal. "Arrest Sarge. Kill him if you have to."

Jubal knew that arresting Sarge would be an express pass to hell. "No white jury is going to send a man like Sarge to jail for killing a black man, even if the black man is wearing a star. Hell, for most white men a black man wearing a star and acting like he has a right to it is a good reason to kill him."

Cletis knew that to get rid of Sarge, he would have to do it. Dutch's hands believed that Sarge had killed Dutch but none of them were brave enough to face him. Cletis believed Sarge could have been prosecuted for Dutch's murder if Skeet hadn't been lynched.

Cody arrested a Mexican suspected of stealing horses. There wasn't much evidence against him; he was a stranger and had no good reason to be in the country, but everyone was edgy with the range war in the background and cowboys would likely have lynched him if they had caught him instead of Cody. Cletis could prove himself a hanging judge before the next election. But a better plan might be to allow the suspect to escape to Mexico if he testified that Sarge had killed Tezel.

"Why would Sarge do that?" Cody asked.

"Ambition," Cletis said. "He wants to own the ranch. He pestered my father to will the ranch to him. Everyone knows he has threatened to quit and take the Rebs with him if he doesn't get his way. How much of a stretch is it for him to kill for the ranch? That's why Sarge and his hands couldn't find the shooter when they heard the shots."

Cletis ordered Cody to form a posse and arrest Sarge. To avoid another battle in the range war Cody rode alone, carrying a message asking Sarge to meet Cletis in his judge's office. It had something to do with the general's murder. Sarge went to Jade Town alone not expecting trouble. He was sitting in Cletis' office listening to Cletis explain why he thought he knew who murdered Tezel when Cody, Jubal and Jade came up behind him, disarmed him and placed him in the roundhouse.

Jade promised Sarge he would keep him safe until he was tried but there was nothing he could do about the trial. Cletis, the judge, would control that because the judge could appoint the jury.

Jade and Jubal feared Augur hands would try to rescue him or one of Dutch's former cowboys would try to kill him. They took turns with one in the suicide hole and the other in the roundhouse with Sarge, switching frequently so the one in the roundhouse could rest.

Word of Sarge's arrest soon hit the range and riders and nesters gathered in Jade Town. When Cletis said it had to be a quick trial, no one objected. Cletis declared that neither Augur nor Rat's Ass cowboys could serve on the jury and appointed plow disciples, most of them new to the county. While Jubal guarded Sarge in the roundhouse, Cody and Jade disarmed everyone in the church house and those loitering outside. There were that many potential killers in town and Jade and Jubal were determined that Sarge would get a trial.

Wilbur believed the only way Sarge could get a fair trial was to move the trial to Menardville or Fort Clark. Gabe had no such concerns. Sarge's contempt of his superiors was treason, which was worse than murder because it destroyed not just a body but the fabric of a moral society. Since Sarge was not on trial for treason he should be hanged for murder.

Despite the testimony of the Mexican horse-thief

and stories of Sarge's violent nature in the Augurville Advertiser not even the newcomers who knew little of county history believed Sarge would ambush his general. However, they feared Sarge and would be happy to be free of him. That was an open door to the gallows.

When Sarge was found guilty, Cody, Jubal and Jade had to force unarmed Augur riders into Curly's club while the members of the jury rode back to their homes or forted up together. Then Jade and Jubal gave their shotguns to Iowa and Mannen and carried rifles to escort Sarge from the church house to the roundhouse.

With Iowa and Mannen backing him, Cody forced the Augur riders out of town, holding one back to return with their guns the next day. When they were gone Cletis declared that Sarge would be hung the next morning. That meant there was no time for even a jiggered gallows. Brother Gabe suggested that they extend a plank from the suicide hole. A rope would be tied far enough from the roundhouse to permit free fall, and the condemned man would be blindfolded with his bandana and forced to walk the plank until he fell and was choked to death. Gabe said he had seen that procedure used on a Rebel sailor who had betrayed the cause.

Early the following morning a few townsmen, three-horse ranchers, and cabbage farmers in town to sell their wares witnessed a handcuffed Sarge brought out of the roundhouse. Sarge asked if he might have a last chaw before he died. A former Dutch cowboy stepped out of the bunch and offered Sarge a plug of tobacco. Sarge bit off a chunk and nodded his gratitude. Cody stood in the suicide hole with a rifle. Jade and Jubal stood on either side of the ladder with shotguns. Everyone waited while

Sarge worked up a cud. Then Brother Gabe followed Sarge up the ladder preaching to him.

"Confess your sins, confess that you betrayed and killed General Tezel because of ambition, confess so that when you strangle in your own spit you will see God waiting to usher you into paradise with Stonewall Jackson, Robert E. Lee, Jeb Stuart, Jeff Davis, Nathan Bedford Forrest, John B. Hood and a host of saints in gray saluting you under a Confederate banner. Die with an oath to the Confederacy on your lips and meet God. Do you have any last words?"

Sarge spat tobacco juice in Brother Gabe's face and Gabe pulled his pistol and shot him. Cletis declared that since he had sentenced Sarge to be hanged, he would be hanged. Cody pushed Sarge's dead body out of the suicide hole. Sarge was hanged but he died honorably shot through the heart. Jubal cleaned Sarge's blood out of the suicide hole.

There were insults, threats, some fist fights but no retaliation by Augur hands against the traitorous jury. When Tezel died, Brine shifted his loyalty to Sarge. With Sarge lynched, Brine no longer knew where he belonged. Like Sarge he felt no kinship to Cletis. But Cletis was the closest thing to the general that Brine knew and Cletis wanted Brine to follow him knowing Brine was as hard to get rid of as cockleburs in a cow's tail.

With Sarge gone, a troubled Brine turned to Brother Gabe. "I dream I kill bad men or lay with whores. Both dreams pleasure me but when I wake up I'm mad but I don't know why."

"You're straddling two horses," Gabe said. "Good and evil. You have to decide which to ride."

It didn't change Brine's dreams or his opinion of Cletis but it gave him a horse to ride. Brine was a killer, not because he liked killing, but because it was the only way he knew to resolve complexity. Brine's thoughts were often tangled.

Cletis ran for the legislature in the next election but lost as his opponent ridiculed him as "the judge who hanged a dead man."

⤵

Caught up in the rapture of the coming railroad with Hoot's stories of businesses springing up beside the track like rain lilies after a rain and promises of an important future for everyone, folks forgot the treachery that aimed the track at Augurville and elected Augurville county seat. Cletis and Cody moved their offices to Augurville to the relief of Jade, Jubal and Wilbur. However, the roundhouse remained as the jail. Some of Wilbur's church members moved to Augurville and allied themselves with Brother Gabe.

The Augurville Advertiser expanded with a section devoted to Jade Town. Brother Gabe's preaching was always reported, along with Gabe's column. Also reported was the decline of Wilbur's church because of the parson's hostility toward business, especially railroading and ranching, the failure of Wilbur to protect his own family, the secret and forbidden marriage of Jade and Rain, and Wilbur's willingness to muddy the white race.

The Advertiser announced that a man named Helmer was the new range boss for the Augur. Helmer, a tall man with pale skin, eyes and hair, knew nothing about cattle and little about men but he knew business, he knew who was boss, and he knew profit and power mattered more than cattle or men.

A photograph of Haskell appeared in the Advertiser with a story of his new barber shop that was the equal of any found west of Fort Worth. There was also an ad for his shop that featured the finest razors and clippers and the most hygienic combs and brushes. An ad in the Advertiser guaranteed a story.

Another ad featured Elvin's wagon sales "offering everything on wheels than was not a locomotive." Hoot wrote that Elvin was building a new store in Augurville and predicted that if the talk of horseless carriages became a reality Elvin would be the first to sell them. However, Hoot opined, in this part of the country, wheels would never replace horses as a means of quick, reliable and efficient transportation.

With businesses, including Mannen's store, moving, planning to move or threatening to move, the Jade Town Council asked Jade to fire Jubal as they could no longer afford him. Jade refused.

Hephsibeth knew her future was close to the tracks and left her son with relief. She moved her business to the old Tejano Saloon in the dirty neck side of Augurville-- bare board floor and walls, coal oil lanterns, no windows and a narrow crib in the back. Hephsibeth enjoyed a business boom with railroad workers who didn't want to fight cowboys in the Augurville Saloon and were attracted to Salvie, who looked in pain even when she smiled.

Ruth and Iowa, Curly, Beneficia and those on Barefoot

Street were fixed in place. Only death could move them. Life was simpler, the streets quieter, but nothing had changed to make them happier. "Jade Town has become so sophisticated that a tumbleweed blowing down the street frightened dogs into barking," the Advertiser reported.

There were no black women in the country and Jubal had been circumspect in regard to white women, including Pearl and Hephsibeth. However, he had made the acquaintance of Beneficia when she was still known as Girl. No one noticed or cared as Girl was judged to be dark enough to be beneath the protection of the law and outside the concerns of society until Skeet was lynched. As his widow and heir Beneficia became a property owner and forbidden to Jubal. There were arguments as to whether Beneficia was white or not but everyone agreed that she was too white to marry a black man.

The Advertiser warned that Jubal was going to marry an anonymous white woman, "further mongrelizing the race." Brother Gabe preached that Yankees, "fearing the absolutism of the pure, still threaten our freedom to live our way of life, with our churches, our schools, our friends, our homes that we hold by sovereign right."

Hoot deplored the aggressive advocacy of "self-righteous outside agitators, racial rabble rousers and pettifoggers who promoted strife, class against class and race against race, bastardizing Southern women. Paid propagandists paint lurid pictures of injustices and inequalities they imagine here while ignoring their landless poor, wretched orphans, unemployed city hovel-dwellers, their piteous beggars on every street."

Brother Gabe declared that outside agitators were

not as harmful as inside traitors, "some of them in the pulpits of our churches." God created separate races and meant them to remain separate. "If God didn't mix them then we have no right to fix what some believe God miscreated. Japheth means fair, Shem means dusky, and Ham means black. To deny that is to deny God."

Wilbur wondered who had given Gabe that misinformation and for what purpose. Hoot invited Wilbur to respond to Brother Gabe. "I believe that all people are created equal and have equal rights," Wilbur wrote.

"Show me in the Holy Writ where God's curse on Ham has been lifted," Gabe challenged.

"The entire New Testament," Wilbur responded. He restrained himself from saying, "If you would read it."

Beneficia, who had been despised by those who abused her and those who closed their eyes to the abuse, had become a cause.

"We will face the wrath of God if we deny the Almighty's curse on Ham," Gabe thundered. "Anyone who accepts the cohabitation of a black man and a white woman is an infidel, dead from the neck up. Amalgamation of the races leads to monstrosities such as Jesus." In his passion Gabe forgot that Beneficia was now regarded as white like Smitty.

Hoot reminded readers that Wilbur had married a white man and an Indian squaw, the cause of much of the lawlessness that followed. When self-called moral leaders were guilty of the worst sins, what happened to their followers? Hoot warned that if Wilbur sanctified the marriage of people of opposite races amalgamation would weaken national security at a time when Spain threatened war if we did not give Spain license to do its nefarious will on helpless Cubans. That was the first time some readers had heard or cared to hear of Cuba.

Wilbur already faced his own insurrection and the news that Spain could land troops on the coast of Texas frightened good Christians into firing him and Brother Gabriel was pastor of two churches.

The Jade Town Council fired Jubal for moral "torpitude." Neither Hoot nor Wilbur attempted to correct the Council. Jubal took odd jobs, janitor, painter, porter, gardener, wood-cutter, well-digger, and volunteer deputy. Because there was no fire in Jade's old shack, Rain often invited Jubal to meals and when it was cold, Rain loaned Jubal the buffalo robe. Jubal never asked where she got it.

Gabe wanted Wilbur's church house. Wilbur had supervised the building of the church house, had painted, cleaned and repaired it himself, lately with help from Jubal and Jade, although neither felt comfortable when the church occupied the church house. Jade encouraged Wilbur to sue for ownership of the church house although Cletis was unlikely to allow it.

Wilbur loved the church house. Like him it was sturdy, humble, honest, put together with skill but without flair, a church house built for the frontier, built to last with appropriate care. It was not intended to impress viewers with the skill of the builder or to inspire worshipers with the builder's lofty dreams. Without the cross the building was as intentionally anonymous as the charity of the pastor. Wilbur had never meant the church's home to be his possession. The idea struck him as greedy if not heretical. How could a man own what was dedicated to God? He would use the parsonage for a school.

Jubal asked Beneficia to marry him to honor her and their union. Jubal could operate the blacksmith shop and livery, and become the father of Jesus. He asked Wilbur to perform the ceremony. Wilbur wrestled with that angel all one night. Because he no longer represented the church but only God, Wilbur decided that marriage was sacred and for that reason he should honor the union of Jubal and Beneficia and pray for God's blessing on their family.

First Jubal wanted an apology from Brother Gabe. Jubal rode to Augurville alone trying to work out what he wanted the preacher to apologize for. Calling Beneficia white? Calling Jubal black? Calling their planned marriage forbidden? Jubal was black and he made no apology for it. If Beneficia was white it was illegal for them to marry, but Brother Gabe would have to explain why and when she became white. And the brother would, by gum, apologize for calling Jesus a monstrosity.

Jubal wisely avoided the Augurville Saloon and went directly in search of Gabe. He found Gabe in the printing shop. Jubal's presence in town was reported to Cletis and Cody. Cody and Brine went to the printing shop and found Gabe on his knees apologizing.

"You're no longer the law," Cody said. "Get your black ass out of this town and out of this county if you know what's good for you."

Years in the army had taught Jubal self-control and he turned to leave. As he walked past Cody, Cody drew his gun and shot Jubal in the back. Jubal turned and fired at Cody knocking off his hat and creasing his scalp. Brine shot Jubal in the chest, although he had rather shoot Cody. Cody fired again killing Haskell who had run out of his new barber shop at the first gunshot. Cody's next shot killed Jubal. Cody shot him two more times to be sure. The newspaper quoted Brine as saying, "Cody don't want no ghosts following him," and editorialized, "Sheriff Cody did his job by saving the county both money and decency."

There was a hearing in Augurville with Cletis presiding. The jury was composed of Augur cowboys, most of them new and bossed by Buckshot Bob under the direction of Cletis. The old hands had left after the death of Sarge but the new ones were also unreconstructed. They found the killing of Jubal justified as it cleansed the country of the black stain.

༄

"Two men dead in a shootout between law men," the Advertiser trumpeted. The entire front page told the story of Jubal's death. "In a deadly duel, a notorious Negro gunman was killed by county sheriff Cody Highsmith." The paper that rarely reported anything outside of the Devils country noted America's farmers and ranchers were producing more than Americans consumed. Cuba would be an ideal export if Cuba were free and there were railroads to transport the cattle to Galveston for shipping.

The Cuban revolutionary party headquartered in New York reported that colonial brutality continued. Cubans were concentrated in death camps and tortured especially Amazonian warriors. Spaniards had resorted to cannibalism.

There was also brief notice of other news--a Negro riot in Florida ended when six colored men were shot and the ringleader lynched, the Reading Railroad had failed, 74 railroads were bankrupt.

There was no way the railroads could fail. Until they did, taking 500 or more banks, 15,000 companies and the nation's economy with them. But the few at the top were rich beyond reason, the richest people in the land. It was a great success story.

༄

Folks in Jade Town did not want Jubal buried in the cemetery with white people. Jade and Wilbur dug a grave on top of a low hill where Jubal sometimes watched goings-on in Jade Town to be close enough to ride in if there were trouble. Wilbur read a Scripture and told of Jubal's contribution to the community and his loyalty to a country that did not repay the debt. Rain and Hannah spoke of Jubal's tenderness to Beneficia and his companionship to Jesus. Jade remembered Jubal as his first partner and friend since his father died. There were also curiosity seekers, the same people who every day charted the progress of the railroad toward the county. Some still believed the train would come to Jade Town.

༄

"Was it all for nothing?" Jade asked Hannah and Wilbur. "Building the church house, trying to save the

Indians, trying to save Mattie, trying to save the water for the town. Was it all for nothing?"

"We did save the water for the town," Wilbur said.

"And we taught the children to read and write," Hannah added. "They will determine the future of the country."

"And they read the 'hate outsiders, hate the Union, hate the blacks and Indians who can never be part of us' sermons that Gabe writes for the Advertiser. 'Loyalty to the Confederate dead that they did not die in vain,'" Rain said.

"We can teach them to read so they can read the Bible and to write and do sums so they can understand their world, we can teach them about love and peace and caring for one's neighbor so they can be good citizens, but we can't make them practice it. There are competing ideas," Wilbur said.

"So Brother Gabe won?" Rain asked.

"No," Wilbur concluded. "It will take a long time but time is on our side. Already some things are better. Jade doesn't follow Indians to kill them; he married one," Wilbur said with a smile. "Other people don't shoot Indians on sight. The children still live in misery and try to escape by drudgery, crime or early marriage, and produce children who will live in misery. But some of them can read and write and that can give them hope. It can introduce them to a better possible world. Men still kill men and their weapons are better but fewer people are shot in the street. There is hate, anger, greed, lust but I have preached against them and now it is better disguised as commerce."

"Will you be moving away?" Rain asked Hannah.

"There are still children to teach," Hannah said. "Since he no longer has the church Wilbur has asked that we be paid for teaching."

"I'm a pretty good carpenter," Wilbur said. "I'm building tables, chairs, shelves,and cabinets, whatever someone wants that a carpenter can do. At last I have gotten to where Jesus began--carpentry."

"There are also the poor and sick on Barefoot Street," Hannah said. "They need someone to minister to them. And those whose loyalty is to the nation rather than the few. Wilbur can preach under a tree. He has done it before. You don't need a church house to have a church."

"Outcasts need a church too," Wilbur said.

"There's talk that Brother Gabe wants to move into your house," Jade said.

"Hannah and I built the house ourselves," Wilbur said. "No one else has ever owned it."

"But the school meets there and the school belongs to Jade Town," Jade said, voicing arguments that he had heard.

"I allow the school to meet there until a school is built," Wilbur said.

"I wish Brother Gabriel would find greener pastures somewhere else," Hannah said.

"He won't leave," Jade said. "He's on the Augur payroll."

"Are you sure of that?" Wilbur asked. "I knew he was a company man, but if cowboys find out he's on the Augur payroll that will be the end of his ministry in this country."

Rain made sure the cowboys did find out but Wilbur was mistaken. They already knew. They assumed all preachers were on the payroll of those in power.

Cletis fumed at delays in track laying as the railroad bosses sought more acreage from him, more cash from businesses. "This ain't no transcontinental race by two big moguls," a mucky-muck told him. "This is a small company linking towns that want to be linked enough to pay for it. We lay the track when we have the money in hand. You'll get all the track you pay for."

Cletis had not paid enough. Unable or unwilling to pay more, he agreed that the tracks could be located a mile from the outskirts of Augurville so that the railroad could sell what had been Augur land to increase the value of railroad shares.

⌐

Curly hired Wilbur to replace the frequently broken chairs and tables in his club and to make it more church-like, more solemn, to put in plank floors, maybe a window. Since Brother Gabe now preached from the church house that Wilbur had built, Curly invited Wilbur to preach in his Paradise Club. Curly's former customers had switched allegiance to Gabe's church where politics had replaced whores and religion had replaced alcohol. The background didn't matter; the message was all. Whether it was the wrath of God or the grace of God depended on the bottom line.

Parson Wilbur found he had nothing to say that Curly's club members wanted to hear, enraptured by the railroad and the fortunes and fun that awaited them at its coming. Curly had no dogma except that a dollar was a dollar. Alcohol, a new whore called Jovita, and railroad gangs kept his club open.

Jovita had been pretty until the teamster she claimed was her husband abandoned her in Jade Town. She limped to Iowa's store but Ruth didn't want her inside it. Mannen had no need for her as he was moving the last of his goods to Augurville. She wasn't educated enough to teach in Wilbur's school. Rain did the family laundry and with Jade's reduced paycheck there was no money to pay for help. Rain and Hannah took turns feeding her. Wilbur allowed her to sleep in Belle's room until Curly offered Jovita a job. She knew what men wanted. She had been treated roughly before, she knew her only chance to endure, perhaps to survive, was to do what she was told and to be sweet about it.

Wilbur held services under the trees and married and buried those who could not afford Brother Gabe. Belle married a former teacher, a recent widower with two small children, and moved with her own child to Belton where she seemed at peace. Rain's and Beneficia's boys became friends. Rain was drawn to Beneficia because Rain had also been an alien.

⌒

Beneficia's livery stable failed in Jade Town and she had no future in Augurville. In addition to buttons and dippers Rain taught Beneficia and Jesus to weave baskets. She gave them stones from her medicine bag, told them to find more like them and she would help them make Indian jewelry to sell at her vacant livery. Since the Indians had been eradicated or removed what was left of their culture became quaint and attractive.

Rain tried to interest Noble in finding pretty stones but Noble thought making jewelry was childish. He liked Beneficia and Jesus but he had no desire to learn Indian ways. He wanted to be a lawman like Jade.

Jesus liked school, although the girls shunned him and curled their lips when they accidentally saw him. He tried to be friends with Pancho's boys, the other outsiders. Mick's boys enjoyed grudging acceptance and ignored him. Jesus ran away from home to work for the railroad where he faced the same harassment he did in school. But this was different, he wrote his mother, they were all men and roughhousing was the link to friendship.

⌒

When Noble asked his father to teach him how to shoot, Jade told him to wait until his hand was big enough to grip a hog-leg. Noble worked with his hands to make them bigger but when he demonstrated he was ready Jade was reluctant. "You're safer if you never wear a gun. If you wear one, be prepared to kill or be killed. Walk away from every argument you can but watch your back while doing it. If you have to kill someone, make up your mind to do it before they do. That will give you time to pull your gun and aim it. A lot of men have been killed by a shot that missed."

Jade taught Noble to shoot straight but not how to

draw. "Take this gun and shoot jackrabbits. That's good training."

"Noble is too young to learn shooting," Rain said.

"Is that what you told your Indian son?" Jade asked, "the one who stole a soldier's horse?"

"That was a way to show skill and daring, manhood."

"To soldiers and cowboys it was stealing," Jade said.

"To soldiers killing is manhood. Braves made raids to get horses as part of their culture like cowboys wearing six-shooters when there is nothing to shoot but each other. Braves endangered themselves but it was a tradition they wanted to hold on to. We fought other Indians over hunting grounds but we didn't burn villages. Soldiers shot Indians the way Noble shoots jackrabbits."

"He has to hit one first," Jade said.

Frustrated, Noble rode to Augurville. Cody always pretended a quick draw with an empty hand when he saw Noble. Sometimes they played they were drawing on each other. Noble knew Cody was a killer and asked Cody's advice. Cody loaned him the first cheap pistol that Cody had owned. It was a humble gun useful for scaring off coyotes but the gun belt had ruffles. The leather had been stitched and stamped and decorated with silver conchos. Wearing it made Noble feel like a real man and he practiced his draw every chance he got, mostly at night when he wouldn't be seen.

The front sight on the gun vexed Noble. He wanted to remove it for a faster draw but he was afraid Iowa would tell Jade. He practiced shooting at jackrabbits but the faster he drew, the more likely he was to miss.

Noble told his parents he was riding out to shoot

coyotes, maybe gone all day, carrying the unloaded gun he borrowed from Jade and concealing the gun borrowed from Cody. Rain and Jade talked about his absences. Jade figured Noble had discovered a nester's daughter. Rain feared he would go to Augurville for a lark, perhaps to a saloon for excitement, meet Hephsibeth by accident. That fear lurked in her heart.

Cody gave Noble tips on gun fighting. "It don't matter how big they are, if you need to kill someone start an argument to give you an excuse to get close, point at them with your off hand so they'll point at you with their gun hand, and that's the time to draw. If you want to be a lawman learn who holds the reins. Take care of them and they'll take care of you. Get catawampus with them and they'll take care of you in a different way."

"You mean kill you?"

"They're back shooters so they'll start talk that will get you fired, get you arrested, get you to move on, kill you if necessary. Jade could have gone places, been somebody but he tripped himself every step he took."

"You mean my daddy?" Noble asked.

Cody shrugged. "I reckon he could be your daddy."

Noble was puzzled. What did that mean? He didn't know Cody well enough to ask him what he meant but he was going to ask his dad when he got home. He stopped by Hephsibeth's saloon. He liked to watch cowboys and especially to listen to them. Few came to Jade Town anymore and those who did spent their time in Brother Gabe's church. He asked for a beer. The bartender hesitated but since Noble was wearing a gun he was old enough to drink.

"Hey, chief, you're young to be holding up your pants with a six-gun. You going to be a killer like your daddy?"

"Jade ain't no killer," Noble said to much laughter.

"You look like Cody to me."

Noble knew who the cold-eyed killer was. Brine. Noble studied whether he and his father had been insulted, whether he should shoot Brine or not. He had never shot a man before. He tried to fix his mind on killing Brine but his mind skittered away from it. He returned home cursing himself as a coward.

Noble was quiet at supper, his head filled with questions he didn't know how to ask. Jade and Rain noticed his behavior and Jade asked if he had a fight with some girl.

"Nope."

Noble knew Cody was the one he had to ask. He didn't look for Cody but the next time he saw Cody alone, he asked, "How can you tell who your daddy is?"

"You know Jesus?" Cody asked, using the English pronunciation. "The harelip kid? His daddy had a harelip. Smitty. That's how we knew."

Noble's mother said he walked like Jade but stood like Little Bear, her Indian son. "I didn't know Jesus had a daddy."

"I killed him."

"Why did you kill him?"

"He insulted me."

Brine had insulted Noble and his father. Brine had intended it. Noble reached for something to stop his spinning mind. "Folks say I look like you."

"Don't mean nothing. Hell, you look like half the

folks in the Devils country."

Noble's mouth trembled and so did his hands. He was confused and scared and about to cry, afraid that was an insult.

Cody saw it too. "I ain't talking about squaw woman," he said, putting his left hand on Noble's shoulder to shove him off-balance if Noble tried to draw. "I'm talking about Hephsibeth."

Hephsibeth? Noble knew who Hephsibeth was. He had seen her in her saloon when it was in Jade Town but had never talked to her. They wouldn't sell him beer in her Jade Town saloon, afraid of Jade, but they would have let him in the room at the back where Hephsibeth kept a whore. Noble knew Hephsibeth had a few special friends, including Cody, but how could Hephsibeth be his mother?

"You think Hephsibeth is my mother?"

"Ask your squaw mother."

Noble rode back to Jade Town in confusion and he didn't like confusion, and he hated Cody for causing it. He liked things the way they were before Cody. He wanted to kill someone to make the world the one he knew but he didn't know who to kill.

"Are you my mother?" Noble asked Rain.

Rain and Jade had talked many times about when to tell Noble that he was adopted but the story was as tangled as a horse in barbed wire where every attempt at release meant danger and pain. How were they to explain that his mother was a whore who didn't want him and that no one knew who his father was?

Rain wanted him to wait and talk to his father or

talk to both of them but Noble was anxious to stand his world upright. "Is Hephsibeth my mother?"

"Hephsibeth brought you into the world but Riley and I are the ones who mother and father you in the world. It's like when you pour milk into your cornmeal mush. The milk comes from the pitcher but in the bowl it mixes with the mush and butter. With people, that's called family and we are your family. You have been our son from the day you were born."

"Is Jade my pitcher father?"

"Jade is your family father."

"Is Cody my pitcher father?

"He could be," Rain said.

"Were Cody and Hephzibeth married?"

"No," Rain conceded.

"My mother is a whore."

"I am your mother," Rain yelled as Noble ran from the house.

⌒

Hephzibeth didn't know who he was. "Salvie in the back room is better for kids your age," she said to him with a wink.

"I'm your son," Noble said.

Hephsibeth gave Noble a slow and careful look-see. "Are you Rain's boy?" she asked.

"She said you were my mother."

Hephsibeth shook her head. "I didn't have no place to raise a kid," she said.

"Rain did."

"If you was a girl I might have kept you. I didn't want another man in the world tormenting women," Hephsibeth said. "The way you're tormenting me."

"Who hit you?" Noble said seeing her bruised face.

"It don't matter. That's what men do, starting with my father. Now you."

"Why?"

"Men don't come to me for love or conversation. They come to me to please themselves. Oh, they talk. About themselves. Their mothers. Their wives, girlfriends. That's when the beatings come. Because I'm nothing like their mother, a good woman who would starve before she whored. I'm nothing like their wives who would never do the things they want me to do. They hit me because they loathe themselves for needing me."

Helphsibeth signaled the bar dog to bring Noble a beer and sat down at a table. "You're lucky you weren't left under a bush for the lobos."

"What are lobos?" Noble asked. He had never seen a lobo but had heard people use the word from time to time.

"Some people call them loafers. They're wolves," Hephzibeth said, "but they're all gone now except in stories to keep kids from wandering off. Hell, when I was a kid we ran wild, all over the settlement and as far as we dared into the country. We didn't worry about lobos. It was Indians we was scared of."

Noble refused to be deterred. "Who was my father?"

Hephzibeth wasn't ashamed in front of a kid she didn't even know. "Hell, I don't know. Your mother and father is whoever wants you."

"Is Cody my father?"

Hephzibeth screwed up her face. "Could be, I reckon."

⌣

Everyone in the country went to see the first train that rolled into Augurville. The depot stood unpainted and unfinished a mile outside Augurville but was bedecked with colorful ribbons and ornamented with displays of produce, scrubbed children, costumed citizens, and Brine and Buckshot Bob tricked out in colorful shirts and bandanas, striped pants, leather vests and garnished with shotguns, pistols and knives. Some buildings had been moved to the tracks, some new stores and houses were being built. Empty lots were laid out, some marked "sold." The closer to the planned courthouse the more expensive the lots.

Boys hawked a collector edition of the Advertiser. The front page consisted of photographs of the railroad men and the county men who brought the train to Augurville, and a drawing of a train emerging from the darkness of a tunnel into the bright light of the future. Another photograph was of a doctor coming to Augurville on the train. A cow town turned railroad center seemed the ideal place for a doctor and undertaker.

Inside the paper was a drawing of a naked woman flinching before leering Spanish soldiers and showing readers more of the backside of a woman than some married men had seen. The accompanying story told of the audacity of Spaniards strip-searching an American woman.

Some readers were more scandalized by the audacity

of the Advertiser selling pornography than they were that of the Spaniards. Hoot defended the story and drawing that came from eastern newspapers as revealing the larger truth of Spanish cruelty and crudity, and lack of respect for America and American women.

Another inside story was of colonial brutality toward the helpless Cuban people with drawings of an old man being whipped and a suspected guerrilla tortured into a false confession that he was paid by Americans to blow up trains and burn sugar plantations.

A six-piece band from Comstock played a tune that some Rebels recognized as "There will be a demonstration with pompous ostentation by the black K.P.s of this great nation." Hoot and the Rebs opposed reconciliation with the North. Yankees and Southerners, blacks and whites serving side by side in the military was repugnant to them. Hands on guns the Rebs told the band to play Dixie.

Dixie and the shouts of the newsboys were drowned out by the ringing bell, chuffing engine, squealing brakes, hissing boiler, screaming crowd. A large flowered wreath above the cowcatcher introduced the engine decorated with painted buffalos and the passenger cars trimmed in ribbons. Boys ran alongside the train and someone inside threw fresh oranges to them.

Women held on to their hats and men screwed down their own, the bankers and store punchers tugging their hats down by both sides, the cowboys and farmers getting a grip at the front and giving it a yank. When at last the steam was released, everyone rushed to touch the glass windows and look at the luxury inside. Parents held up their children to see the dignitaries step off the train, the mayor, judge, a couple of legislators. Cody was first, waving at the crowd and shaking the hands of those who mattered. Brine with a look and Buckshot Bob with his shotgun pushed back the audience until the honorees de-boarded. Cody disappeared in the clapping, cheering crowd.

Jade, Rain and Noble rode to the depot in a trap rented from Iowa. On the way out of Jade Town they noticed that the church house needed paint, a window was cracked, and the door half-open. Rain sent Noble to close it to keep out dust. Doors and window frames yawned at the Tezel house, the biggest in town.

There were other see-through houses, Mannen's see-through store, the barber shop with doors and windows broken or stolen. People and stores were moving to Augurville to be beside the railroad tracks. The Widow Waller Saloon awaited a new tenant.

Noble rode in the back, hiding Cody's cheap pistol rolled up in one of Rain's shawls. His father forbade him to bring the gun he shot jackrabbits with. The shawl was a Christmas present Jade had allowed him to pick out for Rain. "What are you doing with my shawl?" Rain asked, believing he was too young to be taking presents to girlfriends.

"I'm taking it to my mother," he said.

The word stung Rain's heart. She had loved him, cared for him, been his mother and he used the word for another.

At the depot Jade stayed with Rain rather than assisting Brine and Buckshot Bob keeping kids off the track and the train. Cletis had asked Rain to come dressed as an Indian to add color to the event but she was hard to distinguish from the others. While Rain and Jade listened to the mayor, the railroad honchos and Cletis, who was no longer judge but was the hero of the occasion, Noble slipped away.

Noble walked until he was sufficiently distant from the depot to buckle on the gun belt that would show Hephsibeth he wasn't a kid and should be taken seriously. There were few in attendance at Hephsibeth's saloon that was the closest building to the depot. Most would celebrate at the Augur Saloon after the ceremonies. Noble was told Hephsibeth wasn't available. "Wake her up and bring me a beer and be quick about it," he told the bar buckaroo.

The man looked at the shawl Noble had forgotten on his shoulder. To cover his embarrassment Noble placed his hand on the butt of his six-shooter. He wasn't no mutt to be kicked or ignored. "Okay," the barkeep said holding up his hands. Noble nodded, pleased with himself.

A cowboy turned to face Noble. "Nice shawl," he remarked. "Got a girlfriend here?"

"What's it to you?" Noble asked.

"Did you straddle your horse on the wrong side?"

"You calling me a squaw?" Noble asked, hand on gun again.

"What are you tossing your horns about?" the cowboy said. "This is a celebration."

"Don't take me for a kid," Noble said determined to kill or die before taking an insult. The cowboy turned his back to avoid trouble.

Noble saw his mother stumble out of the back room.

She had been savagely beaten and Cody posed behind her in the doorway like an artist behind his masterpiece. Noble was surprised to see Cody, expecting him to spend the day with the dignitaries.

"You beat me because you're weak," Hephsibeth whimpered.

"Bitch," Cody said, hitting her in the upper back. Noble hurried to catch her before she fell. "Get a proper whore, you old hag. Someone not so eager to fork her legs for every man in the county. Sorry bitch." Seeing Noble he said, "You come to see your mammy? Your whore mammy? Yeah, run to your whore son, the little son-of-a-bitch."

"You can't call me that," Noble said.

"You ain't got the huevos of a pullet," Cody said, smirking like a magnate who has just stolen another magnate's company.

Tears of rage and humiliation stung Noble's eyes. His chin trembled. He knew he was going to die but he had to be a man. Noble fixed his mind on killing Cody, remembering to be certain that the front sight cleared the holster, and to aim at a specific place before pulling the trigger.

"I ain't no pullet," he yelled and pulled his gun but it misfired.

Cody fired, the bullet hitting Noble in the gut. Noble doubled over but cocked the hammer and pulled the trigger again. The bullet didn't fire. Then he collapsed on the floor. "Stupid kid," Hephsibeth said, falling to the floor beside him. She rolled the shawl and put it under his head. "This is what happens. If you had just left me alone."

"He drew first," Cody said to those in the saloon. "You saw it. He drew first." He memorized their faces as his witnesses, his stare a warning of what he expected from them.

"He's a kid," Hephsibeth screamed.

"He's your kid," Cody said. "You should have taught him better." Cody slipped out of the saloon through the gathering crowd.

"Better get out of town," Buckshot told him.

"Jade will never kill me," Cody said. He beckoned Buckshot to follow him. "Go to the Augur store. Get behind the flour bags. I'll let Jade see me and I'll run inside. Jade will follow and we'll both empty our guns into him. The second man, got it? I'll be the first." Buckshot nodded.

∽

In one of the boxcars a vendor chipped slivers of ice and gave them to kids along with flyers announcing that an ice maker was coming to Augurville and until it opened ice would come by train. Jade and Rain looked for Noble among the children but did not find him. Jade looked for Brine or Buckshot Bob to help with the search but did not find them either.

The dignitaries had already departed for Augurville and the doctor had ridden with them to seek a suitable location for his office when those far enough from the crowd noise heard a gunshot. The doctor hurried to ply his craft. He saw a crowd outside the saloon and heard that inside a whore had been beaten. The doctor stepped over Noble and opened his bag to stitch up Hephsibeth's torn face and tack down her torn ear.

Jade ran for the trap, Rain beside him, and raced to Augurville with others drawn to gunfire. Jade pushed his way through the crowd outside and inside, grabbed the doctor's arm and told him to do something for his son. The doctor looked at Noble on the floor and shook his head. "I can do something for this one," he said of Hephsibeth.

Rain dropped to the floor beside Noble opposite Hephsibeth, cradled his head in the shawl that had been hers and kissed his face. Jade pointed his gun at the doctor and said again, "Do something for my son."

The doctor turned from Hephsibeth and studied Noble's wound, sniffed it and said, "There's no hope."

Noble began to cry. Rain said, "There is always hope. There has to be hope." The doctor looked at her as though she were another whore and said, "There is no hope." He turned his attention back to Hepsibeth.

Jade put his gun to the doctor's temple. "The bullet pierced his bowel," the doctor said. "Smell for yourself. There is no hope."

"You can do something."

"Nothing can be done."

Noble was screaming in pain, asking for water because his insides were aflame, begging his father to shoot him. "Don't give him water," the doctor said. "Shooting him is up to you."

"Please, Dad, please. Help me."

Wilbur came as soon as he heard, prayed for Noble, explained to Noble that there was nothing those who loved him could do, and read and quoted scriptures to distract him from his agony.

"Somebody shoot me. I can't stand it," Noble cried.

Rain and Hephsibeth wept over Noble. Hephsibeth called for water and cloths and she and Rain tried to cool Noble who was burning with infection. Jade sent Hannah to the train for ice. "He tried to help me," Hephsibeth said. "He tried to protect me. Cody shot him."

Rain wailed in fury and grief. If Cody hadn't told Noble that Jade wasn't his father, that she wasn't his mother, Noble would be begging to ride the first train in the county, enjoying the band from Comstock, laughing at the stiff-collar potentates trying to look important, sucking slivers of ice. After the third hour Rain told Jade she was going to kill Noble if he didn't. "No one deserves to suffer that much," she said.

Jade shook his head. The idea of both fathers shooting Noble and both mothers implicated in Noble's death was off the reservation. Jade and Wilbur crushed ice and put it on Noble's body. Mercifully Noble died after two more hours.

"This is what happens in this business," Hephsibeth cried. "I never wanted to be a whore. I never wanted to get married. I never wanted to have children. I wanted a life of my own. I wanted someone to love. This is what I was allowed." Hephsibeth cried over the misfortune her life had been. Later, Hoot would write that no one knew which of Noble's mothers mourned his death the most.

After Noble died, Wilbur's attention turned to Rain and Hephsibeth. Rain shook off his ministrations and looked at Jade. "Cody won't be alone," she said.

"No."

"But you're going anyway."

"Yes."

"Let me borrow a gun and I'll go with you." Rain would watch for Brine, maybe Buckshot.

Hephsibeth gave Rain the shotgun behind the bar. "Aim for the lowest button on his britches," she said.

Rain took the shawl and put it around her neck. "This is mine," she said.

"Do you want to do this?" Wilbur asked Jade. "Should Noble's death be tarnished by the deaths of others? Blemished by your arrest for killing an officer of the law? Is this the example you want to leave? Two lawmen shooting it out in front of citizens they took an oath to protect? Is this the story you want told of your son's death?"

"What other way is there?" Jade asked. "Cody is a killer. Now he has killed a kid and the law is on his side. You have said there is no perfect justice in this world. What other way is there?"

"Vengeance belongs to the Lord," Wilbur said. "I have to believe that's true."

⤚

The first person Jade and Rain saw was Brother Gabe who sported a gold railroad pocket watch and was armed. He held up empty hands. "I'm no part of this," he said. "Vengeance is yours, saith the Lord."

Jade and Rain walked into the Augur saloon, one standing on either side of the door, Jade holding a six-gun, Rain holding a shotgun. "We're looking for Cody," Jade said. "If that concerns you speak up now." The cowboys turned their attention to their cards, drinks or conversation. Jade and Rain waited beside the door. "No Augur cowboy rides for Cody," Brine said. "We ride for the general's silk shirt son."

Inside a former store that had become the courthouse Jade and Rain found a room filled with dignitaries and Cletis in full gloat at the head of the table. Jade studied their hands. One man had a small bruise under a nail and he clenched his smooth hand to hide it, hoping no one thought it was dirt. None of their hands had held a lariat, a shovel or a gun in earnest. Deciding the fate of others was the sweatiest work they had ever done.

A man and a woman holding guns stopped conversation. "What's the meaning of this?" Cletis asked.

"Cody shot our son and the meaning of this is we aim to do justice. If he surrenders and you let him go, we'll do justice to both of you. Declare your hand now. Cody is going to get a fair trial and you are going to see to it or you and Cody will both get a fair shot at defending yourselves."

Cletis slowly raised his hands. "I'm a businessman. I'm no longer judge, remember?" Hoot and the new judge sat beside him at the table, both of them sporting gold railroad pocket watches and flanked by railroad bosses.

"You and these gents have got justice by the throat but we're going to loosen the grip a bit or a whole lot," Jade said. "Take your pick."

"We want to get back to business," Cletis said. "That has nothing to do with justice."

"Railroad business has more to do with justice than with business. I was once in your business, killing Indians for you, but I did it myself and I didn't steal their land."

"We know you can have us killed," Rain said. "Better get both of us at the same time or we'll follow you until you have one careless moment."

"I move this be old business and we put this behind us and take up new business," a railroad boss said. "I second the motion," said his club buddy.

"New business better be quick because we'll be back to help you gents decide your future," Jade said.

↜

Brine reached Cody first. "Jade is looking for you and he has his shooter face on. And so does his squaw wife. I don't know what they're thinking but I know it's about you."

"Jade ain't going to kill me," Cody said. "I can tell you that. I'm waiting for him."

↜

Jade and Rain walked down Main Street that was narrower than Jade Town's Broad Street, past a horse pawing at the ground, digging its own grave. At the livery stable they found nothing, but the horses seemed restless and Jade was more cautious coming out of the livery, suspecting an ambush. He looked one way, Rain the other. They took separate sides of the street, staying close to buildings, pausing before each door and window, both of them leveling guns at the same opening.

❧

Brine waited outside the courthouse for Cletis to come out. "Jade and the squaw is looking for Cody," Brine said. "And they both got guns."

"We'll rid the country of both of them," Cletis said. "Buckshot Bob is laying for Jade in the store and when he sees Jade he'll empty both barrels. You need to be in the store when Cody gets there or the squaw will kill him or Buckshot. Maybe both."

Brine left the courthouse, turned the corner and saw Jade and Rain coming down the street. Cody fired a long shot at Jade that missed. Both Jade and Rain returned fire, both shooting short. Cody ran for the store. Brine knew what duty required.

❧

"There he is," Rain said. Out of range, Cody leaned against a building, his arms crossed against his chest. Jade nodded.

"You ain't going to kill me," Cody shouted.

When they drew close to six-gun range Cody fired and missed. Jade and Rain returned fire, both kicking up dust. When Cody ran they trotted after him still wary of an ambush.

❧

Brine ran to get into the store before Cody. Cody, hampered by his warped foot, saw Brine running to the store and feared Brine would get to the door first. "Wait, wait," Cody yelled at Brine.

Brine burst through the door and jumped to one side for a clear shot.

"Don't," Cody yelled at Buckshot as he came through the door. Too late. Buckshot, who had taken a stand behind bags of flour, unloaded two barrels of buckshot into Cody's chest. Cody crumpled to the floor, his momentum leaving a skid of blood across the planks.

The door to the store was still open and Jade and Rain stopped outside on opposite sides of the door, uncertain as to what had happened. Both listened, mouths open, breathing hard. "I'm throwing my gun out," Buckshot said, throwing out his shotgun.

"Six-shooter, too," Jade said. The six-shooter followed. "Come out with your hands up." Buckshot slowly came outside and Rain pulled him in front of her and kicked Buckshot's shotgun behind her.

"I didn't go to but I did your killing for you," Buckshot said.

"Brine, what are you going to do," Jade called.

"I ain't holding my hands over my head. I ain't throwing out my gun neither but I'm holstering it. I got no further duty here. I'll come out but I ain't surrendering."

"Come out slowly. Rain's got the shotgun on you."

Brine came out his arms out but not raised. "It was Cody's idea," Buckshot said. "Jade was supposed to be second."

"I done what I was told to do," Brine said, proud of

having done his duty.

"Anyone else inside?" Jade asked.

"I'm a soldier and I ain't talking," Brine said. Buckshot shook his head no.

Leaving the two men to Rain's control, Jade stepped quickly inside and to one side of the door. He surveyed the store for hiding places, then kicked Cody's gun aside and kneeled over him.

"I always said you'd never kill me," Cody said. "I'm dying by accident." He tried to smile. "You'll never hang me neither. No man can ever claim he killed me in a fair fight."

Jade picked up Cody's gun and left him to die alone. Outside he turned his attention to Brine and Buckshot. "What are your plans?" Jade asked.

"I ride for Cletis. If he don't need me I'm headed for Arizona terrortory," Brine said, mindless of the irony.

"Wyoming for me," Buckshot said.

"Then hit the saddle," Jade said.

～

When Wilbur heard the double shot he ran toward the sound. "It may be a trick," the doctor yelled.

"I have to save them if I can," Wilbur said. When he saw Jade and Rain outside the store he slowed. Jade nodded inside. Wilbur went in and kneeled beside Cody. "Cody's dead," he said when he returned outside.

"Outsmarted himself," Rain said.

"Is that enough?" Wilbur asked. "Are you disappointed that you didn't get to do it?"

"It's over for now," Jade said. He and Rain both held guns. "Soon enough it will start again. Some will always resort to violence to enforce their will," Jade said.

"Maybe we can be better," Wilbur said.

Rain and Jade looked at each other. "That was before barbed wire," Jade said as he re-holstered his six-shooter.

⤶

Back in the courthouse only Cletis and board members remained. The others who had invested in the railroad discovered their investment was nearly worthless and left. The railroad had no money to extend its line until the state, and more counties and towns paid them to come. They gave shares to Hoot for ads and stories. The board members sat sullen and silent.

"Now hold on," the railroad boss man said. "Back east there are rumblings of a war and we want to support it. There's a lot of money to be made in war and we believe the federal government might subsidize our line to connect with Galveston or Corpus Christi."

"We want America to ride to war on rails and the trains to float on oil," said the boss's bordello buddy. "We have found oil under Augur land that is now ours. The government might pay us to drill for oil. War is our ticket to riches, more riches than we can dream of."

"The country needs this war," Hoot said, ignoring the gun play outside that left two men dead. "That's the story I'm printing and other newspapers will print it too."

"We're working now to change steam ships from coal to oil," the boss man said. "The coal mines are lobbying for coal. We have to win this battle in Congress or the oil industry will fail. That requires a lot of money."

Cletis tried to hide the smile he felt. If there was oil under the land he traded for railroad shares there was oil under the land he kept for himself. He was going to be rich. With a balance of land and investments in oil and transportation he had a future in politics. If not as an elected official, as the man behind the elected official. The man who could make things like war happen.

Chapter Five

Civilization Comes to the Devils Country

As though missing the Indians and the opportunity for heroism, sensationalism, killing and theft, the nation like a victorious fighter looked for the thrill of battle. Newspapers, even the Advertiser, carried lurid stories of female Cuban prisoners guarded by brutish Spanish soldiers. Artists sketched pictures of starving peasant women and children. A congressman envying other nations colonizing other lands in the name of God and commerce or god as Commerce said, "Wake up America! It's time we grabbed some property for ourselves." Another said, "We are a conquering race. We must obey our blood and occupy new markets, and if necessary, new lands."

Although there were few stories of success by Cuban rebels newspapers reported that the sabotage of railroads, the burning of sugar cane fields and sugar processing plants cost American investors hundreds of thousands of dollars. Investors demanded US intervention. Hoot editorialized that US trade with Cuba was reason enough to liberate Cuban peasants from Spain's cruel control. The president was quoted as warning Spain, "The United

States is not a nation to which peace is a necessity."

The Advertiser announced that Brine had been elected sheriff and that Buckshot Bob was his deputy. Jade, who had been reelected Jade Town marshal, knew Cletis still aimed Brine's bullets.

An ad announced a new furniture store beside the train tracks that sold factory-made furniture cheaper than Wilbur could make it. Another ad announced that the new doctor in New Augurville had a pill for every illness, a salve for every pain. A smaller ad revealed that Parson Wilbur's house in Jade Town was for sale.

Although it didn't appear in the paper, everyone heard that Brine had roughed up a whore singing "Oh the Naval cadet is the pride and the pet of the girls the country o'er."

Brother Gabe had become a popular journalist as well as preacher. He deplored the continual attempts of newspapers to glorify the Union; Southern boys should not have to die for Yankee profit. He warned that if war came and Southern boys had to serve under Yankee officers with foreigners from the mud races, it would mark the final defeat of the once-sacred South. The South would never rise again.

Hoot wrote that railroads meant fewer mule and bull trains, stage coaches and stations, and that men who had few other skills would join cowboys who were out of work and out of luck because fences reduced the need for men on horses. Hoot saw the unemployed as a danger to the nation.

The Advertiser reported repeated brawls and knife and gun fights between gandy dancers, oil men and cowboys. Sheriff Brine and the new judge had asked the governor to send Texas Rangers.

⤚

Wilbur and Hannah said goodbye to Jade Town although they were unable to sell their house. Wilbur had never fit in because instead of representing the majority opinion he told the hard, cold truths of the Bible and what was required of believers. "The building that I designed and helped to build belongs to another. I have fewer listeners now than when I came," Wilbur told Jade and Rain.

"We're moving to the territory where Wilbur will fulfill his calling to minister to the Indians," Hannah said. "I will teach and Wilbur will be both parson and teacher and maybe a carpenter."

"This is a calling in which success, the only success, is that you keep trying," Wilbur said. "The only failure is to succumb to the success the world offers. Excessive wealth, excessive delight in physical pleasure."

"Belle and her husband are going to join us as teachers," Hannah said. "Their children are going as friends and equals. Will the Indians be better because of us? Maybe not but we will be better because of them."

"Listening to me was a gift to me," Wilbur said. "Hearing would have been better but maybe they heard something and in later years when the earthly rewards don't seem so important then maybe they will remember a bit and pass it on to their grandchildren. Will we fail? Of course, because we seek no rewards this life can afford."

No one said goodbye to them as they boarded the train with only what they could carry in their bags.

⤳

Hoot gave more space in the newspaper to Gabe in order to ghostwrite for those who had colorful stories to tell. He anonymously reviewed the stories in the newspaper and the newspaper printed and sold the booklets.

Gabe noted that Wilbur, who lost his church because of his antipathy to business, had lost his house because Jade Town could no longer support a teacher.

Hoot reported that the Good Citizen's League founded by Gabe opposed blacks or Mexicans from getting off the train or staying in Augurville overnight and would boycott unChristian businesses. Women of the league picketed Hephsibeth's saloon forcing men to push them aside to patronize the saloon and brothel that had been the scene of a shooting and perhaps the reason for the deaths of two men. Hephsibeth reopened the Widow Waller Saloon in Jade Town.

⤳

Across the nation the big news was that the new president said, "We want no wars of conquest; we must avoid the temptation to territorial aggression," a noble sentiment. Then the siren call of opportunity wafted over the waves.

The president ordered a battleship to Cuba to protect US citizens, property and investments. The ship's officers saw no sign of rebels and reported that their Spanish counterparts were genial, polite and homesick. The battleship exploded and sank with the loss of more than two hundred sailors.

Spain, the United States and Cuba had long played the imperious husband, jealous lover and abused and unloved wife with just recriminations and fabricated atrocities on both sides. This was the opportunity the jealous lover had longed for. The possessive husband had publicly insulted the passionate lover creating a scandal with newspapers competing to write the most salacious story.

The cause of the explosion of the battleship was unknown and the president appointed a commission to investigate but the American press knew the cause: Spanish treachery. Newspapers headlined, "Remember the Maine, to hell with Spain." A congressman said, "Even if the President's commission clears Spain of all blame, it will make no difference. The people are bound to have a war." American honor and national security required it. Newspapers quoted Theodore Roosevelt as saying, "I should welcome any war for I think this nation needs one." Some newspapers editorialized that America needed a war to open markets for American businesses.

Brother Gabe had a vision in which God declared that He had anointed America for the task of saving primitive nations from paganism and Catholicism and Southern boys would carry the Gospel as well as a bayonet. Privately he told his followers, "The Yankees are training our boys to win the next revolution. They'll bring their guns and training home with them and turn them against the real enemy of liberty, the government in Washington.

Out of work cowboys and teamsters, farmers whose crops had failed, mutton punchers whose lamb crop died enlisted as soldiers or contract workers for a job. Jesus, Pancho's and Mick's boys enlisted for adventure, independence, and freedom for Cubans. Jesus died of typhoid fever in training camp. The Advertiser mentioned his death but few cared and the unreconstructed ridiculed the idea that he was a hero. The news of the day was the miraculous landing of troops in Cuba with the loss of only two drowned soldiers. "The hand of God was on us," a congressman piously pronounced.

Hoot wrote that a former Confederate officer commanding Negro troops in Cuba led them into battle shouting, "Kill the damn Yankees." Other former Confederates or sons of Confederates attacked screaming the Rebel yell. Still, they all fought together against the dagos.

Reporting the triumph of the US Navy in Manilla Bay Hoot crowed, "How do you like the newspapers' war?" Other newspapers pointed out that Manila was the key to the Far East and America had freed the dagos from Spanish occupation. However, politicians discovered that Filipinos were too "uncivilized" to govern themselves and the soldiers were ordered to stay until Americans could do it for them.

The Advertiser ridiculed Aguinaldo as the "George Washington" of the Philippines. Filipinos who had fought beside Americans to drive out the Spanish discovered that they had become the "terrorists" the Americans wanted to eradicate.

A prominent journalist said, "Commerce, not politics, is king. The manufacturer and the merchant dictate to diplomacy and control elections. We did not go to war for the poor, bleeding Cubans but to grab what we could because we're after markets, the biggest markets we can grab - Puerto Rica, Hawaii, Guam, the Philippines."

America itself had become a Robber Baron.

Another journalist warned, "The Monroe Doctrine does not apply to the whole world."

⌇

Jade and Rain received a letter from Hannah and Wilbur about life on the reservation. Living conditions were primitive but Wilbur was building a house for them and one for Belle's family with help from the Indians. They were all teaching and the grandchildren happily ran with the Indians but returned home when quarreling began because fighting usually followed. The grandmothers and grandfathers grieved over their irrecoverable loss but there was resentment, even anger in the younger ones. The food was barely adequate, the water often dirty, and no medicine or sanitary facilities. The Indians wanted to go off the reservation to gather Indian medicine but the soldiers would not permit it.

Wilbur appealed to the government and wrote Christian groups begging for food, medicine, teachers, nurses, doctors. Churches sent teachers who preached but soon returned home.

There was little news outside the reservation except what the Indians told them and that was usually bad--a young man badly injured in a horse accident, three children burned by a fire, sick children in every home. A little food, a little medicine, clean water could produce miracles. Hannah particularly wanted news of the country; Wilbur wanted news about the Devils country.

Rain and Jade composed a letter that Rain wrote. One of Pancho's boys, Miguel, was sent to Hawaii when the

US annexed it, married a Hawaiian woman, came home an alcoholic and was now an Indian. Tomas, Pancho's other son, went to Guam, then to the Philippines. Tomas disappeared on patrol. No one knew what happened to him.

Mick's boys, Pat and Liam, were also ordered to free the Filipinos. Pat died in a Filipino ambush. Liam guarded Filipinos in a concentration camp. More soldiers died in the Philippines than in Cuba but there were no heroes and no parades when Liam came home. Many people, even some in the Devils country, believed that Aguinaldo had been the Filipino George Washington and were tired of the American Empire and its cost to America's ideals.

When Jade asked Liam about the liberation of the Filipinos, Liam said that his army buddies had permanently liberated more than eight thousand of them.

Windmills and the pumps at the spring lowered the water table so that deeper wells had to be dug. There were complaints that oil drilling used too much water and polluted water wells but the complaints came from plow hangers-on or small cow-and-calf ranchers and their concerns were ignored.

The railroad brought settlers and commerce to Augurville. Ice was available to most of the county with a local ice maker. Jade Town had no new residents and few new customers. The county had been quieter since Hannah and Wilbur had left. Jade Town was peaceful "as in dead," Jade added. The Devils country had been pacified. The previous year fewer people had died of violence than had died of neglect.

Wilbur and Hannah's old house had burned down. The church house was vacant but Brother Gabe had built a bigger one in Augurville, a brick house with a steeple and a cross, to which Gabe owned the title. He still preached that Indians could never be Americans, never be allowed to vote, no more than Africans could. It wasn't the color of their skin but their inferior race. It seemed that people liked to hear that.

Mick's life had improved since he took his produce to the Augurville stores and did his shopping there. The railroad offered more and better markets but short haul shipping fares put them out of reach. Pancho's family tried to grow everything they needed because the local market for wool dropped, and the cost of shipping to the Fort Worth market was prohibitive.

Rain wrote little about their present circumstances except that those who had known Rain as a savage and Jade as a killer, still saw them as outsiders, but in a different way, almost in awe.

⌒

The Advertiser declared that America's new hero, Theodore Roosevelt, would lead the American people to great prosperity with further expansion into the Caribbean and Pacific. With the help of the US, Panama declared its independence from Columbia and granted the US the right to construct and maintain a canal linking the Atlantic and Pacific oceans. Some had opposed the war on Spain but with new markets it was now clear that the cause of freedom was right.

There was talk that the federal government was going to set aside oil-rich land for a Naval Petroleum Reserve to supply Navy ships with oil in the event of war or other emergencies.

The Advertiser carried a story from another state about kids using a fake landslide to derail a train, killing two people and injuring two dozen. The father of three boys had deserted them and their mother because the only job he could get was as a tamper on a railroad crew and he could not afford to take them with him and the mother was too sick to live in a tent alongside the tracks. The boys said they derailed the train so their father would come home. Instead, they went to prison, their father went to work on a railroad in Missouri and their mother, who had begged outside churches and the homes of the wealthy to feed her sons and avoid prostitution, killed herself.

Stupid woman, some readers grumbled. If she had treated her husband decent he wouldn't have left her. Others condemned the husband who likely drank every cent he earned.

The president promised a new beginning for Indians in which they would be fully integrated into society as the Negroes had been. The Irish, Chinese and Italians would also make strides to full membership in the American community.

Hoot reported a Spanish influence in the colorful and daring clothing in Mannen's show window. Elvin's stage line continued to expand to towns without tracks. Cletis expanded his holdings in land, cattle and rails. Navy ships were converting to oil and trains would soon follow. If there were another war the oil under Cletis's property would become a national treasure.

Brother Gabe deplored Spanish influence, the mainspring of deceit in business, treachery in politics, immodesty in women's fashion, cruelty in sports, Catholic influence in education, the fecundity of women, and more Mexicans in a visible but secret occupation.

‿

Rain and Jade tried to live ordinary lives. Because Jade wore no gun or badge and Rain dressed as a paleface they were mostly anonymous when they went to New Augurville unless one of those who called themselves "reporters" got off the train. Hoot, happy to oblige, pointed them out to the visitors. The presence of a stranger or two following the marshal of Jade Town and his squaw wife attracted others so that a small crowd gathered. The Augurville Saloon offered to pay Jade and Rain to draw their followers to the saloon, drinks on the house for Jade and Rain, food if they wanted it.

Jade provided security for Jade Town, patrolling the streets at dusk and dawn to avoid thrill-seekers, checking the mostly vacant stores in Jade Town at first light looking for looters, vagrants, vandals. He made certain that locked buildings were still secure. Sometimes fugitives broke into locked buildings to hide in them. When it was cold sometimes vagrants or a drunken Miguel built fires inside the building. Two fires had started that way. Miguel had awakened in time to stop the fire he had started in Mannen's vacant store. The other, in the house that Parson Wilbur had built, was allowed to burn out because there was no wind to spread the fire. Jade Town had nothing to stop a fire from burning down the whole town or fanning out across the range.

Jade found it a relief not to be wearing a gun even after a sheep dipper came home early from chopping wood when his axe handle broke and he found a cowboy in bed with his wife.

The scab herder chased the cowboy around the one room shack with his short-handled axe while his wife screamed. The cowboy had on his hat and one boot and a non-threatening cut on his backside when he escaped through the door only to be caught and killed outside. Jade went to the home unarmed. The axe was outside, buried almost to the eye in a log to clean it and protect it from rust. The wife had no visible bruises but she wept as she scrubbed the blood off the floor and the walls. The cowboy's boot and other clothing were neatly placed outside the door. An old tarp was placed over him to keep off the blow flies.

Her husband meekly surrendered. "I'm going to have to take you in," Jade said. The sheep monger nodded.

"Please let him stay with me tonight," the wife cried.

"I'll come in tomorrow. You won't have to come and get me," the husband said. "Maggie don't like being alone at night. She'll come with me tomorrow and we'll make some kind of arrangement."

"Is that okay with you?" Jade asked the wife.

"Please," she cried into her apron.

They both seemed to want to be together but he wasn't sure why. The husband could kill the wife, maybe himself. They could vamoose and Jade would have to notify Brine and go looking for them.

"Come to the house," Jade said. He didn't want them to be part of Buckshot's show. "Rain will see what can be done for your wife and I'll notify the sheriff. At night you can stay with your husband in the roundhouse until the sheriff comes and gets him. I don't want either of you in there during the day."

They must have spent most of the night in the wagon because they were at his house by midday.

More and more often Jade checked the houses on Barefoot Street to be sure that the sick and elderly inside were able to take care of themselves. Sometimes he had Rain prepare soup that she took to those with nothing to eat and those who could not feed themselves. He missed the fiery Indian who had scalped his heart but enjoyed the loyal wife who stood beside him in danger or drudgery.

Rain had to wash clothes where she was visible to everyone or wash them after dark or in the creek when there was running water. Rain tried to get her laundry done before Buckshot's stage got to Jade Town, and hung the clothes on the line that Jade had strung for her between trees. Visitors wanted to pose with her and her wash pot and hand-made washing pole so she no longer answered the door.

The oddity collectors posed for pictures in front of her house, beside her wash pot, her wet clothes. Sometimes they took things, one of Jade's worn socks, a spoon thrown outside with the dishwater, a rock or a small branch off a tree that had been stripped bare. She had planted and watered flowers that bloomed little bunny heads and souvenir seekers sometimes picked them to press in Bibles or other classical romances.

Memories of her life often caught up with Rain while doing the family wash--white child, Indian wife and mother, alien, half-breed wife to white hero. All had been hard, the loss of her children the hardest. Closest to her heart were memories when she had been Indian again, beside her man with a shotgun, against the odds. She had desired Jade most when she liked him least. Love was somewhere in between. She had loved him most fiercely when she thought they might die together.

Now in her declining years she had become an outlandish novelty to be photographed, gaped at and forgotten.

⤳

Beneficia sat outside the small Augurville depot dressed in a paleface dream of an Indian maiden--fake trader beads on silver-plated brass chains, fake leather clothing that gapped at appropriate places, and low-necked dress that provided glimpses of breast when she bent over to pick up fake silver and turquoise Hopi jewelry. Short-sleeves that allowed peeks of her arm pit when she held up the jewelry for curious travelers to examine. Her backside was revealed, her calves exposed when she bent over to pick up counterfeit Paiute baskets or Navajo rugs.

Behind Beneficia were photographs of her beside a frightful Indian brave in Apache leggings and breechclout, wearing a buckskin vest over bare chest and arms with a feathered Sioux war bonnet on his head, a bow and quiver of arrows hanging from his shoulder and a Winchester in his hands; Brine and the brave standing shoulder to shoulder and clasping hands, Brine and the brave face to face with the brave's knife at Brine's throat and Brine's six-shooter at the brave's heart, Brine wearing a star, a brace of gun belts and guns and holding a rifle in one hand

There was also a photograph of an Indian woman bent over a pot that was purported to be Rain and one of the back of a man who stood in the doorway of a saloon with his hand on his six-gun. A note at the bottom claimed that it was a photograph of Jade just before he entered the Jade Town Saloon and killed three Augur cowboys.

Beneficia hated selling cheap, shoddy goods that cheapened Indian art, and advertising Buckshot Bob's stagecoach ride to nearby Jade Town, the "killingest, shootingest, deadliest town in the West." She had been mongrel, white, black and Indian but always her lot had been selling fake and worthless products for real gold and silver. It was the only kind of whoring Augurville allowed.

For two-bits Buckshot Bob in fringed buckskin jacket, vest and trousers and carrying a double-barrel shotgun would take a photograph of travelers posing with a genuine Comanche squaw. For four-bits he would photograph them between himself and the squaw.

For a dollar Buckshot would take them to the hell-raising town known to the post office as Jade Town, perhaps be able to take a photograph of the traveler standing with Jade, the deadliest lawman in the West, a true Indian fighter and expert marksman with rifle, pistol or shotgun. Buckshot held up his trusty shotgun. "Me and Jade are right proud that we never had to swap lead, both being on the right side of the law."

Buckshot set up the camera and folding stand he carried on his back and took photographs of a woman in suit and hat standing with Beneficia, and a man pretending to kiss her on the cheek.

For another dollar Buckshot would tell them the true story of Jade Town and show them the exact locations where blood was spilled and justice was done, including the sites of two hangings. Included in the tour would be a visit to Boot Heel Cemetery where some of the deadliest killers in the West were laid to rest. All that was required was a dollar for the stage ride to Jade City and a dollar for the story, and at least six passengers.

Buckshot pointed to the worn coach he had bought from Elvin's stage line. Those who wanted to hire their own horses were welcome to trail along. Refreshments would be for sale in the same places where Jade, Confederate hero General Tezel, the infamous dutchman traitor to his own people, murderers, bank robbers, highwaymen, and the notorious buffalo soldier, outlaw and lawman Jubal ate, drank, and some of them died.

After a dusty ride the stage stopped at Jade's shack to see the hole in which Jade and Rain hid while Augur cowboys shot up the town. "Some say they did more than hide if you know what I mean," Buckshot said with a wink.

Seeing an old man shuffling down Barefoot Street, Buckshot called him over. "This is a buffalo hunter present at the Indian raid. His buffalo gun brought down at least seven savages but more likely a dozen. I'll take your photograph with him for two-bits."

Ruth greeted them at Iowa's store. At last Ruth had found her place, a southern lady in crinoline petticoats, a white taffeta silk waist with a detachable collar and a cameo at her neck, a satin-lined green wool skirt bound with velveteen around the bottom, and a short plush green cape appliqued with satin with a storm collar, and a nobby Madrid hat that she wore at a tilt to cover her scarred face. She was not a Texas slattern in gingham.

Ruth offered tea or coffee and cookies or cake, ten cents for either. She shooed flies off the sweets. For two-bits she would provide biscuits, steak and eggs. She took orders and prepared the food while Buckshot told the story of the store--the first store in these parts, selling to freighters, ranchers, cavalrymen, cattle drovers, prospectors, explorers. He told the frightening story of four desperadoes holding up the store, Iowa refusing to open the safe although they beat him and threatened to kill him. Iowa stood beside the safe and told how he gave the bandits the combination of the safe only after one of them drove a knife through Ruth's hand, pinning her to the counter.

All eyes turned to Ruth and the glove she wore on one hand, even when cooking. They imagined the horrible scar that remained the twisted fingers and shuddered at the pictures in their mind of that terrible night. Rather than throw away one glove, Ruth changed hands every day so the gloves would show the same amount of wear.

"What happened to the robbers?" someone always asked.

"Jade and Cody went after them alone, "Buckshot explained, "Chased them for five days, then corralled them in the deep canyons of the brimstone branch of the Devils River, and killed all four of them in a desperate gun battle. They returned to Jade Town with the bandits' bodies, almost dead themselves for lack of food and water."

"I rode with them for a while but had to turn back knowing how Ruth needed me," Iowa said.

With new customers every day, Iowa became the huckster he had been when he met Ruth, only now he wore a gun since it was safe. "If you'll step right this way I will show you what they recovered," Iowa said. "Without the money of course. My wife has already spent that." He was rewarded with a few manly chuckles. Iowa pulled out a drawer filled with rings, watches, earrings, necklaces, bracelets, crosses of gold or silver, all for sale. "If you see anything of your liking, you can buy a piece of priceless history as well as a splendid piece of beautiful and valuable jewelry. Think of the story you can tell. Look all you want to. I'll know if something is missing and Buckshot here has a shotgun if you try to run with it."

A few laughed. Others crowded in to see the display. Some tried on rings or examined watches. Others examined scorpions and centipedes in bottles. One old man on Barefoot Street had been a taxidermist and he sold Iowa stuffed jackrabbits, coyotes, rattlesnakes, a mountain lion, a bear and what Iowa claimed was a mummified Indian baby. "Because you come all this way, these animals are for sale at a 10% discount." Also on sale was a buffalo robe that had belonged to an Apache warrior so fierce that palefaces called him "El Jefe." or The Boss.

Iowa offered more of the beaded necklaces and bracelets that Beneficia had made, authentic Indian arrowheads made by Miguel, photographs of Beneficia, Miguel and Gloria dressed in what easterners believed Indians wore. For select gentlemen Iowa furtively flashed naughty pictures of Beneficia, Salvie, or Jovita bathing or undressing while Ruth distracted the women with small tastings of horehound candy and molasses taffy.

When the customers became restless Buckshot drew their attention to Iowa's array of weapons--Cody's six-shooter with a notch for Eph, Chuy, Jubal, seven unnamed rustlers, four prisoners who had tried to escape and Noble. The army Colt revolver that Jubal used to kill four Augur cowboys. "Jade made Jubal a deputy but men from that race are not capable of positions of responsibility. Jubal stopped peaceful white men and demanded their weapons. He accosted white women and even attempted to marry one. That's why Cody challenged him to a duel and killed him. I'll show you where he stood when he died," Buckshot promised.

"This is the rifle that Sarge used to kill Dutch," Iowa said. Also for sale were weapons picked up after the Indian raid and the Big Shootout between the cow outfits--rifles, pistols, shotguns, bows, arrows, lances, some with feathers. Most of the guns were rusty but some looked suspiciously new. Also for sale, the noose that hanged the woman called Killer and the noose that hanged a dead Sarge.

Last, Iowa showed his prize collection: the Sharps 50 and Springfield trapdoor that Jade used to kill Indians, the Winchester and six-shooter that he used when the Indians surrounded him, the saddle with arrows imbedded in it. No one asked how Jade was in the saddle when an arrow was planted in the seat of the saddle. All were for sale along with jade knives made of dyed onyx with gold-plated handles. For children there were knives made of rubber with green blades and gold handles. And the real prize: the true knife that Jade carried with a jade blade and gold handle. One hundred dollars would buy it for some lucky man. Buckshot Bob winked at Iowa as Ruth pocketed the money for the third real knife that Iowa had sold.

As they left the store with their purchases and headed to the church a screaming Indian in full war paint, fringed buckskin and feathered headdress raced his paint pony full-speed toward them with a lance. Men recoiled and women screamed. "Run for the roundhouse," Buckshot Bob yelled and then shot the Indian off his horse. The Indian fell in a clump and the horse raced wildly back to the stable. While the visitors were catching their breath, Miguel rose and drew a knife and scowled at them. Buckshot Bob stepped in front of the Indian. "You don't want to chouse him when he's wrathy," Buckshot said, but offered an opportunity for folks to have their picture taken with an authentic Comanche warrior for a thin quarter. A picture with the Indian and the horse was four-bits.

"That charred building was the home of the parson who loved savages. His house was burned down by a drunk Indian. The red devils despised the do-gooder more than whites did."

Buckshot pointed at the cross above the church. "The woman they called 'Killer' was lynched from that cross. Some say she killed babies she didn't want. She entertained cow folks while her confederates stole their cattle. The rustlers who did her dirty work decorated cottonwoods. The parson was inside praying for her but he couldn't stop the lynching because he didn't have a gun. Some want to take guns away from folks but they'll get this here shotgun out of my cold dead hands."

Buckshot gave them a look inside the church. "That mark on the floor is where Indians tried to set the church on fire when they raided Jade Town. The parson they had here then wanted to make peace with the savages. Give up everything we won."

Curly's former Jade Town Club, that became the Paradise Club, bore a new but faded sign: Knife and Gun Club. "They called him Curly because when someone provoked him he gave them a look that made their hair curl, same as the pop skull he sold at the bar." Curly glowered at them from the bar where he sold tea in shot glasses and lemonade in mugs, and searched his scalp for a hair to exorcise. "When troubled, Curly pulled loose hair until he snatched himself bald-headed," Buckshot said and waited for a laugh.

"Get yourself something to drink and I'll show you the exact spot Jubal was standing when he shot four Augur cowboys sitting at that table right there. You can still see where a bullet chipped the edge of the table before hitting the cowboy in the lap."

Curly was reduced to selling Bibles, religious charms, tawdry paintings of a glittery Last Supper and a bloody Jesus on the cross. Indians dressed like Beneficia and Miguel kneeled before a setting sun that lighted a cloud forming a cross, Brother Gabriel with an open Bible that he couldn't read in one hand and a pointed finger of the other calling sinners to repentance. Like the eyes of Jesus, Gabe's eyes followed the curious around the club the way Ruth had followed customers in her store.

Religion was a good seller and Curly intended to sell it. "That painting is of Brother Gabriel a gun-toting preacher who helped tame Jade Town," Curly said. "Gabe had been a fighting chaplain in the war against Northern aggression and on one occasion had single-handed saved wounded Rebels from the bayonets and swords of bloodthirsty Yankee soldiers. You can hear Brother Gabe tell that story or you can buy this book and read it."

The booklet that Hoot had ghost-written and the Advertiser had printed and promoted cost fifteen cents.

"And Brother Gabe still fights for what he fought

during the war--opposition to a power-mad federal government that wants to rule rather than serve. Visiting his church is free but if you want to donate to a good cause, the money put inside the box over there will buy pamphlets that appear in every car of the train stating the railroad's opposition to regulation that will put them out of business, and you good people will go back to riding wagons and stagecoaches in this great land."

Curly didn't tell that that Brother Gabe affected a robe that Ruth had made for him with swords forming a cross on the front and the Confederate battle flag on the back.

"Cody was a lady's man," Buckshot said. "When a jealous cowboy named Eph shot Pearl right behind this building, Deputy Cody was pawing dirt to meet the killer in the street outside and shot Eph in the face."

Curly had equipped the shack behind with a plank floor, brass bedstead, clean sheets and bedspread, and a painted mannequin. He pointed out the bullet hole that killed Pearl then had them follow the steps of Eph as he went to meet Cody.

"This place had canvas sides until the Indian raid when they set it afire and drove an arrow through my thigh, right here," Curly said pointing out the spot. "It still hurts me sometimes. I had to shove the arrow all the way through my thigh so I could break off the arrowhead and extract the shaft. That's the arrowhead with part of the shaft still with it if anyone wants to buy it."

"Curly has also written that story and for two-bits you can own a copy and have your picture taken with the author," Buckshot said.

Before leading his group to the blacksmith and livery Buckshot pointed out the spot where Shep, a real sourdough, was killed by a pistolero hiding behind the canvas side of the club. "And right over there is where Cody killed a pistolero called Chuy, wilder than a Comanche funeral, for insulting a good woman. And right there is where Cody killed Jubal in a duel.

"This roundhouse is where besieged citizen fought off a murderous Comanche attack. Jade and Cody stood back to back in the suicide hole up there protecting the women and children inside from flaming arrows. Segundo, a cowboy who rode for the Skillet of Snakes, heard the gunfire and raced to get into the fight. Riding up Main Street with his reins in his teeth and a six-shooter in each hand, he was killed by three arrows but not before he dispatched six of the red devils with his deadly gunfire.

"Sarge, a loyal soldier and later faithful cowboy for General Tezel was hanged from the roundhouse for killing Dutch. Dutch comes here,and then leaves to fight against us, helping Yankees who want to tell everyone what they can do with their own property. Then Dutch comes back and wants to take over the Devils country, cutting Augur wire, stampeding and stealing Augur cattle. He even shot blooded bulls the Augur had imported. When Sarge caught Dutch cutting the wire he rode over to investigate. Dutch shot at Sarge, crippling his horse, but Sarge, a brave Rebel, advanced on foot and shot Dutch dead. The wire cutters Dutch used were found near his body where he dropped them but a rigged jury found Sarge guilty of murder and hanged him from a board extending from the suicide hole. Making him walk the plank like he was a traitor."

The smells of the incarcerated lingered and the audience was ready to leave. Buckshot pointed out bullet holes from the Big Shootout on the viewing side of the Tezel house. "A fight between two cowboys became a fight between brands and when a Skillet cowboy killed one of Cody's friends, Cody shot the Skillet rider. Soon all three cow outfits were smoking it up with the biggest fight between those in the roundhouse and those in the Tezel house." Most of the bullet holes in the Tezel house had been put there by Buckshot to enhance his story.

Some complained that they had not seen Jade or Rain. "I've been watching for them. Maybe we'll see them when we take a look at their house."

"Will we have to walk back to the stagecoach?" one man asked.

"Iowa will meet us with the stage at the Boot Heel Cemetery. But first we're going to take a look at the Widow Waller Saloon, still in business but ladies are welcome inside."

The younger of the two men who had followed the stage on horseback went after their horses. Hephsibeth met the others at the door, offered to pose for photographs and invited them inside. "Have you seen Jade or Rain," Buckshot asked.

"Not yet but they may show up. Until then, come in, have a drink and relax."

Some of the men bought a beer and Hephsibeth introduced Salvie and Jovita who sat at tables with the men. The two women on the tour sat alone in disapproval. Buckshot told how both Cody and Noble loved Hephsibeth while Hephsibeth stood at the bar looking demure. "The three of them had words right where Hephsibeth is standing. She tried to keep them apart but words turned to insults and Noble and Cody pulled guns. Cody was older but Noble had been trained by his father, Jade. Although Noble went for his gun first, his shot missed and Cody shot him in the heart."

Miguel came into the saloon and begged for a drink. Hephsibeth pushed him outside.

"Cody knew Jade would be on the prod and Cody went to Iowa's store to buy more bullets. He saw Jade and Rain coming down Broad Street. Both were armed, Jade with a six-gun, Rain with a rifle. They walked on opposite sides of the street with Rain watching for ambushers. Rain's presence with a rifle distracted Cody and when Jade stepped into the street Cody was slow to notice. Both men drew at the same time but Cody hurried his shot to be ready to shoot at Rain if she shouldered the rifle. Jade's first shot was true. For a silver dollar you can have your picture taken with Hephsibeth and hear her story, how her husband was killed by Indians and she became the plaything of powerful men. If you're shy I will arrange it for you. But first we're going to see if Rain or Jade is at home."

Neither Jade nor Rain responded to Buckshot's call but he allowed consumers to look around the house, look in the windows, examine Rain's wash pot, her milk cow and plow horses and the guineas that came when Buckshot spread on the ground the grain he had picked up at Iowa's store.

"It was on that porch that Rain, holding only Jade's gold-handled knife, turned away the cowboys who come to lynch Killer. And right over there is where the springs used to be."

Obstructing the view of the springs was a pump house. The big spring that had sometimes produced a geyser now barely seeped; the others were dry. Cletis and the railroad bosses formed a company to buy land adjacent to the spring. No one in Jade Town had the money for the prolonged legal battle and Cletis arranged for the company to seize the land through eminent domain. A deep well was drilled into the heart of the springs and the water was piped to Augurville where it was needed by the expanding population, the trains and oil drilling.

"The savages wanted the springs for themselves," Buckshot said. "That's why they raided the town and tried to burn it down. The parson at the church you looked at wanted to be friends with the red devils and now he and his family live with them on the reservation, which makes everybody happy. The parson said Jesus died a pauper and he could too. That's a Christian sentiment I've never heard before."

Buckshot nodded to acknowledge the chuckles. "The Indians come here one last time. Rain and Jade exchanged food for their weapons. That's how the West was won."

The last curiosity on the tour was the graveyard marked with the sign, Boot Hill Cemetery. Buckshot pointed out the graves of some who were buried there and some who weren't. Noble, Jubal, Smitty, Sarge, Eph, Cody, Doby, Segundo, Jefe whose grave was dug up and his buffalo robe stolen. A woman who was found dead and naked beside the creek. No one knew who she was or the cause of her death and no clothes were ever found. Dutch, Tezel, Poteet Monroe, a gambler Cody shot for cheating; four prisoners Cody shot for trying to escape, Chuy, Haskell, the barber shot by Jubal for pulling his kinky hair; a turn-coat Rebel shot by Swede. "Swede disappeared. Some say he became a lawman in Arizona Territory. Some who claim to know say his body was left for lobos to eat and his bones were thrown in the Pecos."

"Who did Jade shoot?" someone asked.

"Cody and at least four but probably six outlaws who made the mistake of riding too close to Jade City. Most of his killings never made it to the cemetery."

The tales grew bigger with Buckshot's telling, a dab of color in a dreary story, but were so inconsequential that it was worth no one's time to correct them until they became metaphors of such weight and import that no one could. Might was right and even when it wasn't it was victorious. Justice was permanent when served by a gun. Freedom was in the draw between the quick and the dead.

After the tour a stage passenger and the younger rider, aroused by the tales of brutality and death, returned to the saloon to get drunk, bed a whore, and catch a glimpse of Jade or Rain to complete the adventure. They also bought drinks for Miguel who told stories about Hawaiian girls and his plans to go to the Philippines and find his brother.

⌐

When Buckshot Bob occupied Jade Town Jade visited Pancho and Mick. Buckshot and his stories had taken over in a way that Indians, cowboys, desperadoes never had. To Jade leaving town to see Pancho or Mick seemed like running away but to stay was to be someone he didn't know.

The creek barely ran in rainy seasons and in drought years the water holes dried up. Pancho's and Mick's crops withered and died or bore bitter, pithy fruit. Mick and his wife lived alone with rheumatism, loneliness, hard work and no children to assist them and no other help or care. They lived on what vegetables and crops they could grow, and occasionally old mutton that Pancho gave them. Liam had come home restless, and unable to settle down to farming sought his future in Mexico. His parents had not heard from Liam since he left. They did hear that he had a Mexican wife and family.

Miguel and his wife, Gloria, lived with Pancho and Aurora. Gloria helped Aurora in the kitchen and the garden, kept a sow, and sometimes assisted Pancho in the field but Miguel was a serpent in their garden of peace, borrowing money for alcohol. Gloria had to give two pigs to settle a debt and once she was so hungry she lay down with the pigs and sucked the sow herself. She refused Hephsibeth's offer to be a whore but dressed as one and served drinks to pay Miguel's bill at the Widow Waller.

Jade also checked vacant shacks in the country. Those who dreamed of the clean cut of the plow or mutton in every pot had lost their land because it was cheaper to ship oranges from California to Fort Worth than it was to ship grain from Augurville to Fort Worth. The railroad that had brought farmers and shepherds to the county by rail sent them to other dreams by mule and wagon.

Occasionally Jade found a body in a nester's shack. He dragged the bodies away, by a rope around the heels if it looked as though the person had died of contagion, and buried them himself, then registered the death. Always he watched for ambushers as before, sensation seekers who wanted to come face to face with a legend and to collect a story to be cherished and passed on to later generations.

⌒

Jade and Rain learned that Wilbur and one of Belle's children died in a fever epidemic on the reservation. There were no medical facilities. Newspapers quoted a congressman as saying, "Fever is nature's way of taking care of these ignorant and helpless people and it saves the government a lot of money."

Now that Buckshot Bob had taken his thrill seekers with him, Jade and Rain sat on their porch watching the last bit of sunlight on Jade Town. The news of Wilbur's death and that of his grandchild turned their thoughts to their own lost children. They would die childless.

They had only each other, for a while, and memories of a past filled with life and death punctuated with horror and violence. And fanciful stories about them that even some in the county believed. Together they had gone to Cuba, posed as Cubans, and tracked and killed Spanish soldiers the way Jade had tracked and killed Indians. Rain bushwhacked and scalped cowboys riding back to the wagon alone. One of the cowboys lived long enough to identify her, long enough without a scalp for his face to slide down over his ears, closing his eyes and wilting his mouth. In a gunfight with four cowboys Jade had avoided injury by jumping from side to side and spinning around while killing all four of them.

Sometimes Jade pondered Wilbur's question in the last letter he sent them. "Did Cody win?" Jade knew Wilbur didn't mean the election or the gunfight. He meant what would the Devils country have been without guns? It was impossible to know but hard not to wonder at the needless deaths, some of them at his hand. The many who had been physically or mentally crippled by guns? The many left lonely and alone. The number made destitute.

If the federal government had not used soldiers to seize Indian lands, if railroads, cities, towns had bought the land they used and had invited the Indians to be a part of what they became, if the government had not given land to paleface settlers but had required them to acquire if from the Indians without violence, if they had not regarded Indians as hostiles and red devils unworthy of a place in the land, in the nation, then Indians might have been pacified without guns.

Advances in machinery would likely have made slaves unnecessary, even unprofitable in two or three generations if they had been willing to wait. But they wouldn't have been equal. They would have traded picking cotton for driving steel, digging coal or cutting timber and would have forever been the mudsill people of Tezel's dream.

Given equal rights they would have aspirations. They'd want a livable wage to afford a family, shorter working hours so they'd have time with their children. With a livable wage there would be fewer widows and orphan girls forced into prostitution, fewer hungry and abandoned children. That was what Tezel feared. With equal rights they would want to participate in democratic society, threatening economic stability and political harmony. Perhaps the government could not be defeated with guns but the Union couldn't have been saved without them.

Cody didn't win but Cletis did, achieving his father's

dream of destroying the government from inside through commerce so that economic and military security required tying commerce, the military and the federal government in tie-fast knots so tangled that they could never be broken. Jade had protected citizens from kids with guns but had done nothing to protect them from the real killers, looters, vandals. A gun was useless against them.

That's why he no longer wore a gun. Few men did, and those mostly for swagger. A gun made them feel bigger but it had come to weigh on him, a burden that he need not bear. If there were one person he could kill that would set everything right he would do it, even at the cost of his own life. But how many would it take? And where would he begin?

He was ending his lawman career where he had begun, unable to bring justice to one person because of all those he would be required to punish.

"I'm glad you don't carry a gun anymore," Rain said, as though reading his thoughts.

Jade hoped he never had to again. He had hidden his guns in a safe place, knowing he could never kill the heart of greed. He could only shoot off the fingers of those made desperate by its grasp.

Glossary

bot flies lay eggs in the nose of horses or inside the front legs. The horse, rubbing its nose on the leg ingests the eggs. The larvae attach themselves to the stomach or intestines until they mature and are excreted as pupae to mature into flies continuing the cycle.

caballero - cowboy, horseman, knight

cabron - literally male goat but idiomatic for cuckold or bastard

cahoots - partnership, throw in with

conchos - literally shell. Decorative ornamentation, usually in silver, on saddles, belts, chaps, etc.

didn't go to - didn't intend

$40 and found - salary and boarding, whatever you could find, sleeping on the ground or in the bunkhouse, eating whatever was available at the main house, the chuckwagon, or carried in a greasy sack when working a distance from the house or chuckwagon.

four-bits - 50¢

huevos - Spanish for eggs, idiomatic for testicles

lamb licker - man who keeps sheep

mad stone - hard, roundish mass found in the stomach of deer and other cud-chewing animals

mongrel - without identifiable class or breed

mudsill - lowest part of the house, usually on or in the ground, that the remainder of the house rests upon. Used by Senator and Governor James Henry Hammond, a wealthy Southern slave owner, to illustrate the need for a lower class of docile inferior people without aspiration or political power as a base for skilled laborers and the aristocracy to grow upon.

On the prod - angry and dangerous

pendejo - literally a pubic hair but idiomatic for idiot or fool

plow boy, chaser, disciple, follower, monger, pusher, slang for anyone who breaks the sod

powwow - talk

pullet - a young hen

scalawag - worthless, no good

screw flies - flies that lay their eggs on live, open flesh. Unlike most maggots, screw worms eat live flesh and if left untended can kill large animals including human beings.

three-horse ranch(er) - small one cowboy outfit

two-bits - 25¢

warble - a lump in the hide of a horse or cow containing the larva of the warble fly

wart(ed) (verb derived from noun worrywart) to annoy, trouble, harass

CPSIA information can be obtained at www.ICGtesting.com
Printed in the USA
LVOW040837290212

270924LV00001BA/17/P